The Call of the Sea
A Collection of Short Stories

From

Leaf by Leaf Press

Published by Leaf by Leaf Press 2021
www.leafbyleafpress.com

ISBN 978-1-9993122-4-4

Copyedited by Kirstie Edwards: www.kirstieedwards.org.uk
Cover Photo © Sara Piper Heap
Cover Design by Branding By G

Foreword

The world of reality has its limits;
the world of imagination is boundless.

Jean-Jacques Rousseau.

I have always had the greatest admiration for short story writers. It is an art somewhat akin to getting an implausibly large ship into an exceedingly small bottle. Literature is decorated with wonderful tales from the likes of MR James, Roald Dahl, Daphne du Maurier and Fay Weldon, to name but a few, so when the small group of writers at Leaf by Leaf Press set themselves the task of pulling together an anthology of short form stories, I was intrigued to see what we would come up with.

Some six years ago, Leaf by Leaf Press was born to provide a framework of support for a group of friends to pursue and complete individual literary projects. Nine publications followed all at least in part as a result of the support and guidance received from each other. What became clear in this period of time was that we all had very different styles of writing and hopefully this will be one of the things that any reader of *The Call of the Sea* will enjoy.

My fellow members of Leaf by Leaf Press and contributors to this anthology are John Heap, Kirstie Edwards, Wendy Lodwick Lowdon, Trixie Roberts, Ron Turner and Vicky Turrell. You can read about all of the authors at the end of the anthology or online at http://www.leafbyleafpress.com The idea of creating this anthology during the first COVID lockdown of 2020 encouraged us to meet online, to keep in touch with each other during difficult times and to pursue a collaborative goal.

The tales included in *The Call of the Sea* are very varied in style, genre, location and emotional tone, which we would like to think will add to the reader's experience. We very much hope you enjoy these stories as much as we enjoyed writing them.

Bernard Pearson

Contents

After All These Years

Ronald Turner

Ted died suddenly while mowing the lawn – his sole contribution to the gardening – about eighteen months ago. In some ways I've found widowhood quite isolating. Our old friends have cut me off, just as certainly as if I'd murdered my husband. I am no longer invited to their social occasions and can only suppose that I was previously tolerated simply because I was married to Ted. Or perhaps they are afraid that a woman on her own might be a threat to their marriages, but as I shall be seventy next birthday, I can hardly believe that.

In other ways I've found my single state quite liberating. I've joined a painting class and discovered a minor talent. I read at the table, watch what I want to watch on television, get up when I like and go to bed when I choose. Most importantly, I can think what I like and express those thoughts without being shot down in flames. No, I haven't started talking to myself: I talk to the birds in the garden. I was doing that two days ago when the telephone rang.

'Hello … Is that Jean?'

'Yes it is. Who's speaking?'

'It's Bernard Chambers. You probably won't remember me.'

I remembered all right. Tall, dark, handsome Bernard, whom I had last seen more than forty years ago, just before my best friend, Megan, stole him from me. My heart began to pound, as they say in those magazine stories.

'Bernard! What a surprise! After all these years.'

'I've come back to Burston Green – a couple of months ago. A chap I met in the pub told me you still lived here. Said your husband had died. Anyway, I thought I'd give you a call … See how you were.'

So Bernard was back in the village, after all that globe-trotting.

'How's Megan?' I asked.

'I'm afraid she passed away … It must be … mm … seven years ago. We were still in Africa then.'

'Oh, Bernard … I'm so sorry.' But I wasn't sorry at all. I had never forgiven Megan. She had taken away the future I had planned for myself as Mrs Chambers. And that sent me on the rebound into marriage with Ted.

'Look, Jean,' continued Bernard, after a suitable pause. 'Can we meet … in the flesh … so to speak. I would really love to see you again. Catch up on all your news.'

That won't take long, I thought, but said, 'I'd be delighted, Bernard. Just tell me when and where.'

He suggested a time and place and after a brief pause, while I pretended to consult a busy diary, I agreed. When I put the phone down I stood in the hallway for a while, my mind in turmoil, before hobbling back to the sink. Then, as I stood there, automatically swirling the pots round in the suds, I looked into the wintry garden and spoke to the few brave birds dabbing about in the frozen soil.

'What have I done? He'll remember me as a pretty young woman. Yes, I was pretty once. Now I'm like your garden. My colours have faded, mostly to shades of grey, my flesh is as crinkly as those fallen leaves and my limbs creak in the bad weather like the branches of that apple tree you love to perch in. Whatever will Bernard think when he sees me now.'

For the next two days, while I made an appointment at the hairdressers, considered what to wear and booked a taxi, I thought back to those years when Bernard was the centre of my life. I'd first noticed him when I was in the lower years at grammar school and he was a lordly sixth former. In those days, he was always being called to the stage during assemblies to receive his cricket colours or take the sports day trophy on behalf of his house. He moved with the grace of a natural athlete and managed a look that combined confidence with modesty.

When he left school I could only read about his triumphs in the local newspaper, scoring a century for the village cricket team or winning the men's singles at the tennis club. Meanwhile I had emerged from the chrysalis of adolescence into an attractive young woman, fluttering about among many admirers until I met Bernard again at the May Ball and gladly allowed myself to be caught in his net. By now, Bernard had become as successful in business as he was on the sports field and had transformed his father's ailing haulage company into a thriving concern.

Our brief courtship was like a fairy tale. We made an attractive couple, dashing about in his MG from one social engagement to the next. We became inseparable and it was no surprise to anyone when we became engaged. Then one day I introduced Bernard to Megan, my best friend, who had just come down from Cambridge with a first-class degree. I saw no danger in this, as Megan was quite plain and not at all interested in sport or a social life. But within a month Bernard had broken off our engagement and six months later he married Megan and they moved to Australia. I never saw either of them again and soon after that I got married myself … to Ted.

On the morning of my meeting with Bernard, I returned from the hairdressers and went upstairs to make a final decision about what to wear. It was while I was standing in front of the mirror, holding up one dress after another, that I began to have some doubts about this reunion. Why did Bernard want to see me again after all these years? Was it more than curiosity? He was a widower now and he had just discovered that I was single again. Was he lonely? Was he looking for someone to share his old age? How would I feel about that? I'd just been freed from one long disappointing relationship. How would I feel if a new one proved just as unsatisfactory? And what if Bernard wanted sex? Ted and I hadn't slept together for at least ten years. Could I cope with a more potent partner after that long abstinence?

At last I chose a simple blue dress, which matched my eyes and as I studied myself in the mirror some of my excitement returned. From a few feet away and without my glasses my face looked quite young again, especially framed by my newly styled hair. I had kept my trim figure and shapely ankles, which my shortish dress revealed. Yes, I was still quite a presentable woman. Bernard and I would make a handsome couple, even now.

I arrived early at the hotel. It was one where Bernard and I had often dined in our younger days. The meals were expensive but I imagined that would be no problem for Bernard. I sat in the lounge and watched the world go by, smiling with the pleasure of being out in it again and at the thought that I was here, at almost seventy years old, on a date. I saw several older men – some with partners, some alone – pass through into the dining room and wondered if I would recognise Bernard straight away – after all, he would be in his mid-seventies now – but when he arrived, just a few minutes late, I knew him at once. A tall man with only the slightest stoop, his hair completely white which showed up his deep tan and just a little thicker round the waist than when I had last seen him. You have aged well, I thought, as he strode through the swing doors as if he owned the place and looked around. He did not recognise me straight away so I stood up quickly, trying not to show the stiffness of my legs, and crossed to him.

'Hello, Bernard.'

I watched while surprise and disappointment were chased by courtesy from his rugged face.

'Jean, my dear. It's so good to see you.'

He took my hands, lightly kissed my cheek and then led me back to a seat.

'We've so much to talk about. But first, let me get you a drink.'

After All These Years

He shouted loudly for service, as if he was still in Africa, and a young man hurried over.

We chatted for a while over our sherries and then went in to dine. As we progressed through the courses an easy intimacy was quickly re-established. The excellent food and plentiful wine helped. Bernard was still such good company and his travels had given him a fund of lively stories in which he usually figured as the reluctant hero. I began to see beyond the weather-beaten mask of the elderly man opposite me, to the young man who was still inside. We became increasingly frank with one another and the revelations tumbled out. I hinted at the unhappiness of my marriage and was pleasantly surprised to discover that his marriage had had its failings too.

'That's the real reason I wanted to see you again,' explained Bernard, and suddenly my heart fluttered with anticipation like a young girl's. 'You see, I have often thought of you over the years and felt guilty about the way I broke off our engagement so suddenly. It was as if Megan had some power over me that I couldn't resist.'

He paused, frowning, as if trying to solve the puzzle and then continued.

'Megan and I had an interesting life together, seeing the world, becoming successful in its eyes. And all our children have done well in their chosen fields.'

I thought briefly about my own childlessness and sighed.

'But there was always a sort of hollowness at the core of our relationship, with so little in common except our family and our careers. I always felt guilty about the way I had treated you and longed to be able to apologise but Megan would never let me contact you. Will you ... can you ... ever forgive me?'

I reached across the table and put my hands over his and whispered, 'Of course ... Of course I can, my dear.'

By the time we had finished our meal and both our taxis were waiting, it was as if forty years had melted away and we were courting again. I felt relaxed, contented and hopeful for the future in a way I had not felt for years. I was sure that Bernard felt the same and I was determined to keep him for myself this time.

'Look, Bernard, I've really enjoyed our reunion. We must keep in contact now. Let's arrange another meeting. Soon!'

We were back in the lounge. Bernard had ordered that same young man to fetch our coats. Then, while he helped me into mine, he whispered.

'Yes, and next time we'll include Ellen.'

My face fell, and he saw my bewilderment.

'Oh, dear! I haven't told you, have I? I married again about four years ago. Ellen came to look after me when Megan died. She's a good deal younger than us of course. But I'm sure we'll all get on splendidly.'

Neville and the Guardian

Bernard Pearson

The stroke had been moderately severe.

'The good news is your speech is unaffected,' the doctor had said cheerily.

Never having been a great talker this was of little comfort to Neville as one side of his body hung limp and unresponsive. He would be using a stick for 'the foreseeable future' as they'd put it down at the hospital.

'Well, that's it then, isn't it. I'm bloody finished,' announced Neville.

'Don't talk daft, Neville,' said his mother, rearranging the one ornament on the mantle shelf in her pristine house.

'Well, I'm not going to ride again and if you think I'm showing my face down the gym again, you must be mad.'

'Oh, but you used to really enjoy it down there, love.'

'Well, that was then and this is now. OK Mam?'

Neville's mother looked at him despairingly. He had always been a strong willed little so and so and he was going to need all of that and more after what he had been through.

Neville appeared to have been lucky when he misjudged a bend while off roading on the reclaimed slagheaps up behind the estate where he lived. He sustained cuts and bruises, after being seen at Accident and Emergency, he was sent home with a tetanus jab and a box of pain killers. It was exactly a month later when coming out of the shower that he started feeling odd with a burning sensation in his head. When he looked in the mirror, one side of his face had gone all droopy, as if he had had very bad news. His stroke was pretty devastating as often the case for younger people.

Muttley, Neville's mongrel dog, arrived at the door carrying Neville and his mum's curry and chips from Micky's café. This was his task every Friday night. Once fulfilled, he knew he would be given the crispy batter leftovers that Mickey always included, especially for him. The dog was a rescue animal of uncertain parentage. Muttley was not a beauty to look at but Neville and he were as devoted as an old married couple and the old mongrel brought Neville a modicum of pleasure in what was otherwise a joyless existence.

'Hello mutt boy,' said Neville, transferring his crutch so he could lean down and stroke the old dog.

'You're going to have to start taking him for a walk soon, Neville. Otherwise he'll go mental.'

'Look Mam! Will you get off my case?' said Neville, retreating to the sanctuary of his bedroom and computer games.

'I'm only saying, love,' responded Mrs Davies, following him to tidy up where there was little need and plumping up already well plumped cushions.

It had been just Neville and his mother in the house since his father decamped to Pontardawe with some girl he'd 'met' over the internet four years ago. Mrs Davies worked part time as a cleaner in the local primary school and Neville, before he had the accident, was about to start as Assistant Groundsman for the local rugby club. His father, having played for the club before going on to play professionally, had helped Neville get the interview. He'd been told they'd keep the job open for him but he'd believe that when he saw it.

'Why don't you come down the club tonight love? It's Quiz night, it is.'

'Oh, is that all I'm good for now? Listening to my old head teacher showing off how much he knows about flags of the European Union and types of pasta? No thanks. I hated him when I was in school and I does hate him now, snidey bugger!'

'Neville!' said his mother. Neville's mother knew when it was time to retreat. Truth be told, she wasn't much of a one for the club but she needed to put some space between her and her son.

The row of miner's cottages where Neville lived snaked along the side of the hills. Most of the houses were identical to their neighbours' from a distance, with their lifeless, darkening grey stone. However, on closer inspection, some of the properties made a statement about their owners with profusions of potted plants and wind chimes and dream catchers jostling for prominence; others though appeared to have unlived in front rooms, devoid of the usual detritus of everyday family life; they were kept by their elderly occupants as well-polished shrines to happier, more prosperous times. Halfway up the hill was 'the club,' a single storey modern building with painted render on the outside in a garish syrupy yellow. The bar was dimly lit with pictures of Abertillery Rugby teams past and present. In one corner of the room was a state-of-the-art fruit machine usually surrounded with a coterie of old men taking grumpy turns.

'We don't see much of your Neville these days,' said Brian, the club steward. How's he doing?'

'Well, you know how it is,' said Mrs Davies.

'Yes; it must have been dreadful for the boy. What can I get you?'

'Well actually, I just popped in for some fags.'

'Thought you'd given up.'

'That was last week.'

Before the bike accident it was at the club that Neville had first set eyes on Sian. She had been at university in England somewhere when her father had got a job in Newport. She had dropped out from her course after a year suffering with anxiety and was now living back in the village with her parents.

One evening, Neville had gone out the back of the club and found Sian crying.

'What's up, if you don't mind me asking?' he'd asked, looking at the young women before him. She wasn't dolled up like most of the local girls. She was wearing a loose navy-blue shirt over a pair of faded but well-fitting jeans. Her blond hair was tied up in a loose pony tail. Even through her tears, Neville could see her large blue-grey eyes. She kept it simple, and that's what attracted him to her.

'I feel like I've let everybody down.'

'How do you mean?'

'Well dropping out from uni … with depression of all things! God you look at all the awful things going on in the world and here I am, weeping and wailing like a two-year-old.'

'You can't help how you feel. No one else knows what it's like to be in your head.'

'Oh, thanks. I suppose you're right.'

'No doubt about it. I know some people say exercise do help.'

'Yes, I've heard that too.'

'We've got a gym here, you know and a pool. It's a bit crap, really, but it's somewhere to go like.'

Neville had no idea what had possessed Muttley to do a runner that night, but when he went to the dog's kennel in the backyard, there was no sign of him. One possibility that occurred to him was that the dog had been taken. There had been a spate of animals been taking and used in organised dog fights, a lucrative and blood thirsty business for a few unscrupulous young men in the South Wales valleys. Muttley was a gentle creature but of fearful aspect with his box shaped head, immense, well-defined jaw and he was deep chested. Blind in one white opaque eye, his nature and arthritic old legs meant, however, that he would be no competition for younger, fitter dogs.

Neville felt his chest tighten as he thought of his companion being ripped to pieces in some dimly lit garage. It would just about put a cap on the year he was having. He grabbed his hood and headed out into the early morning gloom.

Neville and the Guardian

There were, of course, people in the surrounding towns and villages who remembered the day of the disaster well. On the morning of 28th June 1960, in an old seam of The Six Bells colliery an explosion caused by the ignition of fire damp took the lives of all but three of the men working in that particular part of the mine. The Memorial Park built to commemorate the tragedy was a favourite haunt of Muttley's, a place to meet up with like-minded canines and patrol the rough grass and remnants of the old mine workings for unsuspecting rabbits and disdainful feral cats. The elderly Muttley would act more as a cheerleader for the other dogs, barking encouragement as they tore off into the undergrowth and then licking the bottoms and noses of the hunters on their return.

On his crutch, it was a good ten minutes before Neville arrived in the park to search for Muttley. It was late April, just after five in the morning; there was a grass frost and the scrubby blackthorn bushes dripped with dew. Some of the trees on the hillside were faintly tinged in green and the hum of early morning traffic making its way up to Ebbw Vale was the only noise to be heard.

Through the gloom, Neville could make out what was called in the local tourist guidebooks 'One of The Wonders of Wales,' a sixty-foot-high installation of a Welsh miner in a pose reminiscent of Rio de Janeiro's Christ The Redeemer. Bare from the waste up and barrel chested, the steel construction appeared almost ephemeral from a distance and the beginnings of dawn could be viewed between each riveted rib, although the structure became more solid the nearer one approached it.

There was no sign of Muttley, however; to lose the dog would be it, as far as Neville was concerned. He leant against the plinth of the sculpture and looked back on what a mess his life had become. Mind you, it hadn't been any great shakes before the accident. His father, Wynne, had been out of work ever since Neville could remember. He'd spent his time watching daytime TV or down the club. He'd been an affectionate dad, all right, but you could tell he'd somehow had the soul ripped out of him when he had to finish playing rugby. It was then his father's drinking had increased; most of the fridge had been taken up with lager and then he'd have various stashes of vodka hidden around the house, which he thought his wife knew nothing about. In the months before he left, his consumption of skunk had increased and the faint astringent aroma could still be smelt around the house several years after he had left. It made Neville wretch.

Since he'd taken up with the girl in Pontarddulais, there'd been the occasional email enquiring how Neville was and inviting him over to meet 'Layla,' saying how much he thought they'd get along. They had all gone unanswered.

Then of course there'd been his so-called mates, who'd been all over him after the bike crash, but when the longer-term effects of the stroke had become apparent, one by one they'd found themselves excuses not to call for him, even on match days.

'It's only because they're scared love. They'll come round,' his mother had said.

But Neville knew it wasn't fear; it wasn't even disgust. It was embarrassment to be seen with a cripple. Most of them shared an interest in two things: going down the gym and girls. As far as Neville could understand, they now saw him as an encumbrance in both departments. He thought back to his grandfather, Iestyn, who had been working in the mine the day of the accident and had escaped unscathed only to be struck down with emphysema a few years later. Neville remembered him now being wheeled into the club, his ever-present oxygen cylinder strapped to his chair, his pale ghostly skin and a voice hardly rising above a whisper.

Neville closed his eyes and just wished the rotten, stinking world would disappear. All of a sudden, he felt something cold and damp brush against his knee. For a moment he thought it might be Muttley's wet nose, but when he opened his eyes there was no dog to be seen. The sky appeared to have darkened and for a few seconds he felt totally disoriented. Was he about to have a second stroke? Perhaps this one would have the decency to finish him off.

He looked up to see a huge, metal-framed figure bending over him, blotting out the light. Then he heard the sound of grinding metal on metal. Neville found himself placed gently into one of the Guardian's great steel hands. He was about to jump off, but as he now appeared to be thirty feet above the ground, he thought better of it. It must be the meds he was on. Neville then found himself rising further from the ground. To the north, he looked down the wooded valley and onto Brynmawr and the mountains. To the south-west of Cardiff, he could just make out The Principality stadium, like some enormous grey galleon waiting to set sail. To the south and east, he could see the white ribbon of the Second Severn Crossing with its more sedately built predecessor in the far distance. A cold spring shower scudded through the valley and for a moment, Neville clung to the thumb of the figure in whose grasp he sat, letting the rain pepper his face. He looked up again into the eyes of the Guardian, who seemed to smile and then wink at him before gently placing him back down onto the grass.

Neville was in such a daze he started to walk without his crutch to support him. After a few steps, he stumbled and fell. Again, he felt something cold and damp; it appeared to be licking his face. This time it was Muttley.

'Where the hell have you been?' said Neville.

The old dog looked at him cheerfully and proceeded to chew on Neville's crutch, a sign that the prodigal dog was eager to get going.

As they made their way up the hill, Neville glanced back. The Guardian was in his rightful place looking up the valley, arms outstretched in a sign of greeting, supplication or defiance, depending on your interpretation.

The next morning Neville made his way to the gym. His one side might be useless, but he still had the other side and it couldn't do any harm. Sian was there. She'd started going regularly after the night she and Neville had first met. She'd just got out of the shower and her tousled fair hair fell down around her shoulders.

'All right Neville,' she smiled at him, towelling the last bit of damp from her blond locks.

'Haven't seen you down the club lately?'

'No! Well, you know … what with the stroke and everything.'

'Oh, don't be daft man! Anyway, we've missed you. I've missed you.'

'Might see you down there sometime then?'

'Cool,' said Sian. Slipping her bag over her shoulder. 'Mine is a lager,' she laughed.

Outside the gym, Muttley cheerfully cocked his leg on a convenient lamp post.

.

The Call of the Sea

John Heap

It was early morning and Peter Farris, camera bag over his shoulder, was walking along a deserted marine drive in Southport. He was supposed to be working but that morning the light was flat, grey and disappointing. Noticing the bright beads of water collecting on his fleece, he realised that the once soft drizzle was now more insistent and that his waterproof was still in his bag. He looked up ahead to see a brightly painted shelter guarded by a solitary gull perched on the seawall railings. On reaching the shelter, he nodded to the gull but then stopped, startled by the presence of a young woman. After an awkward moment of indecision, he sat down.

She looked across at him.

He removed his jacket from the bag and spent a long time putting it on; his goal of a smooth action followed by a smooth exit was confounded by the awareness of being observed.

But to be fair he was observing too.

At art school he had unwittingly developed an 'artist's eye,' and from even the briefest of glances he was building up a picture of the girl. She was casually dressed, with faded jeans and an equally faded T-shirt, over which she wore a dark tan leather jacket. She looked eastern European; perhaps Polish, and her short dark hair matched her equally dark eyes set above striking cheekbones. Peter had never seen such striking cheekbones.

After lovingly re-fastening his bag, he looked out to the sands. Out there, at a distance almost beyond reckoning, was the economical line that provided both the horizon and the hint of a sea. Southport has a landscape that is based on this line. On the edges of this curving thread are the hills, pale Welsh on the left, dark Cumbrian on the right; in the space between are balanced the ships from Liverpool, the gas platform and sometimes, to the annoyance of the quiet people of this borough, that shimmering symbol of northern class, Blackpool Tower.

'Do you come here often?' she asked.

Peter didn't know how to react to this opening line. He thought that she must be joking, but then they were in an Edwardian rain shelter overlooking a desolate beach at eight-thirty in the morning, so perhaps she wasn't.

'Not often,' he said hesitantly, but on looking across he saw she was smiling.

'I do,' she paused and then said more quietly, 'every day.'

She looked out through the rain to the sea again and they were both silent for a while.

Then she turned and said brightly, 'My name's Maria. What's yours?'

'Peter,' he said and turned to face her. 'You mean you come here every morning?'

'Hello Peter, it is good to meet you,' she replied and then continued: 'I like it here, at least at this time of year, and the view of the sea is good, is it not?'

From a pocket she took out an almost flat cigarette packet and extracted an equally flat cigarette, which she carefully moulded back to shape. Looking across, she saw Peter watching and with a smile she offered it to him.

For some reason he accepted it. She took another for herself, and then moved closer to light them.

'Thanks,' he said and inhaled rather too deeply.

The dizzying hit was immediate. This was his first smoke for three years. He wasn't sure why he'd taken it, but it was as if his life was now something else, different from a minute ago, and that all those old rules no longer applied.

'So Peter,' said Maria, watching him struggle, 'what brings you out here?'

'I'm a photographer. Early in the morning, the air's clear and the light can be fantastic ...' he trailed off as he realised she wasn't particularly listening but was again staring out to sea.

He took another drag on his cigarette and was about to ask her about herself when she shuddered, looked at her watch, stamped her cigarette out and stood up, while zipping her jacket.

'It's turning,' she said, still staring outwards. 'I must go now.'

As she made to leave, Peter quickly rose and asked, 'But will I see you here again, tomorrow?'

She looked at him, as if seeing him for the first time, her eyes struggling to refocus from the distant horizon.

'Maria, the same time tomorrow?' Peter persevered loudly, as if afraid she couldn't hear him above the wind.

'No, I'll be an hour later,' she replied and with that she was gone, enveloped by the gathering storm.

The next day the weather was worse. Peter had been up for hours and ever since their meeting he hadn't stopped thinking about Maria. Yesterday, buzzing with anticipation, he'd walked taller through a world now bursting with colour, life and new possibilities. It was only on the wet and windy journey from his flat, past the silent pier to the deserted shore, that he started to worry. Who was Maria? They'd only exchanged a few words, so would she bother to turn up, especially in this weather?

He arrived at the shelter early. He hadn't wanted to be late, so he'd put in contingency after contingency to avoid it, but now he had thirty minutes. Thirty minutes of shivering self-doubt, thirty minutes to think on the absurdity of the shelter, the rain, this meeting.

He lit a cigarette and looked out in search of the horizon, but in the gloom the exact place could only be guessed at. It was sometime yesterday, whilst going over every word and nuance of their short conversation, that he had discovered the key. He had realised that she'd been talking about the tide turning and he had quickly confirmed that yesterday's low tide would have occurred just before she had got up and left.

But what was this about the sea? Why come out in this weather to witness a non-event? Wouldn't high tide be better? Of course, he'd consulted the tide tables but deep down he knew that she'd felt the tide turn and that Maria was attuned to a more earthly current than a broadband connection.

A seagull arrived on the railing. It may not have been the same one. It watched, waited and nonchalantly defecated.

Peter saw Maria as she turned the corner a good two hundred yards away. She was dressed as yesterday; her leather jacket was fastened tight against the rain and her head was down. He tried to look at her dispassionately, to see her as others might. She was short and whilst slim looked sturdy as she leant into the wind. From this distance she could have been a chunky schoolboy and there was nothing remarkable about her at all. However, as she came closer Peter found it more and more difficult to be objective and when she finally looked up, he was struck with a powerful rush by how beautiful she was. Those eyes, those cheek bones, her sturdiness transformed into strong feminine lines: this was Maria and she had come.

Maria smiled, said her hellos and accepted a cigarette. She leant closer for the proffered light, holding his hand steady, water still dripping from her hair and nose, the drops creating dark grey circles on the concrete floor.

'Thanks,' she said and leant back against the bench, eyes half closed, half open, looking out to the distance.

Maria looked perfectly at ease with the following silence, but Peter was busy inventing and dry running his next lines. In exasperation, and much to his horror, he just erupted with, 'So how come you've this interest in the sea then?'

Taken aback she looked at him, as if not sure whether to take offence at the intrusion, admit her interest or to deny it.

The Call of the Sea

'You know about tides and their cycles, you knew when it was turning, you come here at low tide for some reason and you seem to know a hell of a lot about the sea for a Polish girl.'

Peter was panicking. This wasn't going to plan. What had happened to the smooth enticing conversation he had practised, envisaged, even fantasised about? Why was he being such an arse? Who had said she was from Poland? He awaited the smack down.

It came slowly but steadily.

'Excuse me but I am not Polish. Your phrase 'Polish girl' is meant in a derogatory way is it not? Well, I must tell you Mr Peter whoever-you-are, that I am an educated Russian woman. I know five languages, each of which I speak better than you speak your own English. I know many things about the many things about which you know nothing.'

'But you do know about the sea,' he replied quietly, like a petulant twelve-year-old.

During the silence that followed, Maria gazed again out at the gloom hidden sea whilst Peter concentrated on another cigarette, determined now to keep his head down in the vain hope he hadn't blown it.

'Yes, I do know about the sea.'

Peter kept quiet.

'I am drawn to it.'

'It can be very beautiful.' Peter liked to show his sensitive side.

'You do not understand.'

Wrong again. He allowed her to continue.

'The sea is terrible, it is a curse.'

He couldn't let that sentence hang there. He wanted to know why she thought that, but he would have to tread carefully.

'Why do you think that?' he asked as neutrally as possible.

'I cannot explain; it just is.'

She looked across at Peter and he noticed for the first time that there were shadows under those dark eyes and that she had a tired, lost look that produced in him an almost overwhelming desire to hold her. He glanced at his watch and noted that if events ran as previously, she would be leaving soon. Low tide would be forty-eight minutes later today, so he must make a suggestion quickly.

'Listen Maria,' he said, 'can we walk back together; I'll treat you to a late breakfast down the café if you'd like?'

'Perhaps,' she turned her head as if listening; Peter tried but failed to either hear or see anything through the persistent rain.

'I must go now,' Maria said, standing quickly and without another word, she left the shelter. Peter grabbed his cigarettes and lumbered after her, trying to run and refasten his waterproofs as he went.

They sat facing each other, separated by their bacon sandwiches and coffee, damp clothes gently steaming with the heat of the rushed retreat.

Peter asked Maria where in Russia she was from.

'I was born in St Petersburg, a beautiful city I'm told, but something went terribly wrong and when I was three, I moved with my father to live in Omsk.

'I don't suppose I had your western idea of a happy childhood, but with school and the housework, there was little time to dwell on it. They were exciting times in Russia and I knew that if I studied hard I could get a scholarship in Europe, so that is what I did. I grabbed a chance to study in Frankfurt, get a European student card and travel. I came to Liverpool and now here I am.'

Peter took a sip of coffee; he didn't want to finish it too quickly.

'Is your father still alive then?'

'Yes, well I assume so; he never writes. My father is a good man but like a lot of men back home, he drinks too much. He was never violent though; he just became more and more sad.'

'And your mother?' Peter felt it would be rude not to ask.

'I do not know my mother.' Suddenly angry, Maria finished her coffee.

'I'm sorry.'

'She is the cause of my father's sadness. As I said, I was only three at the time, but I still have a vague impression of the trouble. Then my world was all mixed up and I was on a train travelling through the night. I arrived in a cold place and she wasn't there for me anymore.'

Not wanting to break the moment, Peter mimed another cup of coffee. She looked at the rain against the window and nodded. As he got up to get it, her eyes were cast down and her attention was once again somewhere else.

He brought back the coffee and waited.

Later she spoke again.

'I used to ask my father about her sometimes, especially when he was sad. I would ask why he wasn't angry at her for abandoning the two of us.'

Maria looked up at Peter and continued.

'He said that it wasn't her fault; that she was sick and it was her illness that made her leave. He said that she was beautiful, and wonderful, and kind, and that they loved each other very much, and that she loved me very much too, and that she was very sad to go.'

There were tears in her eyes now and Peter grabbed her hands across the table in a spontaneous gesture of support. She didn't remove them but said quietly.

'Peter, I am ill too.'

*****

Peter was at his computer. A Dire Straits CD played quietly in the background and Maria was asleep on his sofa. She was wearing one of his fleeces and some tracksuit bottoms and every so often Peter would glance over as if to confirm to himself that she really was there.

She was, and it had all happened perfectly naturally.

Still holding her hands, he had tried to re-assure her that everything would be all right, and that she wasn't ill, or if she was, that it wasn't serious. He had suggested that they should go back to his flat, dry out their wet clothes and get warm. If she was ill, that was exactly what she needed and anyway there was only so much coffee you could drink.

Earlier schemes had evaporated, fantasy firmly ousted by reality, and despite himself Peter had acted honestly. She was upset, they were both cold and he understood that neither of them wanted to say goodbye. Maria agreed.

To avoid any awkwardness at his flat, Peter had organised things quickly. He had given her some clothes, shown her the shower, got changed himself, lit the gas fire and put some soup on the hob. By the time Maria had showered and changed, he had a mug of chicken and vegetable ready for her. A quick discussion pinpointed Dire Straits as one of their few musical crossovers, and they had sat on his sofa in front of the fire.

They had chatted a little while and he had learnt that she was Maria Anosovich, she was twenty-two and she had a degree in Modern Languages. She didn't have many friends, certainly none in England, and considered herself a bit of a loner. They didn't discuss her illness, the sea or her mother; she looked too exhausted and very soon, all warm and soup-filled, she had drifted off to sleep.

At his computer, Peter was searching newspaper scans from St Petersburg. They had taken some time to find and he certainly couldn't read them, but whilst it was a long shot and Maria had been vague, he knew the timeframe, between nineteen and twenty years ago, and he had a name, Anosovich, so it may well be possible.

He started at the earliest and worked forward, looking blankly at page after page of unedifying script, his eyes vainly scanning for the word Anosovich. He was nearing the end of his search when he saw the photograph. Maria's unmistakeable eyes complete with shadows were staring out at him. They were in the photograph of a man who Peter assumed was her father, Петро Anosovich. It wasn't a flattering photo; the man had the look of a prisoner, a desperate prisoner.

Peter printed the page out.

He was so pleased with himself that he wanted to wake Maria immediately, but resisting the urge, Peter went to the kitchen and made a Bolognese sauce to have later. She was still asleep when he had finished so he quietly left the flat to get some wine.

Outside the rain had stopped and the sky had cleared. It was now a fresh spring evening, yet Peter began to worry. It wasn't the fact that he'd left a stranger alone in his flat, but that in his excitement he hadn't thought about how she would react to him raking up her past. The article was bound to upset her. What on earth was he thinking?

He decided to buy two bottles of wine.

On returning to the flat then, it was a blow to find her standing with a cup of coffee reading his printout. He was right; she had been upset. However, her anger had quickly passed for what she was reading was chillingly familiar.

'Perhaps I should've asked beforehand,' offered Peter from the kitchen as he was putting the wine in the rack.

'Yes,' she said coldly, 'but that is not important now. This is.'

She explained to Peter that he was right; the article was about her mother's disappearance. The original thoughts had been suicide; her doctor had reported frequent bouts of depression and her father had alerted the police immediately she hadn't returned from her customary shore-side walk. But then two days later they had found her clothes washed up on the edge of the Baltic, and her father had come under suspicion.

'Why would that change things?' asked Peter

'Because,' she paused to reread a paragraph to make sure she had it right.

'Her clothes, her shirt, her jeans and her jacket were found with their buttons all fastened.'

'Weird … but that …'

'No Peter, you do not understand. Her clothes were inside each other. As if fully dressed, my mother's body had simply dissolved.'

Peter was silent as he tried to think of explanations, but he couldn't and now wasn't the time for lame suggestions.

Maria continued, 'Apparently, according to my father, my mother had been fascinated by the sea and over her last few weeks this had turned into such an obsession that she was compelled to make a daily pilgrimage to see it.'

'Ah,' Peter replied. There was rather too much to think about.

'Does it not remind you of anyone?' she asked rhetorically.

It was time to talk about her illness. It was time to get to the bottom of it all. Peter went to the kitchen, opened a bottle of wine and poured out two generous glasses. He returned, passed her one of the glasses, sat down on the sofa and motioned for her to sit down beside him.

Maria shook her head and started pacing, glass of wine in one hand, the printout still in the other.

'No wonder he moved to Omsk. I do not know of any place that can be further from the sea. Perhaps that is why I only started to feel this pressure since I came to England. You are never far from the sea here. You are surrounded by the sea and there is no escape from it on this little island, no escape.'

'And another thing,' she thrust the printout in Peter's direction, 'here they quote some … some old crone … some charlatan,' Maria was getting angry again, 'who is apparently convinced that my mother must have been a mermaid. A mermaid for God's sake! She was my mother!'

With this she uttered something Russian, finished off the glass and sat down.

Peter hadn't even tasted his wine so swapped his glass with hers and went to get the bottle. This was a lot for him to take in and in truth he was having trouble keeping up.

When he returned, her face was still furrowed but she was quieter.

'You never said your mother was dead,' said Peter.

'I do not know that she is. A body was never found so she is still officially missing. My father feel's she is alive, that she just swam off into the sea. But me, well, do you know how cold the Baltic is in March?'

'No.'

'Very.'

She nodded at Peter's cigarettes on the table and with his permission she grabbed one and lit up greedily.

'Maria, you say you're ill. Exactly what's wrong with you?'

Peter had done it; he had asked the question that he didn't really want answered.

She took a deep drag on her cigarette, paused, exhaled and began.

'I do not know what's wrong with me. It started with headaches. I would wake in the morning with a pain on one side. At first I thought it was drink,' she raised what was left of her wine, 'but on the other side my limbs would be numb as if I had spent all night sleeping on them.

'Sounds like your circulation,' said Peter.

'Perhaps, but it is becoming more extreme, and more painful and it is linked to my other problem.'

'Oh?'

'You know; this problem with the sea. Peter, it is more than a fascination as reported in that paper; it is a need, a physical need. I need the sea; I feel it in my head, in my bones, in my gut. But, and this is the scary bit, I believe the sea wants me, that it is waiting for me, and that is not good.'

She finished off her wine again and as Peter didn't immediately replenish it, she shrugged and continued.

'It seems the change of the tide, that moment of slack water is the worst. That was when you first saw me, err … yesterday? I go down to the shore to catch the low tide. It is far enough away then; it is not too dangerous. I cannot go at high tide.'

'And this is associated with your other symptoms?'

'Yes, the pain at night is somehow linked to the time of the tide and I often have nightmares; I promise you I can wake up screaming.' She gave Peter a warning look and he understood that she was planning to stay over.

'What can I do to help?' asked Peter.

'I do not know. Probably nothing. Keep an eye on me? Perhaps that is all I need. It has been getting worse over the last month. I do not know how long I can resist. I do not know how long I want to resist. Just smelling the sea is a release. I really want to escape into it but I know it would take me.'

'Right!' Peter needed a timeout. 'How about something to eat? Do you like pasta?' With that he left Maria, who was emptying the last of the bottle into her glass.

Alone in the kitchen he gathered his thoughts. What he'd heard was disturbing; Maria seemed to be reliving the death of her mother and he wasn't convinced that 'keeping an eye on her' was going to be sufficient. Still, he wasn't going to give up that easily and besides, it looked like she was staying over.

The pasta didn't take long and soon he returned to the living room with two steaming plates of spaghetti Bolognese and the second bottle of wine under his arm.

Maria was leafing through one of Peter's portfolios. She was particularly intrigued by a set of photographs showing several metal figures set into a beach, all looking out to the distant horizon.

'Where is this?' she asked.

'That's Crosby. It's an installation by Antony Gormley. There are a hundred identical statues, casts of Gormley himself and they're spread out over the shore. It's really impressive.'

Peter put the plates and bottle down on the coffee table and went back to the kitchen for cutlery and pepper.

'The way they are all looking out to sea is quite unnerving though.'

'Yes, that's the point I think, it's called "Another Place",' shouted Peter from the kitchen.

'Oh.'

On his return Maria was now inspecting his large DVD collection and picking out 'Syriana', she asked, 'Peter can we just be normal this evening? Say, watch a movie, just forget about all the weird stuff and relax whilst we can?'

'That's fine with me,' said Peter trying not to sound too relieved, 'but are you sure you want to watch that? It's pretty heavy, complicated stuff.'

'Yes, I need something involving.'

They ate with their plates on their laps. As the movie unfolded, Maria was quieter and whilst she drank more than her fair share, she lacked the recklessness of earlier. After finishing their food, she brought her feet up on the side of the sofa and snuggled against him. He in turn put his arm around her, trying not to concentrate on the feel and the scent of her body. A body that was now so close, he was finding it extremely difficult to follow the convoluted plot.

'Peter?' she started.

'Yes?'

A pause and then, 'What the fuck is going on in this film?'

She looked up at him; he looked down at her cute grinning face and he had to kiss her.

'It'll take a long time to explain,' he replied smiling.

'Well, let us forget it then and go to bed.'

With that Maria leapt up and made to the bedroom, taking off her top as she went.

It had just gone four when Peter was woken by Maria muttering to herself. She felt very warm against him, a bit too warm, so he removed some of the duvet to help cool her down and carefully got up and made his way to the kitchen for some water.

On his return she appeared even more restless, and he could tell something was wrong even in the dim light from the hallway. He opened the door wider and was shocked by what he saw: one side of her face, the closest side to him, appeared red and swollen, her forehead beaded with sweat, whilst the rest of her face looked drawn and cold, bones visible through blue translucent skin.

'It is too deep, too deep, I cannot go there!'

Still asleep Maria had started to shout. It took some time for Peter to wake her and then when she came around, she was confused and frightened; her eyes scanned the room attempting to recognise and remember where she was.

Eventually she settled and apologised saying, 'Sorry I woke you, was I very loud? What was I saying?'

'I was awake already,' Peter replied, 'but your face?'

She reached up and touched it gently and replied 'It is tender. I suppose it looks terrible. As I said yesterday, one side is swollen whilst the other feels numb. Do not worry, Peter. It will subside soon. I just have to get moving, redistribute the fluids.'

She rose to her feet gingerly and hobbled off to the bathroom.

He was making some coffee when Maria came to join him in the kitchen. She looked tired, but her face was much better and she had changed into her now dry jeans and T-shirt. As Peter handed her a coffee, she attempted to kiss him on the cheek, but somehow the easy friendship of last night had been replaced by an awkwardness that hung in the air about them.

They sat on opposite sides of the kitchen table, sipping their coffee quietly, each occupied with their own thoughts. Maria spoke first.

'It is quite scary is it not, the physical stuff?' She gestured to her face. 'All the rest, the sea and the like, is easy to brush off, a state of mind, a depression, but not the swelling. That is rather too real.'

'I'm sorry Maria. I'm tired.' Peter took another slug of coffee. 'Yes I suppose it was worse than I'd thought. Did it really coincide with the tide?'

'Yes and last night was a big one.'

She looked at Peter, who was just looking at his coffee, either vacantly or thinking things he didn't want her to see; she suspected the latter. Perhaps filling the silence would stop him thinking too much.

'I have tried to work it out, but it does not make much sense. You know all life has come from the sea? Well, I get the feeling that my body, its blood, plasma and whatever other fluids are in there, has forgotten it's no longer part of the sea and that it is desperate to get back to it. I believe I am actually having tides within my body.'

Maria was right; Peter was busy feeling sorry for himself. There was always a catch somehow, but he looked up after she had finished talking. Not having paid much attention, he grunted non-committally and said, 'If I'm to keep an eye on you, then we need to go and get some of your gear. Later though, we should wait till it's light.'

'I'm not holding you to anything you know,' replied Maria and seeing no response, went on, 'and to be honest, I would rather go back by myself, sort out what clothes I need, water the plants. It will take a few hours, so I would rather go now. I am over the worst and will not be affected again for a little while.'

'OK, if you're sure that's what you want.'

'Yes I am. A bit of space would do me good too, so I will see you soon OK?' Without another word she grabbed her jacket and left.

*****

A quietness descended on the flat as Peter finished his coffee looking at the door through which Maria had left. He collected the plates and glasses from last night's supper, did the washing up and checked he had the necessaries in for scrambled eggs for when she got back. Placing the DVD back into its case and the case back in its alphabetical place, he looked around his living room and whilst now there was little evidence of Maria, there was still an echo; a tangible feeling of her absence. Life and excitement had been to this place and now it seemed flat and dead in comparison.

He sat on the couch, flicked on the television, settled down to catch up on the news and before long had fallen asleep.

He awoke with a start and checked his watch to find it was almost eight. Maria had been gone for hours, so she should be back soon. He switched off the TV and rising from the sofa went to make some fresh coffee. He sat at his desk, turned on his laptop and whilst waiting for it to boot, he picked up yesterday's print out. He could make out that her mother had disappeared on the 20th March and realised that this was exactly nineteen years ago today.

Peter opened up his browser to search for more information on tides and found hundreds of pages on the topic. Perhaps here was the key to Maria's sickness. But where was Maria? Why wasn't she back?

He soon found out that the vernal equinox occurs on about the 20th March and is associated with exceptionally strong tides, known as equinoctial spring tides. He pondered on the fact that one of the biggest tides of the year would happen today. Last week he wouldn't have been interested, but now he wondered why people weren't kept informed of such important events. Maria had been telling him how her condition had been growing worse; perhaps it was all building up to this equinox and some sort of crisis.

Two clicks later and Peter was hit with a dread that snatched at his stomach. He had stumbled onto a thing called the Metonic cycle. Here was the link between the mother and the daughter and all the confirmation that Peter needed. Today was indeed the crunch and he had just let her go off on her own. He reread the text several times: 'The Metonic cycle, a period of nineteen years after which the new and full moons return to the same day of the year.'

Today was the first Metonic anniversary of her mother's death. The tides, the Earth, the moon and the sun, in fact it seemed the whole damned solar system was out to get her, and he had no idea where she was.'

He lit up a cigarette and tried to think. He didn't know where she lived and had no way of contacting her; the only thing he had was the shelter. If she didn't return to his flat, then perhaps she'd go there. Peter looked at his watch and did a bit of mental arithmetic. Low tide, Maria's shelter appointment wouldn't be till after ten this morning. By eight-thirty, there was still no sign of Maria, and whilst there was a chance that she had just fallen asleep, he doubted it. Peter had a shower; for some reason, he always felt he could cope better when clean. He then forced himself to make some breakfast and had some more coffee and yet another cigarette.

It was time to go. He would be early but he just couldn't wait any longer. He felt that if he could only get her through today, she would be safe. He reached the shelter and looked out. The sea was not to be seen, and the beach, whilst not as empty as on previous occasions, still held only a scattering of dog walkers.

Sat on the bench, Peter could feel something strange in the air, an absence, a sense of waiting. The sea was too far away, creating a vacuum of space and a palpable tension. He felt the sea was stretched to its limit and was ready to snap forward, releasing its waters back up the sands. It was as if the whole Earth had inhaled a massive breath but was only holding it with difficulty and soon it would exhale with a terrible ferocity.

The seagull wasn't there and Maria never arrived.

It took some time for Peter to accept this. He went over the tide times in his head. He knew she should have been there so he gave her another half an hour, just in case he was wrong. But he knew he wasn't.

Peter needed to be doing something so he started to walk, south under the pier and then by the empty funfair. If Maria had wanted to avoid him, there were plenty of other shelters, but the sands stretch for over fifteen miles and soon the futility of the task overwhelmed him and he stopped.

He decided to retrace his steps and pass by the café where they had shared a late breakfast.

She wasn't at the café. He went back to his flat. She wasn't there either.

He hung up his fleece, picked up today's junk mail from the floor, walked to his desk and started to file away papers that had accumulated there. He picked up the portfolio and saw the photographs Maria had been so interested in; it was worth a try.

He slammed his front door shut and started running to the station. He needed to move quickly, but everything was frustrating him, his unfit body and the queue at the ticket office. Nobody knew or understood his situation; even the train obstinately remained at the platform for fifteen minutes. It was a slow train and at each stop the sliding doors would open, pause for a few minutes and then close again, perfectly timed for the convenience of non-existent passengers.

When the train arrived, Peter was up and out onto the platform quickly; a couple of seconds of orientation and he was walking towards the beach. Being off the train and actually doing something helped and he started to breathe again. He arrived at the shore suddenly. In Southport there's a build-up, an increase in seaside paraphernalia as you get closer, the promenade, the pier head, the lake, the miniature train, and then the funfair: one knows the sea is coming. In Crosby, one goes through a tidy suburb, turn a leafy corner and it suddenly opens out to an almost overwhelming space of sand and sky that feels out of place after a mile or so of closeting privet hedges and tidy lawns.

He walked across a small green, and down to the seawall, the sand and Gormley's figures ahead of him. The sea is usually closer here than in Southport but on that day, it was still little more than a smudge. The distances of the sands were magnified by the human scale of the statues and the people amongst the statues created their own silhouettes, further multiplying their number. Peter walked along the sea wall looking at all these figures. The further out they were, the more difficult it was to differentiate between art and reality and to begin with, he couldn't see anyone out there but statues. Slowly though their movement betrayed them and once his eye was in focus most could be removed from consideration quickly; they were too tall, too male or too something else; others however took longer to dismiss. About half a mile away he saw someone, standing still, looking out to sea, their arms open to embrace the wind. He started to run, but he wasn't nearly fit enough and after only a few minutes, he had to stop and walk until close enough to shout her name. Then the figure turned and looked at him. It wasn't Maria.

He wasn't giving up yet and in the distance, he saw two figures together, both resolutely still, water gathering at their feet, both looking out to that 'Other Place.' He stared intently, but from this distance it was impossible to say whether the shorter one was Maria or not so he started towards them. Too tired to run, especially after the last disappointment, he could only walk, avoiding the wide snakes of sea water making their way up the beach. Progress was painfully slow and the sea was almost to the figures' knees and still they looked out, and still he was too far away to be sure. But as he got closer, whilst one figure remained still, he could tell the other was occasionally looking down and shifting their feet, and now it was looking a lot more like Maria.

He started to run again, splashing through the water that had by now encircled him. Eventually he got within fifty yards and shouted her name.

'Maria!'

She looked around.

He moved closer but between them was a fast-flowing river of encroaching sea water. Peter tried to cross but within a few yards the cold water was grabbing his legs and he was having immense trouble keeping his feet firmly on the sand. He stopped, the water slapping at his thighs.

'Maria, don't do this!'

'How did you find me?'

'That doesn't matter. Listen, today is the worst day. Get through it and things will improve. I promise.'

'Was it the photographs?'

'Yes. Come on Maria, let's get back.'

'Are they not magnificent? Gormley understands. He knows there is Another Place.'

'No, he doesn't. It's just a name he made up.' It was getting difficult to hear each other over the breaking waves.

In front of him Maria was holding onto a statue, but Peter had no such support and as the water rose he was finding it increasingly difficult to remain standing.

'Peter, it was good to meet you. I am sorry we did not have longer.'

On hearing that Peter lost his footing and fully immersed he swam as hard as he could, attempting to reach Maria, whose head was just above the water.

'Maria!' he shouted, but his view of her was now intermittent as he moved up and down on the waves; on a crest he could see her, but then had to wait, faced with a three-foot wall of dark grey water. The tide was rushing in. This was the biggest tide of the year and Peter couldn't stop it.

'Maria!' he shouted again and with one last effort he got a little nearer to her. She was now holding Gormley by the head, her legs splayed out in front of her. A few yards further out was a seagull, floating serenely, just watching and waiting.

She looked out to the horizon and with a big breath shouted back to Peter.

'Peter this is wrong. I am not ready. Help me!' Maria lost her grip and she was gone.

Peter started to search for her, but the current was too strong. He was tiring rapidly. His jeans, tight against his legs, were sucking the heat and the life out of him. From the top of a wave, he had one last look and then turned towards the shore.

He knew he wasn't going to make it; his legs were useless, incapable of movement, just a drag. He started coughing, taking in as much water as air with each desperate breath and stupidly counting. A drowning man goes under three times; he was up to seven. He was cold, so very cold. As his efforts weakened, however, the less he cared. He felt comforted by the inevitability of it all, the fatality of the situation. He coughed less and less and as a wave of fatigue swept over him, he allowed himself to close his eyes; he could sleep now.

The sea was rocking and caressing him, back and forth, up and down; he was floating in the ultimate cradle, an isotonic resting place, a return home. Peter knew everything was well with the world. The moon pulled the tides and the tides were the lungs of the Earth, their endless harmonic motion, the breath of the planet.

Bang.

'Wake up! My mother is dead.'

Bang.

'Wake up! There are no such things as mermaids.'

Bang.

With silted eyes, Peter saw Maria's fist once again smashing into his chest.

Bang.

'All right, I'm awake!' he shouted silently.

*****

On a warm summer evening, Peter and Maria sat on the sea wall, watching Gormley's men appear one by one, their nature exposed by the retreating tide.

In the months following those events, Maria had found it difficult to describe the intense need she'd experienced and somehow this lack of words had made it more difficult to remember, that lack of memory reducing the solidity of the events, the time becoming more dreamlike than real.

They were both silent. There was no longer any talk of the sea or her mother's death. Nothing would be achieved by discussing it further. The sea had welcomed Peter and it had rejected her.

There were other important things now. Maria was pregnant. She carried a daughter, growing safe and secure within her own special bubble of brine.

And this was their last visit to the shore; they were moving to Wolverhampton. They had discussed this move calmly, without reference to residual fears, only an unspoken acknowledgement that it was for the best.

They nodded to each other, stood up, turned their backs on the sea and walked away.

At seven forty-eight, Maria's child turned to face west.

In the End There's Only You

Vicky Turrell

I am on my own staring out of the window. I am on my own, even though there are people all around me. It is raining.

The young girl brings me my pot of tea for one. The tide is going out.

I pour my tea from the white pot into the white cup and sip quietly. Then I look out of the window again. A mist smothers the view.

There's a young girl opposite me snuggling and laughing with her boyfriend.

There's a family planning what to do now it is raining. They settle for the cinema and run off in a hurry, as fast as the raindrops racing down the window.

The young couple grab their jangling hotel keys and smooch off.

It is getting dark. The café is closing.

The lights go out – and so do I.

On the Cloud

Trixie Roberts

My friend, Brenda, called today. She usually does on a Wednesday after she's been to the market. I was really pleased she'd stopped at Simon's shop and bought some of his fresh pies; otherwise we'd have had nothing for lunch. I'd run out of time to do any baking as I'd spent all morning trying to work out how to use this new mobile phone my grandson, Jake bought me. He knows all about the latest gadgets, phones and tablets and talks about music by streaming. When he was here at the weekend I said,

'But Jake, streaming is a way of selecting children for classes in school and tablets are what I get from the doctor.'

'You should call them pills, Nan, to save you getting confused but not *the* pill mind,' and he laughed.

'What do you know about *the* pill, young man?'

'Lots,' he says, 'We did research before Jessica went on it.' Jessica's his girlfriend.

'This phone's easy, Nan. You'll soon get the hang of it. You need to have it with you at all times, especially now you're getting out and about more since your knee operation. Just in case.'

'Just in case of what?' I said.

Without turning a hair he replied, 'We don't want you having another fall and not being able to get help.'

Jake means well and he tries really hard to get me to understand how to use the phone but it's going to take a lot of practice.

When Brenda arrived, I could smell the fresh pies.

'I'm so glad you brought those pies; I've had no time to bake this morning.'

'Well, I nearly didn't as there was such a queue but I couldn't resist the smell as they came out of the oven. I got some of those biscuits you like too – the ones like a currant sandwich – Vivaldi biscuits. Anyway, you could have texted me on that new phone of yours to remind me.'

'Oh, I've not got that far yet, Brenda. I'm still working out how to turn it on!'

'Come here, I'll help,' she said and in no time she'd got it going and was trying to explain how it does its tricks. This is the point where I'd rather be doing something else so I went to put the kettle on for tea before the pies went cold.

'You're very good at this, Brenda,' I said when I dared to creep back into the sitting room.

'Oh, not really. Young Sally tries to teach me something new each time she visits, so a few things have sunk in but I only want to use my phone to call and send text messages.'

Sally is Brenda's granddaughter. Like Jake, she's not only a tech wizard but they both seem to be surgically attached to their phones. Brenda said,

'Sally is never without hers, she's either talking to it, listening to it, typing on it or taking photos of herself, her friends and heaven knows what else with it. It's like an affliction.'

'You mean, addiction,' I suggested.

'Whatever,' Brenda muttered. 'I asked Sally, "What happens to all those pictures? How do they fit on to that tiny phone?"' She said, "Oh, I don't let them take up space on my phone, Gran. I send them to the cloud. They're all on the cloud."'

'On the cloud?' I said, puzzled.

'Yes, Dolly. On the cloud. I know, I know. It's a waste of time asking these kids any questions because the answers don't make any sense.'

'But, shouldn't that be *in* the cloud?'

'Apparently not.'

'But they could fall off,' I said.

'Well, yes,' said Brenda, 'I suppose it's just a way of speaking. Like in hospitals when they say someone's "On the ward." That's silly too. We all know they're *in* the ward, usually *in* a bed, *in* a room called the ward but we say "On the ward." Perhaps *on* the cloud is the same thing and they're really *in* the clouds.

'But where do these photos go when it's a clear sunny day? And what would happen on a bad day if there's a cloudburst? Would everyone's photos come falling down? Where would they land?'

Brenda laughed.

'Well, I'd go out and gather them up and see what other folks are up to, although endless pictures of other people's weddings would get a bit tedious. I'd like to see what our Sally's up to when she's out with her friends.'

'And,' I added, 'there's that seedy looking guy up the street who, I'm told, photographs young women in his front room. They would be revealing. I wonder if we could get Jack Sharp, you know, the head of the Planning Committee. I wonder if anyone's thought to hide a camera in that hotel at the back of Viaduct Street where, everyone says, he takes his secretary.'

'Oh, that would be great ammunition to force a change at the council, or – maybe – material for bribery. If only we could get those pictures down from that cloud. Eh, Dolly is that tea brewed yet? Those pies will be cold.'

'Never mind, Brenda. I'll just pop them *on* the microwave.'

After we'd eaten our pies, Brenda started to give me a lesson in how to use my phone to send text messages. I began to get the hang of it but it kept showing the wrong words even when I was sure I'd typed the right ones.

'Oh, that's called 'predictive text,' said Brenda, 'and it's a right nuisance. It thinks it knows better than you, what you want to say. The oddest words come out. I was texting Sally the other day and asked her if she knew *Alice in Wonderland.* She texted me back and said, 'Where's Sunderland, Grab?' I think she meant

'Gran.' Apparently, you can switch that off so it only shows what you really type but I haven't got that far yet.'

We carried on typing and I sent her a text that said, 'Your tea's gone cold.'

It's not only the phone that gets its words wrong, Brenda sometimes gets hers mixed up too.

'Did I tell you about my neighbour, Janet?' she said after she had drunk her cold tea.

'No, but I can see you're going to.'

'Well, she met a bloke on the internet ...'

'Hang on, Brenda. Wait. Wait. How do you meet someone on the internet? Arrange a date on a cloud?'

'Don't ask me, Dolly. I suppose you go for a meal at a virtual restaurant.' She must have seen my look. 'Never mind, Dolly, let's not go into that. I don't know how you can get to know someone you can't see or hear.'

'Yes and what if these couples do eventually meet and they're nothing like they imagine. I suppose it's no worse than a blind date. Anyway, what happened to Janet?'

'They communicated by text – for ages but then he cooled off. Janet wondered if he had lost interest or if he was suffering from text-ile dysfunction.'

'And ...' I said to Brenda, 'another thing I've noticed is how careful you have to be with your fingers on these tiny buttons.'

'Oh, you're right. Just when you think you're progressing nice and steady, it takes you by surprise and sends the message before you're ready. Maybe that's what happened to Janet's bloke? Whoosh ... premature communication.'

The Cannibals of Nesscliffe Hill

Wendy Lodwick Lowdon

Mary Barnet was dressed, clothed in several layers of woollen garb due to the cold, and was already in the salon although it was at least half an hour before the arranged time for Jane Lytton's arrival. There was so much to discover and to discuss. Mary paced the floor impatiently and considered what she already knew.

The news of the rescue of a reclusive and debased family found living in a cave on Nesscliffe Hill had been known in the neighbourhood for more than a week. Initially the two men, one woman and two children were housed in the lean-to at the back of The Black Gate Public House in Oswestry. Their desperate need for clothing and sustenance had been well-publicised and it had seemed the Primitive Methodists, led by one of their many ranters, would nourish the family but use their destitution to further their cause. Their influence had been thwarted by the vicar, who had claimed the family as one of his flock on the basis of where they were found. He had duly visited the family with some of the largesse donated by a number of Christian women. Mary herself had sent a small basket of biscuits, half a dozen boiled eggs and a tunic suitable for a young boy. She knew Jane had supplied woollen stockings and pairs of clogs.

At the last church service, which had been extremely well attended, the vicar had been full of praise for the donors but had said nothing about the manner of the reception of their generosity. In fact, he had said little more than that they must pray for the souls of those rescued this winter from certain death.

Mary had been apprised by her husband soon after that unsatisfactory Sunday service some of what Reverend Mitchell Hepple, vicar of the Parish, had said to his dear friend, Squire

George Barnet, about his eventual visit to the family immured in the rear of The Black Gate for several days. He had delegated one of the churchwardens to make daily visits with food until his own visit could no longer be delayed. A guard had been appointed to prevent the family trying to leave as they seemed reluctant to appreciate their surroundings.

'George, they smelled abominably of grease, wood ash and offal. Not surprising, of course, but still most unpleasant. They were dressed in layers of stained motley clothes and the woman wore pantaloons under her smock and a man's jacket over it.' Mitchell Hepple's report had taken place while relaxing in front of the fire after sharing a generous supper with his host; he had been drinking port and paying his way with a bit of tittle tattle. He knew most of what he told his friend would be relayed to his friend's wife and thence to the parish. 'Bowls of water and a piece of lye soap were provided at my instigation, a sensible action before giving them clothing, but they were thrown to the ground by the taller and thinner man in a passion. He gobbled and growled at me like an animal. I tell you, George, I was glad the guard was between us.'

The vicar, Mitchell Hepple, had not said the thin man had thrown the water at him and his jacket had been splashed and his new brogues stained by the assault. He had also not informed the Squire that, although he could not understand the utterances so infested as they were by dialect and idiom, the guard had been able to translate the speech.

'He says you are liar and a devil in dress-up.' Tom Wall, the guard, tried to keep his tone neutral. 'He says you told him to trust the Squire would do right by him. He didn't but instead supported wicked Farmer Jarndon.' In the dank room, the baby had begun to scream; never-the-less, Tom had continued with his translation. 'He says you beat him from your door when he came to you for help afterwards.'

Mitchell Hepple shuddered as he remembered the way the guard and the adult members of the family had stared at him.

The baby had continued to scream. The vicar had been jumped into a denial. 'I did not.'

'You did,' said the guard and the shorter man together. 'I remember it well,' the guard had declared. 'That was the time you preached about how sinful it was not working and electing to live like a beggar. You told us to drive the idle from your door and not to encourage beggary by the giving of alms.'

Mitchell Hepple had felt isolated and affronted. In the warm comfort of the Squire's library, he had sought to reposition himself as the beleaguered benefactor. 'The squealing baby made it almost impossible to think,' he had told George. 'That inadequate mother did little to soothe it at first.' He took another large gulp of his second glass of port. 'And then she just flopped out a breast and fed the brat.' George had given an appreciative chuckle. 'No modesty at all; she was absolutely brazen. She even blamed you!' George garbled a few words in a throaty disapproval. 'She stared at me and hissed like a veritable snake. It was a truly depressing experience.'

The vicar had not related to his friend that he understood the penetrating whisperings of the woman all too well. She said her child had died of want for lack of the charity and justice he had promised. She had cursed him. She had pronounced that any existing progeny he had would die; that sterility would ensure no others and that he himself would die of a painful wasting disease. The vicar, a superstitious man, had been very shaken by the fervour with which she had delivered her hex. 'I took out my book of prayer,' he told George, 'and the tall man spat upon me. I fear this family to be heathen in mind and practice.' He had chosen not to relate his fear of contagion from the cadaverous and consumptive man and his fear that the seeds of her curse had been immediately enacted. 'Still, I will endeavour to do my duty and take further donations to them.' Secretly, he had determined to keep as much back as he could and to send his maid to The Black Gate in his stead.

Mary, within a day, had heard most of what George had heard concerning the case of the ungrateful, filthy family.

However, since the vicar had broken bread with George, there had been further developments and it was about these, which had resulted in the family being moved to Oswestry prison, that Mary was restlessly waiting to be apprised in detail by Jane. She heard the crunch of the brougham's wheels on the gravel and hovered by the salon door. She tapped her foot impatiently while Jane was greeted by the butler and the front door was closed. She heard the carriage drive away because Jane was staying for luncheon and would not require it for some hours.

At last, the door was opened and Jane was ushered in. She and Mary raced through the formalities, Mary dismissed her butler with the instruction to serve food at twelve-thirty and then the two women were finally alone in the parlour. They perched themselves on the chaise lounge, because the heavy material of their dresses and the corseting prevented lounging, and rushed into speech.

'Cannibalism!' they exclaimed together.

'I can hardly believe it,' exclaimed Mary.

'But you must,' said Jane emphatically. ' My Bingo,' Jane always referred to Barney Lytton thus, 'has assured me the evidence is irrefutable.'

'Tell me all,' implored Mary. 'I have heard but snippets and I have not been able to speak to anyone from whom I could gather detail and George is being uncharacteristically tight-lipped. I am sure my maid knows more than I and it has been so frustrating and difficult not to beg information of her.'

Jane laughed but then quickly became serious in her demeanour so she could properly describe the latest news concerning the barbaric practices concerning the family who had lived in a cave and were now incarcerated in the dark of Oswestry prison. 'Shortly after their rescue, the Sherriff had instructed two of his men to investigate the cave and the environs more thoroughly but inclement weather and reluctance on the part of the men to return to such an inhospitable part of the county had delayed their dreadful discovery.' Jane related to an agog Mary how Ben Honiley had become agitated and suspicious when he found a couple of large bones near to the cave and how he had declared them to be human. 'Bingo says he is an ex-soldier and he has had experience in seeing human bones from which the flesh had been stripped.'

'Human bones!' Mary squeaked as she raised her scented handkerchief to her nose.

'Human bones!' confirmed Jane. 'And in the cave,' Jane continued with her iteration, 'the men found evidence that the bones were those of a gentleman because of the quality of the scraps of cloth.'

'They ate a gentleman?' Mary gasped.

'So it would appear,' replied Jane.

'A whole gentleman!' Mary repeated in a pale voice.

Jane choked back a laugh by pinching her leg. She knew her friend had in mind the corpulence of most of the gentlemen of their acquaintance.

'Eventually the Sherriff's men found a wallet with a letter of introduction to the local apothecary concerning an ailment of a delicate nature from a doctor in Montgomery but the poor man never reached Shrewsbury.'

They paused to shudder and to exclaim. They shared their imaginings of how the savage attack on the lone horseman had occurred. They commented on the desolation of the forested land between Oswestry and Shrewsbury and how it lapped the road along which few travelled without company and those also usually employed a tough with a mastiff and a cudgel. They spoke in thrilled voices about how the gentleman must have begged for mercy from the dreadful killers and how they had ignored his pleas. In whispers they considered the horror of his last moments as they fell upon him and devoured him alive.

Then Jane dragged the conversation back to reality. The Sherriff had told her dear Bingo that he had sent a message to the poor gentleman's people. Jane was unable to tell Mary, because she did not yet know of the substance of the exchange the Sherriff had had with the cannibals.

The guard, now in situ at Oswestry prison and less sympathetic since the gruesome discovery, agreed for a small fee to liaise between the Sherriff and the tall thin man who spoke for them all. Indeed, the boy who was scarcely more than a toddler, had not spoken at all since the family had been imprisoned and lay bundled in all the clothing the adults could spare. The tall man, husband and father it turned out, claimed they had found the gentleman dead and his horse long gone. 'We'd have et the horse for sure but it were well and away.' The Sherriff felt a qualm because he knew his neighbour had found a horse, a pretty mare saddled and bridled, early in the winter and had not searched hard for the owner.

'We was starving. I'd no luck with the snares. Sure, the man had money in his wallet but where were the likes of us able to spend silver shillings before the spring fayre? We'd no choice but to eat 'im,' the thin man declared.

The Sherriff rocked back on his heels and then stepped a little closer to the bars that enclosed the family from the cave. 'No choice? No choice! You could have come into the poorhouse. You could have sought charity!'

'Like to die of your charity,' hissed the woman. 'We'd heared there were old folk and young who died of want this winter. We decided we'd rather eat the meat provided.'

'But why not a sheep?' the guard, Tom Wall, suddenly shouted at them. 'Why choose to eat a man?' The baby, shocked out of sleep, began to sob and wail.

'Morrell got transported for stealing a sheep. You made us stand at the crossroads to watch the prison wagon pass that would take him to the convict ships. He had five childer he was desperate to feed but you banished him anyway. We figured we was better to eat the man what was dropped by our door.'

Meanwhile Jane and Mary had agreed to lay aside the stomach-turning topic of cannibalism and to speak of fashion and local entertainments over their meal. As soon as they were again ensconced in the salon with the fire refreshed with logs and charcoal, however, they resumed their conversation about the cannibals.

'I heard they ate a child.' Mary was really feeling reluctant to venture on to this topic but to not know would be worse.

Jane said, 'Indeed. Bingo could hardly bear to tell me. They found the Miller's child's dress in the cave.'

'Oh,' sighed Mary. 'That poor mite! Oh, there was a hue and cry for a day or two when she disappeared. The vicar gave a couple of sermons about God's will and the example of Job and the necessity of returning to one's duty, in this case milling flour.'

'Yes, and they had the consolation of still having four. The Miller's wife still wailed a lot despite being told to count her blessings and I see she has been too sick to come to church for the rest of the year.'

'Everyone thought she'd fallen into the mill race and been swept away down the Perry River. But now they think she was eaten?' Mary was appalled and actually paled as she uttered these words.

'Well, Bingo says the Sherriff reported they had not eaten her.' Jane sighed as she felt obliged to report the denial. 'But their depravity is so deep that any right-thinking person must think they are lying.'

The Sherriff had not thought they lied. He had asked the cave family once more about the Miller's child and the discovery of a grave. 'We didn't kill her. I done found the clothes. They was ripped and in a heap by the old oak. Still they did to wrap our boy and the babe. She never needed them no more. The cold had already killed our eldest. We buried the little girl as soon as the ground had softened.'

'You claim you did not murder and eat the Miller's child?'

'There are other monsters what live in this place,' sneered the thin man. 'Him what killed the girl and Squire George Barnet who listened to none about the true nature of his rich neighbour.'

'The Squire? Who?'

The thin man named the murderer of the Miller's child as Mr Jarndon, a wealthy farmer.

'Why? What?' The Sherriff was beginning to feel he had lost control of the conversation. He wished he could ask the guard to leave but he could barely understand a word without his assistance, the accent of the thin man was so thick. 'Jarndon is dead; he died when he took a fall from his horse! You are besmirching the reputation of a landowner of the county.'

The thin man began to rock backwards and forwards. Spittle formed in frothy bubbles at the corner of his mouth. 'Jarndon killed that little girl. We found her body 'cos we saw him riding out of a copse. Oh, and we've had reasons a plenty afore that to know he was a wicked man. Ask any of his tenants!'

A dreadful silence fell as the Sherriff scrambled to take in the scope of the horrors before him. 'It's nonsense,' he suddenly declared. 'You are a cannibal and offended most foully and must have no moral or legal right to make any sort of accusation against one of our own.'

'Oh, he was a killer all right. He killed that girl and he right enough has killed us with his robbery and cruelty so we had nothing. You and Squire Barnet upheld his claim to our land, you protected that monster and you says he could take our land.'

The Sherriff stared in astonishment at the filthy emaciated man, whose voice was loud and fierce and who pressed against the bars of the cell as if he would push himself through.

'I be Walter Pick, Sherriff. I be Walter Pick! We ate a fat stupid man who fell dead off his horse.' Abruptly, the thin man lunged and thrust a grappling hook of a limb through the bars and grabbed the Sherriff by the wrist, dragged his hand to his mouth and chewed on the soft flesh.

While the Sherriff shrieked and tried to tear his hand free, Tom Wall thumped and thumped on any part he could reach through the bars with his cudgel until the thin man fell bleeding and half-conscious to the floor.

Later, his hand bandaged and weak from a cupping, the Sherriff told Bingo Lytton about the family called Pick. He said he thought they had left the region some two years ago after Jarndon had bought their land.

Bingo had related the further particulars of the case to his wife, Jane, several days after her visit to Mary Barnet. 'It seems the Pick family were cheated out of their land, though the Sherriff maintains he was assured by the Squire that Farmer Jarndon had paid the family properly. Jarndon was mad to have the canal run through his property for the rents and trade benefits he thought would accrue and Walter Pick was the fly in the ointment.'

'I remember the family,' Jane replied wonderingly. 'I saw them many times at our church and a neat and tidy family they were; very demure in their manner and voice. I thought there were two older children.'

'It appears one died.'

'They didn't eat her too!'

Bingo shook his head. 'No but they killed Jarndon. I spoke to them in person, well with the brother, Brent, as Walter Pick is knocked about so much, he can no longer speak. I think the boy is dying but the doctor refuses to attend.'

Jane focused on another issue. 'Jarndon was crushed in a hunting accident and died miserably of his injuries a week later.'

'It seems the horse and rider were brought down deliberately and then the horse was induced to roll on Jarndon. After he was dead, they desecrated his grave and dismembered his body. Do you remember all the fuss about badgers in the graveyard. It was the Pick family seeking further vengeance. Even his death couldn't satisfy them. I think that was the moment their monstrous proclivities overcame them.'

'Do you think …? Jarndon and, and …' Jane stuttered her question.

'Oh, no my dear, of course he didn't,' soothed her husband, who privately thought Jarndon had been justly accused. 'His family had been here for generations, although not for much longer as I hear his family are selling up and emigrating to North America.'

'And all because of the baseless accusations of the cannibals! Such appalling behaviour! They will hang?'

'Oh, yes. They are sure to be found guilty of heinous crimes. Oh, indeed yes. They will be taken to London for execution.'

When Jane Lytton and Mary Barnet met again, for luncheon a couple of weeks after the trial, their discussion centred around whether they could attend the execution. It was such a long and arduous trip and even with a variety of further entertainments to consider, both women decided against the venture. They spoke in hushed whispers of the dreadful scene as the adults were conveyed to the prison cart to commence their journey to London. The boy had indeed died and the babe was taken forcibly from the mother though she screamed and wailed and fought like a banshee. No one in the parish would bear with the babe for fear of contamination so she was sent to a family in Chester, where she would be strictly raised.

'And the Sherriff has had his arm amputated. The bite festered. He is still in precarious health. I have noticed the vicar coughs often. I have implored my dear Bingo, despite the relationship meant to exist between him and his spiritual advisor, to avoid the man. Jane looked at her friend defiantly.

Mary shuddered. 'I too am resolved to advise George to limit his contact with Michael Hepple as well.' In her heart she was chillingly afraid that she may be too late with her admonition. The vicar had been a visitor just the previous day and he and George had spent a long time in the study.

'Oh Mary,' sighed Jane, 'It does make it very quiet to have so many of our company depleted by illness, death or absence.'

Crossing Paths at Christmas

Kirstie Edwards

Once, long ago, my Christmas had accidentally become commercial. People spent money on gifts and paper and cards to give to one another and gaudy decorations to hang around their homes. Relations who hated each other came together to eat turkey with gravy and vegetables, and they pretended to care, sitting round hideously dressed pine trees with tacky, flashing lights. Televisions would blast adverts with short pauses for programmes and huge chocolate tins would be passed around, with only hard toffees on offer.

But one day, a very strange thing happened. As I walked into Sainsbury's, a woman wearing a Santa's hat gave me a free lucky bag and wished me Happy Christmas. In the bag was a piece of white paper, rolled up with a red ribbon tied round it. Curious, I slipped off the ribbon and opened the scroll. On the paper were the words, 'Look into their hearts.' A woman shouting distracted me.

At the customer service desk, a dragon of a lady with deep wrinkles and straight grey hair poking in random directions was scowling and spitting at a bright young assistant.

'I've been waiting fifteen minutes in this queue,' she screeched. 'Call this service?'

Red reindeer antlers bobbed around merrily on springs attached to the young assistant's headband. The more she tried to nod, the more the antlers bobbed. 'Yes, yes' they bobbed, laughing at the old lady.

But the old lady's voice was not merry; it was mean and harsh and the bobbing antlers annoyed her.

'Yesterday, he bought them,' she spat. 'Only yesterday and look at them now. Heads dropping off and no scent at all. I want them replaced.'

The customer service phone rang and the merry assistant picked it up, apologising to the dragon.

'Charming I call that. Charming. I'm here and you see to someone who's somewhere else.' She banged the flowers down on the counter. The few heads of pearl white roses still clinging to their stems broke away. 'I'll report you, I will.' She stomped over to the magazines counter and pushing through the queue there, asked to see the manager. Impatient shoppers threw their eyes upwards in anger at her queue-hopping. Antler head, bobbing wildly now, quickly replaced the phone and ran over to where the defiant complainant stood.

'Don't you think you can get away with this now that you're afraid I'm going to report you,' the woman screamed. Her gnarled hands still held the bunch of headless stems.

'I'm sorry; I had to take the call. Let me change the flowers for you.'

The manager arrived and asked if he could be of service. He took the elderly lady aside and asked if she would like a seat.

'I don't need to sit. Are you ageist or something?' She was shouting now.

As I watched this scene, two small clouds appeared, one over each of the women, and drizzle started pouring down on them. It was an unusual sight in a shopping store. Alarmed, I looked around to see whether anyone had noticed, but everyone continued with their shopping, dropping cranberry jelly and Bisto into trolleys, punching PIN numbers into card readers, chatting to acquaintances they came across in the aisles. 'Deck the halls with boughs of holly' was chiming through the store. I turned back to see rain splashing off the antlers and drenching the spikey grey hair, but the argument continued, one voice angry, one voice sad and the manager's voice calm, so calm. I walked towards them to touch the rain, and as I did so, I looked into the old lady's eyes.

With that single, unplanned glance, I stepped through a door in the universe, into a small, dark bedsit. There was a gas fire in one corner, with two well-worn armchairs in front of it. In one was an old man, still, with his eyes closed. I was standing in a doorway and next to me was a small kitchen area, with a Formica table, kettle, toaster and a fridge. It was very cold. The fire was not burning and the light was not on. A double bed lined the other side, with old blankets strewn across it. I thought I was dreaming. I thought of my own home, my two children, my lovely wife. Dusk swept round this cold, dark room. I shook my head to wake myself, but I was still there. Frightened now, I called over to the old man, but he didn't hear me. It must be a dream. He was so still, so quiet. Flower heads were sprinkled on the floor around his feet. I walked over and touched him. Stone cold. Hard to the touch and stone cold; he was dead. Panicking now, I ran to the door and called out. But once through the door, I was back at Sainsbury's looking into the heart of the old lady, the old lady who was still standing under her cloud of rain.

I turned to antler head and opened my mouth to speak, but as I looked into her eyes, I was again taken to another place. This time, I was in a hospital, in a private room where monitors were bleeping, and a little girl lay tucked under crisp, sterile-smelling sheets. A man sat by the bed, holding her small hand, resting his head next to her small body. He stood up and dialled a number.

'Daddy's phoning mummy sweetheart,' he said as he punched the digits in. 'Mummy will be so glad to hear the news. She couldn't speak with Daddy before for some reason, but she will be so glad. Alicia's on the mend, aren't you honey?'

Nobody answered his call.

'Mummy mustn't be at her desk. We'll ring again in a moment.' The little girl smiled at her daddy. I looked into her eyes and was taken to a zebra crossing outside a school, where she lay on the ground, bleeding from her head and mothers and children were screaming. I shut my eyes quickly and opened them. The phone was ringing at the customer service desk. The manager was apologising to the old lady, who was still angry about her flowers, and antler head was watching the phone, her fingers fiddling nervously with her wedding ring. The rain continued to pour over both of them.

I walked over to the desk and answered the phone.

'Is she OK?' I asked.

'Who's this?' Alicia's daddy asked.

'I'm a customer. I just answered the phone. Your wife is busy, but you can give me a message.'

There was a confused silence at the other end.

'Is she OK?' I asked again.

'Well yes, she is actually. Thank you. Yes, please give Mary the message. Thank you.' He hung up.

I walked over to Mary with her bobbing antlers. The manager was talking in low tones to her. Her antlers and hair were drenched now. The old lady was choosing new flowers.

'You're always on the phone and that's the second complaint from a customer today, Mary. I'm going to have to put this on file.' He was a tall, blank looking man. He could just as easily have been telling her that he was going to cook baked beans for tea tonight.

But his words affected Mary. She didn't look merry anymore. She looked sad and forlorn. She looked scared. Her eyes were bright. She said nothing.

'I hope you don't mind; I answered the phone. It was ringing,' I butt in. 'It was your husband, Mary. Alicia can come home. She's OK. She's lucky isn't she, I mean after the accident? Did they catch the driver or was it a hit and run?' I asked.

The manager looked at me, raising his eyebrows, confused. I avoided his eyes. He turned to Mary.

'What's this about Alicia? Did she have an accident?' His voice no longer held his calm, detached tone. He frowned, waiting for her to answer. I moved away then. Her manager knew what was going on in her life now, so perhaps he wouldn't feel the necessity to put anything on her file.

I walked over to the old lady. She stood staring at the flowers, where her husband had stood the day before, choosing her anniversary flowers. Flowers which had fallen from her husband's hands, as he sat in his armchair, waiting for her to return from her singing group at church. This was how she had found him, when she did return.

'These are the ones he chose for you,' I said. 'These are what he wanted you to have.' She took the flowers from me, saying 'Yes, that's right.' The anger from her voice was gone; no fight left now. Her spikey hair had lost its spikes in the rain. I put my arm around her.

'Would you like me to come home with you?' I asked. She said she would. So together we returned to her dear husband of fifty-two years. Together we called for a doctor and together we contacted her family. Within an hour, her granddaughter arrived. But before she did, as we sat together in that little bedsit, with the gas fire glowing and hot tea steaming, chatting quietly about her lovely husband, I felt something I hadn't felt for a very long time. The room was filled with love.

You never know what's going on in people's lives, but if you look into their hearts, you might be surprised. And if you look again, you might see the love. If you look really carefully, you might even see when the rain is falling on the people around you.

So is my Christmas still commercial? No. But I'm still spending money on gifts and paper and cards to give and gaudy decorations to hang around our home. I'm glad my relations are coming to eat turkey with gravy and vegetables, and I don't need to pretend I care. We will sit round our hideously dressed pine tree with tacky, flashing lights. Televisions will blast adverts

with short pauses for programmes and I'll take the hard toffees,
if that's all that's left, and I will smile.

Drowned

Ronald Turner

'If you'm gadding off again next Sat'day you can take our Jason with you. He hardly sees his dad these days.'

So Saturday comes. Breakfast time. Sheila scowls at me over the toast. She'd like to resent my weekly disappearance but she's too damned glad to see me go.

Jason, our lad – whatever possessed me to agree to that name – has had his ears plugged into some aural garbage ever since he got up. And this Saturday, he's up five hours earlier than usual so his mood is best not described.

At twelve years old, Jason is plump and pale with fair hair cut so short you'd think at first glance he was as bald as his dad. Of course he wears the obligatory earring. The only thing he's particularly good at is being a pain in the arse. He doesn't want to come with me. I don't want him to come with me. But his mum says he has to, so he must.

We pack our lunch, struggle into extra clothing, pick up the fishing gear – at least I do – and make for the bus stop. Sheila calls after us down the street.

'You look after our Jason mind. I don't want him drowned. And if it gets bad come 'ome. Don't sit there all day in the pouring rain like you usually do, you daft sod.'

It's raining at the moment. The sort of cold, thin drizzle that seems to suit this place. But there's a small break in the clouds to the west, which is promising and the growing brightness gives a sheen to the wet pavements. The Saturday traffic fizzes past.

Jason starts complaining. He's good at that 'an all. The rain's getting down his neck, his bag's too heavy and he can't understand how I can go past a shop without buying summat.

After that crap he listens to all the time, his favourite thing is spending money.

The bus pulls in just as we get to the stop. The driver moans about all our clobber. Seems like it's one of them days when everyone wants to have a good moan. He has another go when I haven't got the exact change for our fares. I'd like to give him a mouthful back but I can't be bothered. I just want to get away.

Soon we're settled snugly at the back of the bus and by the time we move off the sky has got lighter still and it's almost stopped raining. I feel my spirits rising because we're heading in the right direction: that is, out of Pipton.

If you've ever been to Pipton you'll know why I get out of it as often as I can. Half of it, where the factories used to be, looks like an abandoned scrapyard. The other half – where people live – is a pathetic mixture of Victorian back-to-backs and post-war high-rise hovels. So I get out and I usually end up in Bridgeville, which is where we're headed today.

About an hour later, we get off the bus near the bridge and walk down some steps to the towpath. It's stopped raining now but the river is high and flowing fast. Not the best of conditions for fishing. The riverside path is sticky mud.

Jason is silent, astonishingly so. He just plods along behind me. Mind you, I'm carrying all the gear and his bag as well, rather than put up with his whining. But for once he seems to be taking in his surroundings. You don't know how unusual that is. I've often thought of Jason as the kind of lad who, if he climbed Everest, would want a comic to read on the top.

We reach my usual spot about a mile down the path. Jason seems quite interested in all the preparations. At last I'm all set and the sound of the baited hook plopping into the water for the first time is music to my ears. I ease back on my stool, feel in my pocket for my tobacco and make a roll-up. But by the time I've inhaled a couple of times Jason has started to fidget. He starts chucking bits of twig into the river and I tell him to stop. How does he expect me to catch fish if he frightens them off?

There's a few minutes peace then he takes out one of them computer games and if there's one thing that really drives me up the wall it's the inane bleep-bleep noise those things make. That's the kind of sound I come here to get away from. So I tell him to switch it off but he doesn't, so I tell him if he doesn't, I'll chuck it in the river and of course he tells me I just told him off for chucking things in the river. Then he adds that his mum bought him the game and if I threw it away she'd have a fit. I mutter, 'Sod your mum,' under my breath but he hears me and we have a right old ding-dong. This is suddenly interrupted by the disappearance of my float.

However, the little bugger – whatever it was – just takes a quick nibble at the bait and swims away. Jason gets fidgety again. After a while he goes off to explore. I tell him to watch what he's doing and not get drowned or anything, but I'm glad when he's gone. Now I can slip into my usual fishing frame of mind. See, I'm not really bothered whether I catch anything or not. I'm content, absolutely content, just to be here, to be still, to be alone and let my thoughts drift along, like leaves on the water.

*****

The flood water laps right up the edge of Draper's Copse. Our summer cricket pitch has turned into a beach. The valley has become a bay.

'Well,' says Gerald. 'Where's this boat then?'

He turns accusingly to Eric. Little Eric is nine years old but smaller than me at eight. His dad was killed in the Falklands before he was a year old. Now Eric sometimes makes things up, especially about his dad. But this time he has the proof. He opens the old cardboard box and lifts out something wrapped in tissue paper. He unwraps it reverently. Even Gerald whistles with admiration. It's fantastic. A scale model galleon with all the sails and ropes and guns and everything.

'My dad made it,' says Eric proudly. 'Mum says I can have it when I'm older. I pinched it off the top of the wardrobe.'

Now that he's proved his point, Eric would like to wrap up the little galleon and put it back where he got it from, before his mum finds out. But Gerald grabs it.

'It looks OK,' he sneers. 'But I bet it don't sail.'

Eric turns pale and his lips press tightly together but he says nothing as Gerald lowers the galleon onto the water between two molehills. He needn't have worried. The little ship sails magnificently, rising and falling on the gently rippling water, swaying and turning as the light wind catches in its sails. Just like the real thing. I narrow my eyes until all I can see is the little boat and I can imagine it leaving Plymouth on its way to deal with the Spanish Armada. Then Eric lifts the little vessel out of the water and lays it gently on the grass.

Gerald suggests we build a harbour. He is in his element, planning it out, making us fetch and carry. We are all so engrossed in this project that we don't notice the clouds thickening and the breeze getting stronger. By the time we remember the galleon, it has been lifted by a larger ripple and is drifting away on the floodwater, bobbing dangerously on ripples that have become small waves. Water has got onto its deck and it is listing badly. With every second the rising wind carries the stricken galleon further away.

Eric screams and plunges into the water. Gerald gives chase but stops when the water reaches his thighs. None of us can swim. He commands Eric to come back. Eric hesitates, then turns back to his precious boat and splashes on. The water is up to his chest when he catches it. He holds it above his head and we cheer with relief. Suddenly Eric slips and disappears under the water. When his head pops up again, he is twenty yards downstream. Then he disappears again. We hold our breath and watch in horror. He does not reappear. Gerald begins to cry. We all run home, wailing with terror.

*****

Drowned

The year after Eric drowned, my family left the valley and went to live in Pipton. My dad had taken a job at Eccles and Pratt making steel pipes. Much better paid than farm work and none of that 'tied cottage' nonsense. Mum was delighted. Our new home had an inside lavatory, a gas supply and neighbours. And the place was theirs as long as they could pay the rent.

I was heartbroken. Never a day passed without me wishing I was back in the valley. I hated our cramped new house with no view but next door's washing. I hated the crowded streets and the silly park which tried to pretend it was countryside but you mustn't do this or that or else, 'By Order.'

Gradually the pain eased and I got on with growing up. I left school at fifteen and joined my dad at Eccles. I played soccer and darts for local teams. I drank a good deal and discovered girls. One of those girls was Sheila. Soon we were going steady. Then I got her pregnant. In those days if you got a girl pregnant you were expected to marry her, so I did.

At first, we lived with her parents, then we were offered a brand-new council flat. That's where Jason was born and where we still live. Jason grew up, went to school, got bigger, noisier and sillier. Sheila had a hard time giving birth and couldn't have any more kids, so she spoiled rotten the one she had. He became the centre of her world while I was pushed out to the horizon. I can't say I minded much because Sheila had changed. She didn't smile any more, except at Jason. And she didn't talk, instead she whined. She started to smoke, only a few at first, then a packet a day, then more. Her face assumed a permanent frown, from the smoke in her eyes and from worrying about all the things we couldn't afford.

For a couple of years, I went on trying to make it work. I did all the overtime I could get and gave Sheila most of the extra money. She saved until she could afford a little car. When she passed her test, she started going places with Jason. I wasn't included and didn't want to be. That's when the hobbies began.

First it was DIY. But it didn't take long to decorate our tiny flat and put up a few shelves. Then I got an allotment. I began to spend more time away from the flat, digging, planting, hoeing or just watching things grow. But Sheila said she was allergic to pollen and couldn't have flowers in the flat and she wouldn't use the vegetables because they had dirt on them, so I gave up. Next, I took up fishing and started coming back to the valley. I loved it. Not so much for the fish, because I hardly ever caught anything, but for the memories. Those childhood days came back so clearly. Those days before …

*****

By the time we got back to Pipton it was dark and drizzling again. Smoke merged with the low cloud to form a grey ceiling which reflected the orange glow of the streetlights.

Jason had hardly spoken on the way back. His silence and the way he kept glancing at me made me nervous. I was surprised when he said how much he had enjoyed the day and even more surprised when he asked if he could come next time. At first my selfishness made me reluctant, then I managed a smile and suggested that we might get him a rod of his own. He smiled back, then that worried frown returned, reminding me of his mother. Suddenly he asked, 'What did you mean, Dad?'

'Mean? When?'

When I came back and you were still fishing. I was trying to tell you about this bird I'd seen. Really big it was with all these long feathers in its tail. But you didn't seem to hear me. You just kept saying the same thing over and over.'

'Old age, Jay, or the first sign of madness. Anyway, what was it I kept saying?'

'I don't know. Well, I'm not sure. But it sounded a bit like drowned … drowned … drowned.'

The Slugs Are Back

Vicky Turrell

Well, to be honest the slugs never really went away. It was a wet winter with hardly any frosts, so the slugs did not dwindle as they normally do.

If you have a garden, you will know about slugs and the damage they can cause.

Only the other night, I planted out some little seedlings and the next morning when I went to see them, they had half their leaves chewed off. All my hard work – I was so dispirited.

I try not to use slug pellets because I don't want to damage wildlife.

We have thrushes in the garden and their numbers are dwindling fast; they eat slugs and snails, but there are only two thrushes left.

What else eats slugs? Well, we have a hedgehog, a duck and frogs. We normally have plenty of these but this year there have not been any frogs, for some reason, and the hedgehog can only eat so much. It's not enough.

Our duck has gone lame, so is not a lot of use on the 'eating slugs' front.

To add to my woes, I have heard that the Spanish slug is coming to our shores and it is much bigger than our own slug. It lays twice as many eggs and it doesn't mind hot weather – not that we get much, but even so.

What am I to do?

Well, I have heard that slugs are partial to beer, so I bought a bottle of cheap stuff. My plan was to fill dishes with beer, deep enough for slugs to drown in. Then all I had to do was to sit back and wait.

But feeling low about my slug bitten seedlings, I drank the beer myself – just to cheer myself up, you understand.

I forgot about the slugs that night.

But this morning my seedlings have been eaten completely.

Gulp!

The Overlooked

Bernard Pearson

'That's the thing with this type of property; you get fantastic high ceilings,' said the young estate agent looking down at his clipboard. 'No worries about bumping the old noggin,' he said to his client, a tall, gangly, middle-aged man in a dark blue blazer and expensive looking cream-coloured trousers.

'How long has it been on the market?'

'I'm not really sure to be honest; it was with another agent before us.'

'I think it might be just the kind of place we are looking for,' said his client.

His wife, however, seemed less sure. She was attractive, although one might never have guessed it from the way she was dressed in a faded, wrap round cardigan as favoured by tv cops in the nineteen seventies, over a shapeless, brown maxi skirt with her hair tied back in the severest of buns.

'I'm not sure I really like the idea.' She gazed up at the galleried area on the next floor with a raised platform area, which the estate agent called the mezzanine, but was quite obviously where the pulpit had been.

'I happen to know the vendors are open to offers and may be quite flexible. If you get my drift,' the estate agent said helpfully.

'Well, my wife and I are definitely interested.'

'What about the garden?' the woman asked.

'Well, the grounds are wrapped round the property as you'll see.

'Come on honey; imagine the parties we can throw here.'

The idea of a man like her husband holding wild parties amused her.

'Can we take a look outside then?'

To the rear of the property was an area enclosed on one side by the chapel itself and two thirteen-foot high boundary brick walls, while the back of the grounds were bounded by an almost sheer rocky outcrop of the hill above, down which small rivulets of rather sludgy looking water flowed. There was only one small window high up on this side of the building.

'Yes, that was for the organ loft apparently; still easy enough to put in a few windows and the views at the front are to die for,' said the estate agent.

'Will the head stones be removed?'

Besides one of the walls was a row of six smaller than usual gravestones.

'No. As part of any leasehold sale, the purchaser agrees to maintain the area. But, of course, this is reflected in the price.'

The woman pulled her quilted jacket up around her neck as a sleet shower scudded in from the black mountains.

'A bit like a prison exercise yard,' she muttered to herself.

Sarah and Greg Linderman, or as her friends called him, 'The Hot Yank,' had met on a hydroelectric project high up in the Rockies. Sarah was on her gap year working as an intern. He was the programme director, fifteen years her senior and just coming out of an extremely messy divorce. But he had courted her patiently and discretely through university. She had gained a scholarship to one of the Ivy League colleges and even when she opted to do her Masters in London, Greg would travel from wherever he was in the world to be with her, helping her out with course fees. Her friends, while finding him easy on the eye, thought him rather stuffy East Coast, but it was this old fashioned demeanour that Sarah had in those early days found attractive.

Sarah had been preternaturally intelligent from an early age. In both the arts and the sciences, she had excelled. Boyfriends had been low on her priority list. It was not that there had been a lack of interest. She had no shortage of suitors, even in the sixth form. But books and formulae won the day. Her father, Doctor Hugh Parry Dawes, had been an eminent musicologist. He had died when she was eight years old. Her mother, Penelope, was a professional singer, who was now in semi-retirement after becoming something of a minor celebrity.

So Greg, as he usually did, got his way and despite Sarah's misgivings, a couple of months after viewing the Top Ebenezer Chapel, they were moved in. The property lay one and half miles above the hamlet of Llansharrod, up a single track. The front aspect gave views right across the hills to the west and out towards Hay-on-Wye to the east. It made for a very large house with four good sized bedrooms and an enormous open plan area, where most of the congregation would have sat. The flat they had shared in London was a lot smaller than the chapel and their furniture seemed a little lost in its new setting.

'Oh, don't worry honey; we will go into the big stores in Cardiff and fix up the place real grand, you'll see.'

In addition to her academic achievements, Sarah had inherited her parents' love for music and was an extremely accomplished pianist. Her mother insisted that now they had the room for it, Sarah should take possession of her father's Bechstein grand piano. Greg had always encouraged her playing. He particularly liked Sarah's rendition of Chopin's Nocturnes. He would sit and listen to her playing for hours at a time. Greg was not a musician himself; however, he was very strict about how music should be played. The first time he hit Sarah was when she played a wrong note during one of Mozart's more challenging piano sonatas. It was a glancing blow and for a moment she had felt as if she would topple from the piano stool. Afterwards, Greg would be stricken with remorse swearing that it would never happen again, but then of course it did. A piano lid slammed on her, a glass thrown at her face, a knee thrust in her stomach, and afterwards utter contrition. To begin with Sarah, being the academic person she was, saw Greg's aggression as a problem for her to solve. She made a note of all the triggers, times, dates and Greg's mood prior to the incident.

There were periods of calm and tranquillity: these coincided with Greg's long business trips overseas. It was during such times that Sarah could follow her own interests. She had forgone having a career as such. Greg made it clear that he needed her at home and that he hated the idea of her being stuck in some office somewhere. For Sarah, giving up any idea of working her way up the greasy pole of business, or academia for that matter, was no real hardship. She had a sense of her own worth, knew that her IQ made her among the top one percent of the population. She would be perfectly happy pursuing her hobbies for she, like her husband, could be obsessive. She would paint and investigate the local history of Llansharrod.

Whether it was her strong desire for motherhood and her growing vague sense of loneliness affecting her subconscious or something else entirely when first it happened, Sarah was unsure. Greg was in Mumbai attending a conference on robotics. It was one of those oppressively hot August days. She was sitting reading by the window near the front door, when she thought she could hear children's voices coming from outside. She peered out of the window and down the lane towards Llansharrod. There was not a soul to be seen. She returned to her book and the voices continued but seemed to be coming from somewhere to the rear of the chapel. Perhaps it was village kids up on the mountain; they seemed to be chanting something … something in Welsh.

'Ein Tad yn y nefoedd, sancteiddier dy enw.' Sarah recognised it from her childhood holidays with her devout Great Aunt Nerys; it was the Lord's Prayer.

The Llansharrod Historical Society met fortnightly at The Clytha Arms in the village it was attended by about half a dozen people, most of them incomers from England. Tomas Pritchard, however, had been born in the village and returned there on his retirement from a Librarianship at the University of Wales in Aberystwyth. Tomas was a tall, sparse man in his late seventies, with a somewhat out of control white beard and a watchful demeanour.

The Overlooked

The village it turned out, had ancient, pre-Norman roots, centred around a fifth century, theological college. Later, developments saw quarrying and small-scale mining in the surrounding area. Tomas Pritchard was extremely well versed in everything there was to know about Llansharrod. Existing members of the historical society did little to hide their boredom as he held forth on various facets of village development over the centuries. Sarah, however, was fascinated by the amount he knew. He struck her as a kindly man with an air of disappointment with regards to the cards that had been dealt him in life.

'So anyway, how are you settling at the Ebenezer?' asked Tomas at the end of one of the meetings.

'Really well, thank you. It's such an idiosyncratic place to call home.'

'Idiosyncratic? Interesting choice of words,' commented Tomas.

'Well, you know, quirky, having been a chapel and all that.'

'Oh yes, I see what you mean. Don't forget if ever you need to know more about the Ebenezer, give me a buzz.'

'Why, is there a lot more to know?'

'Well, you know how it is,' said Tomas. 'Anyway, it's nice to have a new face coming to our meetings.'

*****

'Well, Mrs Linderman, you'll be pleased to know there are no bones broken,' said the young doctor. How did you say you'd sustained these injuries to your fingers?'

'The wind blew the front door shut on them. It was my own stupid fault,' lied Sarah, reliving in her mind Greg's vicious latest attack and his parting remark.

'Sarah, you know when you disappoint me there are always consequences.'

Afterwards, and once she had been sure that he had gone, she had hurried down to the bus stop. Her fingers throbbed with pain and two of them were turning a kind of iodine purple. She put the injured hand self-consciously under her coat and gave the bus driver the fare. She had been grateful for small mercies; she was the only passenger and could sob quietly without intrusion from good Samaritans. She had been in two minds as to whether to go to the hospital but she couldn't bear the thought of her fingers being out of commission.

'Oh, is that right,' said the nurse, a middle-aged woman, who looked as if the world now held few surprises.

'I'm afraid I'm accident prone.'

When the young doctor had gone off on his rounds, the nurse pulled a card out from a pocket in her uniform.

'Well, here's a number you can ring if you want to talk to anyone when you have another of those accidents.'

'I told you it was the door hinge,' said Sarah curtly.

'Caught your eye as well did it?' said the nurse looking at the ruby red and black bruises on her face.'

'Hey, look I'm OK, really I am,' said Sarah.

She was relieved to be on her way out of casualty, when she saw Tomas Pritchard across the car park.

'Hello there, you look as if you've been in the wars.'

'Hello Tomas, never mind me; are you OK?'

'Oh, you know, not bad all things considered. The doctor says I'll live, worse luck. Now all I need to do is get a life. Can I give you a lift back to the village?'

'That's very kind. My husband has the car.'

Greg, who could have afforded half a dozen cars, had made the decision to be a one vehicle family on what he maintained were environmental grounds. The fact that due to there being a highly irregular bus service, Sarah's opportunities to travel independently were severely limited was for him, an added bonus.

'So you were going to tell me how you hurt yourself.'

'Was I? Well, that's all boring stuff. I want you to tell me about the Ebenezer Top Chapel,' said Sarah.

'What is it that you want to know?'

'When it was built would be good for starters.'

'During the great religious revival of the first half of the nineteenth century.'

'Don't places like that usually have the year they were built on the front?'

'Yes you are right, of course. However, the Ebenezer was a Primitive Gospeller's Chapel.'

'Why does that make a difference?' asked Sarah.

'Dates were immaterial to them as "the Word" was eternal,' Tomas explained.

'Oh right. So when did it shut up shop?'

'Around 1926, I believe.'

'Why was that? Falling congregations?'

'Well, of course the Great War had taken its toll of the men folk.'

They turned off the main road and into the village of Llansharrod.

'So it's been derelict all that time, until the developers who we bought it from converted it?'

'Well, yes in reality; people have rented it and used it for storage though.'

'But, otherwise it's been ignored, right?' said Sarah.

'Well to be honest, chapels are two a penny round here, most have been converted for English second homes and the rest bulldozed for building land. It's cultural vandalism really.'

'Oh, is that right,' said Sarah.

'Oh, I'm so sorry. Of course, I was talking about the developers and I didn't mean your chapel. To be honest it was a gloomy place. Nice to see it being used again, really.'

'Don't worry. Besides; it doesn't really feel like a chapel now, apart from the garden at the back that's a bit different.

Tomas' car pulled up outside the Ebenezer Top Chapel.'

'Thank you so much and see you soon,' said Sarah as she got out of the car.

When she got in through the front door, she found herself surrounded by huge bouquets of flowers.

'I am so, so sorry honey … Can you forgive your bad boy just one more time?' said Greg, clasping his hands together in supplication.

'I don't think I've got enough vases for all these flowers,' said Sarah.

'So, I'm forgiven?'

'Come on! Once I've got these flowers in water, we'd better eat.'

Sarah winced when her bruised fingers were splattered with cold water as she filled various vases and other receptacles with the flowers. It was when she went looking for more jars for the flowers in the utility room at the back of the house that she heard the children again. She recognised the tune; it was in Welsh, 'Arglwydd, arwain trwy'r anialwch' or 'Lord, lead through the wilderness' in English. She hurried back inside and closed the door, not wanting Greg to hear the singing and not really wanting to hear it herself.

The days were getting warmer and Sarah spent more and more of her time under the portico of the chapel reading and painting. Among the many things she had enjoyed and excelled in at school was art. She was working on a landscape of the valley as it opened out to the south: the river meandering its way down towards the Wye and ultimately the Bristol Channel. The fields had a reddish tint to them and the combine harvesters would soon be making their stately way down the lanes around Llansharrod.

The Overlooked

Sarah became more and more absorbed by the picture. She would spend every spare minute trying to get every detail right, how she wanted it. The muted tones of the valley through her brushwork were transformed into an exuberant explosion of vibrant primary colours.

Greg's aggression towards her diminished for a while. He was involved in an ambitious proposal to put a barrage across the Severn and so in what little time he spent with Sarah at the chapel he was very much preoccupied.

At night, when Greg was away, she sometimes fancied she could hear children's voices again, wafting in at the open skylight. She began almost to get used to it and found it companionable in a way.

The next meeting of the Llansharrod Historical Society took place in the evening of what had been an exceptionally hot late summer's day. The last of the great hay carts had rolled up from the valley, squeezing through the narrow streets of the village and on to the farms halfway up the mountain. Tomas and the others had decided to hold the meeting at the front of the pub in the small beer garden. Sarah was late she'd been working on her landscape painting

'Hello Tomas. Sorry I'm late,' she whispered. 'Can I get you a drink, to say thank you for helping a damsel in distress the other day?'

'That's very kind, pint of lager if that's OK,' said Tomas.

The main agenda item was the effect of the Spanish Flu Pandemic of 1918 on the village. The situation had been exasperated by all the doctors and nurses still being at the front.

'There was a song they used to sing, my dad told me,' piped up Gwen Evans at ninety-seven years old. She was by far the oldest resident of Llansharrod and was a founder member of the Llansharrod Historical Society. She was sitting under one of the pub umbrellas fanning herself with a beer mat.

'Ah yes I think I've got it:

I had a little bird

Its name was Enza,
I opened the Window
And in-flew Enza.'

'So were there fatalities from flu here in the village?' Sarah asked.

'Oh yes, several,' said Tomas.

'My cousin, Lottie, was one of them,' said Gwen.

'Oh, I am sorry.'

'She's buried up at your place, her being one of "his,"' said Gwen enigmatically.

*****

The harvest had been completed in the nick of time as the weather broke that night. Torrential rain and a spectacular thunderstorm illuminated the black mountains with lightning. Water poured through the village as Sarah ran back up the lane to the chapel.

There was a message on the answer phone from Greg. He had been called up to London for a meeting of the project group for the barrage and would be away for two or three days. Sarah climbed into bed and despite the storm fell into a fitful sleep. She woke suddenly. The storm had passed and light from the moon streamed in through the long windows at the front of the chapel. She looked at the alarm clock and it was nearly two am. She went down into the small kitchen to make herself a cup of tea. As she walked back into the cavernous living area, she felt something brush against her head. Reaching up, she felt what appeared to be the end of a rope and above her. Illuminated by the moon and swaying from the gallery balustrade, she could see quite clearly a noose gently swaying to and fro.

The next morning, the air was clear and the temperature had dropped. There was a fine view down the valley and she put down the events of the night to a bad dream. Sarah was eager to get back to work on her unfinished canvas. However, a call from her mother in Cardiff delayed her starting work. Her mother had phoned to explain that she was fine, but the doctors thought she must have had a slight stroke.

'Thankfully, darling, the instrument was not affected by this,' Sarah's mother meant her voice, 'and the nurses are all absolute sweeties.'

Sarah knew her mother would not be telling the whole story, so she hurriedly put on the dress her mother had given her last birthday and let her hair fall loose around her shoulders, the way she knew her mother would like, and walked briskly down to the bus stop.

As luck would have it, Gwen Evans was there, leaning on her cherry wood walking stick, in a crocheted, tea cosy of a hat and a sheepskin coat that smelt of wet dog.

'Well, good morning Sarah. Wasn't that a terrible storm last night?' The word terrible was drawn out as much as possible to give it its full effect.

'Hello, Gwen.'

'Where are you off to today then?'

'My mam's; she's been taken poorly.'

'Under the doctor then is she?'

'Actually, she's in hospital.'

'Oh, well that's probably the best place for her. Like the company, when I'm there, see.'

'Oh,' said Sarah.

'I'm not being funny but a morgue is more alive than Llansharrod. Worse in the winter of course.'

'Gwen?' said Sarah.

'Yes, my lovely.'

'You know last night, when you were talking about your cousin being one of "his," I was curious; who did you mean? Was it God you were talking about?'

'More like the devil,' said Gwen quietly, while looking out of the bus window.

'Oh right, not sure I'm quite with you.'

'The Reverend Caleb Darrowby-Jones, late of this parish, well of any parish really.'

'So, where does he fit in?'

'Oh, I was too young to remember really, but everyone had heard the rumours.'

'What kind of rumours?' asked Sarah.

'Well, the thing is love, in those days no one questioned authority. If you were a teacher, policeman, politician or man of the cloth, it was assumed you were somehow above the rest of us poor mortals. So Darrowby-Jones took his shabby little secret to the grave.'

'Sorry, I'm not with you.'

'Well it turned out the man who espoused the gospel was in fact a bully and a child molester.'

'But surely ...'

'Apparently he ruled over the congregation of the Ebenezer with a rod of iron. No one dared question him. Of course, most of the men had been killed in France. And, well, let's just put it this way: the fight for women's rights hadn't come to Llansharrod and children, of course, were to be seen but not heard. My how things have changed, cariad.'

'He sounds a dreadful man.'

'Would you like a mint imperial?' said Gwen rummaging in her capacious handbag and pulling out an extremely crumpled, white, paper bag

'Oh thank you,' said Sarah.

'Yes, a terrible business. The flu epidemic proved very convenient for him in that it killed off those poor mites, taking any chance of him being brought to justice.'

'So, he lived into old age?'

'Oh no love, there's a happy ending to the story.'

'How do you mean?'

'He killed himself, in the chapel.'

'Oh God! How?

'Strung himself up by all accounts. Oh, I'm sorry love! Stupid old woman that I am.'

'Oh, don't worry,' said Sarah finding herself trembling ever so slightly.

'Are you cold, my love? Never any heating on this old bus. Might as well sit in a freezer.'

'I'm fine, really.'

'The fact is, it's lovely to see lights on in the chapel.'

'Thank you.'

'Tell me love, is it right your husband's American?'

'Yes, we met over there.'

'There's lovely! I knew an American boy during the war. He said he came from Boulder. Colorado … quite apt … in a way. He was a bit of a rolling stone really … rolled away from me anyway. Oh, here we are! This is my stop. You'll be changing in Abergavenny for Cardiff, won't you.'

'That's right. Take care, Gwen.'

'You too, Sarah,' said Gwen, looking up from the bus stop. 'If ever you want a chat, you know where I live. Look to the future! That's what I say. The past is bugger-all use to anyone.'

When Sarah reached the hospital, Penelope Parry Dawes was sitting in a chair by the side of her bed trying to do a crossword, using the hand she never wrote with.

'Sarah, my darling! How nice to see you and you look lovely but you shouldn't have come all this way. I'm perfectly all right.'

'Mother, you've had a stroke. What kind of daughter do you think I am?'

'The best Sarah. How are you enjoying that chapel of yours?'

'It's a beautiful place, Llansharrod. We still haven't got you up there to see it have we?'

'Oh, you've shown me pictures of it, sweetheart, and you know I'm not a great traveller these days. Anyway, tell me how do you fill your days? Such a brilliant mind, darling; aren't you dying of boredom?'

'Oh no, I love it. Greg's away on business a lot and I've got involved in the village. Oh, and I'm really getting into painting.'

'So, things are OK?'

'Yes I'm fine, Mam, I really am,' said Sarah.

'Because, if they're not.'

'No, its fine, Mam. Now you get yourself better, you hear me!'

'Men are just big children darling. You have to work round them. Outguess them.

'Yes, Mam, that's what you've always told me.'

'Your father was difficult,' but I never let that stand in my way.'

'Daddy was an angel, Mam, although I wish he'd been around a bit more. I had so little time with him.'

'Oh, he could be angelic, I grant you,' said Penelope, pulling her Kimono-type dressing gown around her with her one good hand and looking out of the window of the ward lost in thought. 'But there were times when he could be … well obdurate.'

Momentarily Sarah felt like telling her mother everything … how Greg could be charming and attentive one moment and then fly into an ungovernable rage the next. How she lived in fear of doing or saying the wrong thing, and also how she used to believe that she, and she alone could cure him of this behaviour.

The bus journey home seemed interminable to Sarah. A fine, dank, mist hung over the mountains and the passengers who got on the bus almost without exception remarked on the chill in the air. The countryside they passed through had mostly been reclaimed from the mining industry. Soon snaking blackened cottages gave way to the ever-increasing ridges, 'the humpbacks' Sarah called them because they always reminded her of the other whales breaching the waves of land, where England and Wales rolled into one another.

Usually, once Sarah got to this part of the journey, she would sit back and enjoy the views, but today she was worried about her mother and something else was giving her a sense of unease.

The bus dropped her at the bottom of the little lane that led up to the chapel; the hedges were full of small cobwebs glistening like jewels in the drizzly rain. She found herself hurrying in part due to the rain but also due to a gathering sense of anxiety.

When she got to the door, she found it unlocked. Greg had returned.

'Hi, honey! I was worried about you.' Why, you have dolled yourself up, haven't you?' said Greg disapprovingly.

'Sorry, I didn't expect you back; I had to go down to my mother's. She's been taken poorly.'

'Oh really, so that's where you were,' said Greg suspiciously.

'Would you like me to get you something to eat?'

'It's OK. I fixed myself something, but honey ...'

She knew what was coming and swayed so that the back of Greg's hand only just caught her cheek. He moved towards her and kicked her standing leg from underneath her, causing her to fall backwards against the island in the middle of the kitchen.

'Next time, let me know where you are! Do you understand! There's such a thing as cell phones you know.'

The mobile coverage in that part of Wales was patchy at the best of times. Sarah had forgotten to take her phone with her, but she dared not tell him that.

Sarah pulled herself up on the kitchen unit. She looked at him quizzically as a mother might look at her child over some minor misdemeanour. Greg stormed out of the chapel. She heard the car start up and made a note in her computer file named

'Greg's triggers,' listing 'keep in contact.' Then she went to the bathroom to bathe the bruises from this latest outburst. As she looked in the mirror on the front of the bathroom cabinet, she saw in it a reflection of something outside the chapel. It was standing by the side of one of the graves. It was small and grey, with sallow, soulful, eyes and appeared to be reaching down holding something ... that looked like another arm sticking out of the earth. There was also the sound of children again. This time they were laughing as if their attention was taken up with some game.

Sarah shut the cabinet door quickly, locked up and made her way down to The Clytha Arms. There was one thing she needed more than anything else and that was a very strong drink.

Tomas Pritchard was sat at his usual place.

'Hello there! How's it going?'

'It'll be better after I have had a drink,' Sarah replied.

'You haven't been having another of those accidents, have you now?'

'Tomas, can I ask you something and you've got to promise not to laugh.'

'OK, you have my word.'

'Do you believe in ghosts?'

'Of course I do! Living in Wales, it's like asking do you believe in rain?'

'I am a rationalist; I believe there is a solution or an explanation for everything.'

'But you are also a Welsh woman, so what you feel and what you know to be true are often two rather different things,' said Tomas before draining his pint.

'That's a bit sexist, if you don't mind me saying,' said Sarah.

'Oh no, I include us men too! We call it the thin place, where the past and present are caught up together,' explained Tomas.

'The thing is, it's the chapel. I really think it might be haunted.'

'Well, it doesn't surprise me much, given the history of that place. Seen a spectre of the old preacher spitting fire and brimstone have you? Dirty old pervert that he was,' said Tomas.

'What exactly did he do?'

'You wouldn't want to know, Sarah.'

'Well how did it all come out?'

'The story goes, it was little Nerys Roberts, one Sunday when Darrowby-Jones was sounding off from the pulpit about eternal damnation. She just got up and said it.'

'Said what?'

'She said she wasn't going to hell because she might be unlucky and run into him.'

'Wow that was brave!' said Sarah.

'Yes, it was, poor dab.'

'A couple of weeks later, sadly, she died. Last fatality in the village from the flu epidemic. They said her outburst was from having the fever, said she'd been ranting and raving about what Jones had been doing to her and the rest of the village's children. The thing is, from what Gwen says, they were all in denial about the abuse and still scared stiff of Darrowby-Jones. Anyway, a few years later, he goes and tops himself.'

After three large glasses of red wine, Sarah made her way unsteadily up the hill. It had been raining heavily and the sky remained dark and forbidding.

As she got up to the chapel, she began to smell burning. Who on earth would light a bonfire in this weather, she wondered. She went in and saw Greg's house keys and briefcase, but he was nowhere to be seen. The smell of burning became stronger.

There was something else ... something missing. The easel from which she worked was empty; her painting was gone.

The back door of the chapel was slightly ajar; she could see a figure shrouded in mist and smoke. It was Greg standing by the side of their metal bin, which was where the fire was coming from. He was methodically ripping her picture into small pieces, placing each carefully into the flame.

'Hello, Sarah.'

'What the hell are you doi…' she screamed.

'I thought that we had a deal, that you would be here when I came home. You were not.'

'So why don't you just hit me? Like you usually do?'

'It has been necessary to physically chastise you, but this appears to have become ineffective and since this daubing of yours seems more important to you than our marriage, I am disposing of it and in futu…'

Sarah had turned on her heels and walked back inside. Noticing Greg's keys on the sideboard, she slammed the door shut. She was damned if he was ever going to touch her again and it would take him awhile to figure how to get out from behind the building. Serve the bastard right, she thought.

The light was fading fast and showers were blowing across the valley like shoals of tiny fish. Sarah marched down the hill knowing that the spell Greg had had over her was broken. So, it was in a state of elation that she returned to The Clytha Arms.

The next thing Sarah could remember, was waking to the smell of bacon and eggs and a large mug of black coffee on the unfamiliar bedside table beside her.

'Get it while it's hot, cariad.' It was Gwen Evans calling from downstairs.

Sarah struggled into her still damp clothes. When she arrived in Gwen's kitchen, she found her perched on a high stool agitating some frying bacon with a fish slice.

After an enormous breakfast and two cups of coffee, Sarah was just wondering whether Gwen would mind her having a couple more hours of sleep at her place, when she heard the siren of an ambulance roar past the little cottage.

'Well, I don't know what's going on! A police car went up ten minutes ago. We haven't had so much excitement here since Old Morag Jenkins' barn went up a couple of years back. I'd go up and take a look, but my legs are bad this morning.'

'No, I'll go. I'll let you know what's going on, if anything.'

Sarah's head was thumping as she made her way through the village.

As she turned up the hill, she saw various emergency vehicles parked outside the chapel and a stretcher being lifted into an ambulance. She tried to steady herself against some iron railings and then stumbled and fell heavily onto the tarmac.

'Can you hear me? What's your name love?'

A paramedic was kneeling besides Sarah.

'Where … what's happened?'

'You've had a fall, love. Have you been drinking?' said the young man, sniffing suspiciously at Sally's clothes, the same ones she wore the previous night in The Clytha Arms.

'Well, yes actually, a great deal. Where's the ambulance gone?'

'Hospital, there was a chap up at the chapel taken bad.'

'You OK?' said Tomas who was standing on the other side of the road.

'Yes, I'm OK but now you're the one who looks like they've seen a ghost.'

Tomas didn't answer. He just zipped up his fleece. To Sarah, he seemed to have aged ten years over night.

Sarah visited Greg every day. Apparently, he was in an awful state when they found him. It had been Tomas who had found Greg. He had heard screaming coming from the chapel. When he got there, the front door of the chapel was open and he unlocked the yale lock to the back door with Greg's keys from the sideboard. Greg was covered in mud when Tomas eventually got to him. His finger nails were bleeding. They reckoned he'd been trying to climb up the rock face at the back of the chapel, having been unable to get in through the locked rear entrance.

To begin with, the police thought that Greg had been assaulted and suspected Tomas, but the hospital confirmed that Pritchard was suffering from congenital heart failure and any physical exertion would have probably killed him. They concluded therefore, that foul play was not a factor.

Greg drifted in and out of consciousness. He seemed delirious most of the time he was awake. When Sarah asked him whether he wanted anything for the pain, all he would say was 'Just make them go away.'

Ten days after he'd been admitted, Sarah got a call to say Greg had passed away in the night.

'Was it peaceful?' enquired Sarah, who had felt a strange emotional numbness at how things had turned out. She could tell by the hesitation in the nurse's voice before she said 'yes,' that it may well not have been.

When she arrived at the hospital to pick up Greg's belongings and the death certificate, she was greeted by the young registrar, who had treated her in Accident and Emergency.

'I really am very sorry, Mrs Linderman. I don't think there was any more we could have done for your husband.'

Sarah looked at the death certificate, which read '*Influenza.*'

'Greg died of the flu?' she said incredulously.

'Exacerbated by exposure and shock, we think, and it was an extremely uncommon strain of flu,' said the doctor.

'How do you mean?' queried Sarah.

'A type of Spanish Flu. Don't see much of it these days. Now, can I get you anything, a cup of tea or coffee?' asked the doctor.

'No, I'm fine. I really I am,' Sarah replied.

Late for the Wedding

Trixie Roberts

The Reverend Smeek guesses something is wrong when, behind him, he hears the urgent tap tap tap of high heels on the stone floor. He turns and sees court shoes carrying a tall woman dressed like a wedding guest.

'Excuse me. Are you officiating at the Hayley–Bridgeman wedding?' The woman looks flustered.

'Er, well there are three weddings today,' the clergyman replies trying to remember which is whose.

'I mean the twelve-thirty one. I'm Judith Dell, a friend of the bride. Something has gone wrong. You do know a friend of the couple is going to play the violin as she walks down the aisle?'

'Oh, is he, er, she? Oh, I think I remember something being mentioned ...'

'Kieran. He's called Kieran. Well, that was the plan but he's just phoned to say he was halfway here and realised he left home without his violin. He's had to turn back. Now he's on his way but the traffic's bad. He thinks it'll be another forty minutes at least before he arrives.'

'Oh dear.' The clergyman looks at his watch. 'Oh, dear. It's after twelve already.'

'Is there any chance of delaying things a little?' Judith asks with more hope than expectation.

'Er, well, not really. You see I have the Parfitt–Chambers wedding at one-thirty. Can't really keep *them* waiting – the bride's father's a JP and gave very generously to our restoration fund. Oh dear.'

'Yes, yes, I understand.' Judith continues in the manner of one not accustomed to having a problem remain unsolved. 'Is your organist here yet? We did ask for him to be here as the whole programme isn't to be violin music.'

'The whole *programme?'*

'Well, between you and me, Kieran has a somewhat limited repertoire. He's playing the bridal introduction to fulfil a sort of promise, I think.'

The clergyman decided not to question further and said, 'Well, Mr Stretch should be here by now. I hope he's not been held up as well.'

'I was thinking; if Kieran doesn't make it, perhaps the organist could play for the bridal procession and save the day?'

'Well, you'd need to ask him – Ah! Here he is now.'

Mr Stretch, carrying a clutch of sheet music, strides down the aisle and greets the vicar who introduces him to Judith. The vicar looks at his watch again.

'I'll leave you two together – I have one or two things to do before the ceremony.'

By twelve-fifteen, the churchyard is filling with a mix of wedding guests, local people who habitually turn up to see every wedding at the parish church and weekend visitors, who are taking in the church and grounds as part of one of the town walks described on a leaflet from the tourist office. The sun is shining. The bridegroom, best man and ushers go into the church and take their places. The organist starts to play the general-purpose pre-service pieces. Everything is calm.

At twenty-eight minutes past twelve, Joanna Hayley and her father arrive at the church and with the bridesmaids get into position at the back. Joanna can hear the organ. She is expecting to hear a violin start to play at any moment but it doesn't and there's no sign of Kieran. As she walks round the back of the church looking for him, she recalls a nightmare that has recurred in recent weeks, where she arrives for her wedding at the wrong church. She knows this is the right one. It is the church she has walked past nearly every day of her life. She knows this is her wedding. She comes back into the church and one glance up the aisle confirms it, when she sees her mother's hat. Like so many mother-of-the-bride hats, it's conspicuous because it adds about a foot to her mother's normal height. It's also vivid turquoise. They shopped for days to find that hat. Why? By next week it will be in a box at the back of the wardrobe, a few months and it will be in the Oxfam shop. A one-day airing and no more wearing.

Judith rushes up to Joanna and explains about Kieran's delay. Joanna feels desperately disappointed. She and Kieran were music students together. Good friends. He always promised he would play at her wedding. They even discussed whether she would walk down the aisle to Mozart or Schubert. Then, at last New Year's party after she and Will had named the day, Kieran said he would definitely be there and would practice 'something lively.'

'Nothing too mad, Kieran,' Will had warned. 'We don't want to upset the parents.'

'Oh, the parents and their bourgeois sensibilities,' Kieran objected. 'Why do parents always dictate how things are to be done? Whose wedding is it anyway?'

'Look we've already been through all this at home,' said Joanna. 'Will and I would rather have a small, quiet do, but the family want a grand occasion. Only daughter and all that.'

'There are loads of people coming who we've never even met,' added Will. 'Friends and relatives of Joanna's mother and her father's cronies from the golf club. But they said they would pay for everything. So we're just going to grit our teeth and put up with it.'

'Sounds like they could do with livening up a bit. Perhaps we'll agree on a piece everyone will be happy with and then I'll work on an unofficial version.'

'Kieran, behave!' Joanna had said. 'Your playing is the one element of the whole wedding I've insisted on having. Don't mess up! You don't know how hard I've had to work to convince my dad that you won't play anything as brash even as Paganini.'

Since then, Kieran had given every appearance of behaving himself. He'd even shaved when invited to Joanna's home for her parents' summer garden party and to discuss plans.

'So much for getting my way over the music,' Joanna thinks. 'He can't even arrive on time. Kieran's playing was the one thing I wanted. What I didn't want was to be covered in ivory satin and seed pearls and a veil which makes everything look like I'm seeing it through a fog.'

There's a bang and shuffling is heard near the door. Someone says:

'Be quick, be quick, the bride's ready. Everyone's waiting.' Kieran stumbles into the church. Judith's high heels can be heard running up the steps to the organ loft. Joanna beams. Mr Hayley frowns at Kieran's shambolic appearance.

'I made it. Jo, you look gorgeous. You know, I thought I'd have all the local constabulary after me the way I shot round that bypass. Had no idea where the church was. Will gave me directions the other night but I'd had a few pints by then. We'd already done The Red Lion and The Black Horse – and moved on to the Last Man Standing. That's what Will was – he seemed totally sober. Didn't want to let his Joanna down. Can you imagine – his stag night and he's on orange juice and lemonade? I hope no one's policing that double yellow line outside.'

'Young man,' fumes Mr Hayley. 'Are you quite ready?'

'Sure.' Says Kieran. 'I can see it's time for everyone to lighten up. Remember what we agreed last New Year, Jo?'

Joanna takes a deep breath but has no chance to speak.

'We'll show them. Everyone's been keyed up for months over these wedding preparations and you and Will not wanting to say anything for fear of upsetting the family.'

'I beg your pardon, young man,' spits Mr Hayley.

'Well, it's their wedding for heaven's sake. So you think you're getting Mozart? Well let's see – it's OK, Jo. Everyone will enjoy this.' Judith's footsteps are heard coming down from the loft into the church. The organ stops.

Kieran starts to play – it's a quick staccato Irish jig. It's loud – the pure sound of the fiddle bounces off the ancient stones of the church. Everyone starts to smile. Mr Hayley looks horrified but Joanna takes his arm and he reluctantly finds himself swaying from side to side with her down the aisle. The little cousins – pageboy and junior bridesmaid – take the cue and twirl each other round behind them. The guests, somewhat confined by the pews, clap and stamp their feet, but Will's best man, Joe, grabs Joanna's mother and the turquoise hat wobbles while she is spun round. The ushers wave and shout 'Yippee.'

Reverend Smeek looks more bemused than ever but relieved that the proceedings have started at last, taps his feet and grins at the animated congregation. One of the ushers, who has always fancied the chief bridesmaid, dashes back down the church to grab her and twirls her off her feet.

When the bridal party are still only halfway down the aisle, Kieran changes key and tempo but the new piece is equally magical. It rises up and out of the belfry and radiates all around the churchyard. The people outside hear the music. Its spirit falls down on them like confetti and they instinctively join in the dancing. The local ladies waiting to see the bride and groom stop their chatting and start to conga round the gravestones. Passing National Trust members in sensible shoes hum and move in time to the rhythm and the carer of an elderly gent in a wheelchair spins him round. The church caretaker's dog joins in by barking in time to the swooping of the pigeons who have left the belfry and are flying above the churchyard in formation.

Joanna reaches the front of the church and sees Will. He is somewhat breathless after a twirl around the font with his mother. Like all mothers besotted with their sons and in dread of losing them she has been ambiguous about his marriage. She has been affected to the point of dressing for the wedding entirely in black. Now, she is flushed, panting and, for the first time that day, her face is no longer long. She even looks across the aisle and gives a little nod of approval to the turquoise hat.

Bride and groom stand by the altar. Kieran's fiddle falls silent. Everyone breathes deeply. The Reverend Smeek seizes his moment.

'Dearly beloved …'

Invisible Man

John Heap

I sit at the back of the self-service restaurant at college. Dinnertime is approaching and the queues are building. I watch nervously as first the tables then the individual chairs begin to be taken up. I must leave soon, but my time amongst people is limited and I'm torn between the desire to remain and the very real fear of interaction. I must leave soon.

I notice the young woman in the queue; she's exchanging happy animated banter over some tray mix-up. She's short and slim yet there's power in her stance, strong thighs and hips, a solid being.

She emerges with a coffee and moves amongst the tables, as if looking for someone. She comes further into the restaurant until at last there is nowhere else to go and so she sits at my table. She doesn't acknowledge me.

Tables are filled now, young people talking robustly about last night's exploits, their adventures, their relationships, their lives, the rising tumult emphasising the quiet of this table at the back.

In this still place, I seize the rare opportunity and examine her. She sits opposite but askance, the angle exaggerated by her frequent scanning of the room. Perhaps her mouth is too wide, her skin too dark under her eyes, but in profile she is beautiful and she shines so very brightly.

Absentmindedly, she's struggling to open her milk carton and manages to spurt half its contents across the table. She looks around and her dark eyes focus on me.

'Oh, sorry about that. I didn't see you there.'

'Not many do,' I incautiously reply.

'Sorry?' she asks, but she's already losing interest and her eyes turn to the room again.

How can I explain? I wasn't always ill; I used to have friends too, even a girlfriend once. I used to be someone, someone solid.

In the beginning, it was unremarkable things. For example, it would take longer to get served at a bar, moving through a crowd became difficult and buses would pass me at the bus stop. Small things indeed, but they had their effect and I became quieter and more withdrawn. Eventually my friends stopped ringing and then my girlfriend escaped.

I got depressed.

And then I had trouble shaving.

Whenever I turned my head, I felt my reflection fade.

At first, I thought it was my eyes, the light or the mirror, but it wasn't. I soon discovered that if I looked at my reflection sideways, I couldn't focus on it: it became translucent.

Imagine a net curtain. If you look at the curtain you see it, but look at the scene beyond and it disappears from your consciousness.

So I'm a net curtain. How do I explain that!

'I'm an invisible man,' I blurt as she's getting up from her chair.

She looks directly at me and in a movement too quick to avoid pats my hand saying,

'Don't be silly, you just have to be more assertive.'

I feel the shock of that fleeting contact, an electrical discharge. Like the first touch of a long-desired woman, but not quite the same. This is different.

Something terrible has happened and she hasn't yet noticed.

She is leaving the restaurant now but is caught by the queue at the door.

She is there for some time.

I watch her repeated attempts to get through become increasingly half-hearted. Then she turns, head down, to go the long way around.

I continue to watch as she fades into the distance.

The Dream House

Ronald Turner

The last rays of summer sunlight caught the ancient stonework, setting it aflame. A magnificent scarlet rose clambered up one side of the porch and sprawled across the wall right up the eaves. The cottage was set in a large, overgrown garden with the merest wisps of a hedge dividing it from the surrounding fields. They were not more than thirty miles from a busy metropolis yet up here among these hills it was a different world. The only other building in sight was the spire of a church in the nearest village showing above a thick wood to the east. It was the perfect retreat. Even before they looked inside, they knew that their search was over. They had found their dream house.

This was the nineties, when young executives were keen to spend some of their considerable earnings on a place where they could invite their friends to gaze admiringly at the location and skilful renovation of their country property. The formalities took forever so it was mid-October before the deal was completed and at last they were able to take time out from their busy lives to go back for a second look. There was no access to the cottage by car and they were shocked to find that the lovely meadow they had strolled across in July was now a ploughed field. They stumbled across sticky furrows and had almost reached the cottage when Fiona cried out, 'Oh look, James!' He followed her gaze to where recent unseasonable storms had demolished the rotten porch and brought the rose bush down with it.

Too cold and depressed even to glance inside they hurried back to their car and drove off rapidly in search of Dan Williams at Hillside Farm, who owned the land on which their dream house stood. Soon they were sitting in front of a roaring fire, sipping a single-malt and feeling much more cheerful, when Williams began to talk about the cottage.

'I don't suppose them agents told you that Pleggs' Cottage is cursed. No one but them Pleggs lived there for as long as anybody knows. The last Plegg, old Jed, died more'n twenty year ago and there's none 'as dared to live in the place since. If I was you, I'd cut me losses and leave well alone.'

'So what exactly is this curse?' asked James sceptically. He did not believe for a minute in such hocus-pocus and the warmth of the fire and the whisky had rekindled his vision of their dream house.

'The story goes that when they was building the cottage – hundreds of year ago – they'd just set the main beam in place when this young girl – one of the family – come up from the village with a flagon of ale. While they sits sharing bread and cheese and passing the flagon round the little'n goes playing about inside the roofless walls. Suddenly there's this almighty thump and when they looks inside the main beam is back on the earth and the only sign of the girl is a tiny white arm sticking out from under it. When they finally managed to lift the beam again it were 'ard to tell which were corpse and which were clay.'

Although the room was warm Fiona could not avoid a shudder.

Williams continued, 'Mind you, I reckon that's a load of cobblers. Them Pleggs was an odd lot. Probably made up the story to keep visitors away.'

In spite of his dire warnings, Williams sold them enough land, at a considerably inflated price, to make a proper driveway to the cottage. By the end of October, they had put their city centre apartment up for sale and moved into a caravan next to the cottage from where they could supervise its restoration.

At first everything went well. They found an architect who specialised in restoring ancient buildings. He took one look at the cottage and practically danced with joy.

'But my dears, it's an absolute gem. Definitely early seventeenth century. Just look at that main beam. Must be at least a ton of oak in that. Absolutely splendid.'

The Dream House

James and Fiona were rather alarmed, however, when he presented his plans, which demanded that the cottage must be almost entirely demolished before the work of restoration could begin, but his enthusiasm was infectious and they agreed to go ahead. By mid-December the stone tiles had been removed and the slow demolition of their dream house reflected the mood of the fading year.

A few days before Christmas Fiona met an old school friend in town and over several reunion drinks told her about the cottage. Sally, an archivist by profession, was thrilled, especially by the story of the curse.

'Would you mind if I did a bit of research on your cottage, Fiona? I'm fascinated.'

So it was arranged for Sally to have access to any documents she needed and the demolition proceeded. By January, the roof timbers had been taken down, carefully numbered and stored. The first floor was similarly treated. Then a trench had to be dug outside one of the walls so that it could be underpinned. It was while the mechanical digger was making this trench that fragments of bone were unearthed. These were too small and crumbly to be recognisable, except that they were human and several centuries old. It was at this point that things began to go wrong.

Firstly the weather, which had been relatively mild that winter, worsened dramatically. For two days it snowed without stopping and the cottage was completely cut off. Then the gas supply to the caravan ran out much sooner than expected and the caravan walls seemed to shrink to the thickness of cardboard. James and Fiona spent most of each day in bed, fully dressed. Naturally, all work on the cottage ceased. Everything mechanical froze.

The shell of the cottage stood out bleakly against the leaden sky. At night it began to assume an ominous resonance. A bitter north-east wind seemed to be drawn in through the glassless windows where it moaned around inside the walls and seemed to cry out, 'Let me be! Leave me alone!'

Throughout January the weather remained fiercely wintry. Still no progress could be made on the cottage. James and Fiona were unable to get into work for a week. At this rate they would both be unemployed before the spring.

One morning Fiona woke with what appeared to be the inevitable cold. She remained in bed, sneezing and shivering. By midday her condition had deteriorated rapidly. When James discovered that he could not get a signal with either of their mobiles, he set off through the snow to the village and found a doctor.

Doctor Davies was extremely put out at having to walk through the snow, now thigh deep in places, and made it quite clear that he totally disapproved of 'townies' buying up property and sending the house prices soaring beyond the reach of the locals. But when Davies saw Fiona his manner changed abruptly. By now her fever was extreme; her temperature had risen dangerously, her face was glazed with sweat and scarlet patches stood out on her cheeks. All her limbs ached and she complained about some powerful swellings under her arms.

The doctor completed a thorough examination and announced, 'Your wife must leave here at once. Go back to the village and phone for an ambulance. Mobiles are useless up here because of the hills. No time for questions. Go! Now!'

Once more James set off through the snow to make his phone call. It was already dark by the time he got back to the caravan, exhausted and rather frightened. Doctor Davies had left a message to say that the air ambulance helicopter had collected Fiona and that he had gone with her to the nearest hospital.

James realised that it would be impossible to get to the hospital that night, so he decided to load up the car and leave next morning to stay with friends until the weather improved and work could begin again on the cottage. He was sure that Fiona would soon recover with proper treatment and he was determined that they would see this project through and have their dream house in the end. So he snatched a simple meal, opened their last bottle of whisky and prepared to get through the night.

He was woken in the early hours by shouting and what sounded like the thump of wood on wood. He felt awful! In fact, he seemed to have developed similar symptoms to Fiona. His limbs ached and he was shivering and sweating at the same time. Then he noticed the whisky bottle lying two thirds empty on the floor. He poured the rest away in disgust.

It was when he looked up from the sink that James saw a light moving about near the demolished cottage. He put on his coat and staggered out into the freezing night. But it wasn't freezing now. In fact, it was quite mild and the snow had melted away. The night air even had a different smell.

He approached the cottage but came to a sudden halt when he saw that the light, a paltry flickering flame like that of a candle, came from one of the bedrooms. But there were no bedrooms! Then he shuddered violently as he realised that this cottage not only had bedrooms but a thatched roof. The more he stared, transfixed, the more he became aware that this was not the same cottage at all, yet it stood in exactly the same place.

James felt sick and dizzy. As he stood swaying, trembling, unable to shift his gaze from this impossible sight, he noticed that something was happening near the front of the cottage. Another light appeared, much brighter, then another and another. These were flaming torches, which caught the faces of an angry mob as they surrounded the dwelling. Suddenly one of those torches was flung through a doorway, where the door itself had been broken down. The voices rose in a cheer, then faded rapidly as the mob hurried away. James wanted to rush forward and stop whatever it was that was happening but found that he could not move. He was here and yet not here. He was able to watch but not to intervene.

In a moment the ground floor was ablaze, the flames catching instantly on the straw strewn floor and the wooden furniture inside. The fire roared as it was fed by the wind drawn in through the open doorway and the flames rose rapidly to the wooden beams. Then James heard other voices and screams of terror, which suddenly intensified as flames began to lick upwards towards the thatch. A woman came to a window, her long hair on fire, her face twisted with fear and pain. She was holding a small child in her arms, preparing to drop it to the ground. James saw the little body falling towards him and knew that it must land on him, but instead it seemed to fall through him and he felt nothing. The shock was too much. He collapsed onto the ground, where he was found next morning, lying in the snow, almost dead with exposure and babbling incoherently about fire and murder.

*****

After a few days Fiona was able to leave hospital: in fact, her symptoms had begun to disappear as soon as she left the caravan. It took longer for James to recover as he was suffering from mental stress as well as hypothermia, but eventually he joined Fiona at her parents' suburban home, where they stayed while they tried to put their lives together again. Their apartment had been sold and all the money sunk into the restoration of Pleggs' Cottage but they both knew they would never return to that place. Perhaps one day, someone would buy the site and do something with the ruins, but for the moment they did not care. One morning they received a letter, in an envelope, which had been readdressed several times.

Dear Fiona and James,

I have been looking into the history of your cottage and have made some surprising discoveries. Firstly, the name, which is not really Pleggs' Cottage at all, though there have been Pleggs living there since the eighteenth century, when the cottage was largely rebuilt. They inherited the name or corrupted it from a previous dwelling on the same site. The original name was not Plegg, but Plagg or even more likely, as you will see from the information below, Plague!

It appears that in the middle of the seventeenth century, a family came northwards to escape the plague, which was raging at the time. The villagers did not exactly welcome them, but some more Christian soul suggested the abandoned cottage across the meadows. The grateful family stayed there in self-imposed isolation until they could be sure that they had not brought the plague with them. Unfortunately, a child in the village died soon after from an illness with similar symptoms to the plague. That was enough for some of the villagers. One spring night a band of young men crossed the meadows and set light to the cottage. The whole family perished in the upper room, except for a little girl, who was found a few days later, dead of exposure and with both legs broken. She was quickly buried, just outside the cottage walls.

All this sounds rather macabre, I know, but it must add to the fascination of your cottage. I hope that the restoration is going well and eagerly await an invitation to your dream house.

Sally

Overheard at the Late-night Chemist

Vicky Turrell

Paracetamol, please.

Here, Paracetamol.

Thanks.

...and ... a urine specimen bottle, please.

Urine specimen bottle, coming up.

You can't keep it a secret can you? Even under the cover of darkness. It's embarrassing and it has to be me that comes because I'm the only one that has a car.

You're lucky to be able to drive at your age.

Yes, but I get all the rotten jobs, don't I?

Hasn't she got a bike?

Well, yes, but, as she said to me, you can't cycle for a specimen bottle with that sort of problem, can you?

That's true. It could make her worse, what with the bike seat, all in the wrong places. I see what she means.

At least that's my good deed done for the night.

It could be you needing help one day.

Maybe it could, but who would get a bottle for me? I'm the only one that can drive and she hasn't got a light for her bike.

In Our Times

Wendy Lodwick Lowdon

'You took your time!'

'Ah, the days when I could shimmy through the mob and wave a smile and a wad of cash and get an early serve are long gone.'

'The queue was long, then?'

'Yeah, but not in terms of people, only three ahead of me, but then one of them ordered seven pints.'

'Seven! How did he swing that in this day and age? The SD lot will be all over him!'

'Naahh. Apparently, he takes them upstairs to the landing; it's a part of the pub where the residents can social distance and talk to each other. It's ...'

'Hey, what is it with using the coaster as a lid? I thought the plan was to put your glass on them?'

'It's the latest wheeze whereby bar staff are instructed to protect the beer from contamination ... any heavy breathing or coughing while transporting the amber nectar and the lid takes the damage.'

'Guess I just flick it onto the table with a fingernail then? Then what?'

'It'll be collected after we leave by minions wearing blue gloves, stored for three days and then be trotted out as a lid once more.'

'Can't help but admire the ingenuity of creative drinking. I mean look at this place. Who'd have thought we'd be in a pub with Social Distancing still laying down the law. Yet we've booked this table, which is the regulated two metres long; we're sat at either end and we'll able to have a drink together for forty minutes before surrendering it to a deep clean and another couple of desperados.'

'You know I'm real grateful even if it is just forty minutes. Drinking on my own was bloody awful and the beer tasted sour. Good to see you, my friend, good to see you!'

'Hmm. Where'd did you say those seven pints were going?'

'Up to the residents – they've found a position which fulfils SD but where they can sit on the carpet and see each other and yarn.'

'I wonder how they distribute the beers? Do you think they're using the method popularised by that TV café; you know where the waiter puts the tray on a high table and the drinkers take turns to squat-crawl over to the table and take their drink without ever letting more than the whites of their eyes show above the surface.'

'Yeah, that was a funny skit. You know the man with the seven beers said something funny just before we did the SD do-si-do, so he could leave the counter with his tray.'

'What did he say?'

'He said if SD kept on much longer, eulogies wouldn't hold many surprises anymore. What do you reckon he meant by that?'

'Well … it's a thought. It's probably pretty true in the circumstances.'

'Yeah, but what did he mean?'

'Oh, come on! You've been to funerals where you don't know the deceased all that well; well, you've been around them for years, but you just know them through the job or something and drinks for a couple of hours once a week. At the funeral, some person you've never seen with your dead friend gets up and starts to talk about the past.'

'Yeah! And it all comes out in this tidy little story, polished up for the event.'

'But you find out stuff! You hear about losses and successes your old friend had never mentioned but that sort of explain a few twitches and the reason why he stormed out of one of the company meetings.'

'Or you make connections. You realise the weedy bloke was her cousin and the high stepping drape of shawls was her aunt and that's the Sunday commitment she'd never dodge 'cos they'd come through for her when the going was tough.'

'Or you find out they'd had a love child or were the founding member of the anti-something club or they ran away when they were ten and caused a nationwide child hunt.'

'Yeah, I get that but what's the connection to my man with the seven pints?'

'Well, these days the distractions in the pub have been muted. You know, the big screens are scarcely wound up much above a whisper, so drinkers, forced to sit miles apart, can talk to each other. There's no sport except reruns so nobody really bothers with that either.'

'Yeah, and you've had a few months to realise the most popular songs and TV are crap but the link to eulogies is …?'

'In the early days of 2020, if the music was blaring and the commentator shouting urgently about a game, you'd stick your head right next to someone else's and bellow a bit of nonsense in their ear.'

'Yeah! And spray spittle and warm beer all over their face in the process and then flick your attention back to the main event. Do I miss those days?'

'But now, with SD you can't get up close and personal without a permit and promise to household, so you have to focus and really concentrate on what's being said.'

'And what's being said is now in sentences and even paragraphs instead of fragments. I get the drift but I'm still struggling here to make the connection!'

'Those men boarding in the pub are listening, probably for the first time, to the longer story about another person's life.'

'Ohhh! No surprises at the funeral, then?'

'Sort of disappointing in a way, isn't it?'

'Don't worry. I'll keep a few gems to myself to have trotted out on the day that'll make your eyes roll.'

'Not you, mate! You're an open book!'

'Yeah, you wish. You'll have to wait until I answer the call to find out if that was indeed the case. Cheers.'

Flower Power

Trixie Roberts

If you walk through this neighbourhood on the fringes of the port's city centre on any evening, you will see an elderly couple sitting outside their flower shop. You will nod the normal courtesies and pass on without comment. The neighbours and people familiar with the place remember the old couple as having been there forever. No one can remember a time when they were not arranging or serving flowers during the morning or sitting under the veranda after siesta, waiting for evening customers.

The wife, Elena, had arrived in the port as a young woman, in the years after the revolution when everything was in turmoil. She had travelled from an inland town, beyond the mountains, where her parents had died in a plague. The plague was the sort that arrives out of the deep blue sky with the summer wind, rising heat and all manner of insects. Elena had nursed her family but was the sole survivor. She decided to make her way to the coast and perhaps find a ship to travel elsewhere. Before she left, she visited Anna, the wise woman of the village who helped families through life's major events.

'I helped most people here into the world, including you, Elena. I've laid many of them out for burial; too many since the devil sent that plague that took your mama and papa.'

'I shall miss you, Anna, but I must see what the world can offer me. There's nothing left here.'

'On the road, if you are in difficulty, always seek the help of a wise woman. You must look after yourself. Send me word from time to time to tell me how you are.'

Elena had few belongings and no map. She just knew she had to keep going west. There were not many family possessions to sell as most had been burnt because of infection so her little money had to stretch a long way.

On her journey, Elena learned many lessons about life on the road. How to find shelter from the midday heat and when to rest; how to hide her money to avoid theft; the kindness of goatherders in the mountains when she lost her way; despite Anna's advice, the things she was forced to offer in exchange for lifts. As she neared the coast, she discovered plants and flowers unknown in the dry plateau inland. They were all growing wild and the scents and colours were unlike anything she had ever seen. The people she met had no interest in them; they were not edible so had no value. But Elena was intrigued and began to understand their power.

By the time she arrived at the port, her money was almost exhausted so she joined the girls waiting by the dockside for sailors, newly paid. It was the only way she knew of making a living and the girls were friendly and welcoming. It was the next best thing to a new family. She explored the town too and one day, returned to its outskirts and found patches of ground where the bright flowers and grasses grew. She picked some and wove then into a band which she tied round her hair. The scent was warm and musky. That night she had a very wealthy customer. When in his hotel room, she untied the flower band to loosen her hair and left it on his pillow. He paid her very well. Elena became very friendly with a co-worker, Carla. Carla was rather plain and because she didn't show great enthusiasm for her work, she struggled to get clients. Elena made her a corsage from the sweet-smelling, ivory flowers of jasmine and that night, one of great heat and a large, low moon, Carla had men following her all round the port. Elena made bands, corsages and bracelets for all the girls. They were happy to pay a few cents for something that would enable them to earn a lot more.

'Do you have gardenias, today, Elena? That huge cargo ship, *The Cotopaxi* is due in this evening. Last time you gave me gardenias, the engineer paid me enough to feed everyone at home for a week.'

Flower Power

'I'd like those red ones. They look good wound into my black hair.'

By morning, the flowers had faded, been crumpled, their scent disappeared, so the girls needed more before evening. That was how Elena started her business. Word got round so she was asked to make floral arrangements for christenings, weddings and family parties and she was always invited. Because she collected the flowers herself, she charged a lot less than the town's florists. Their prices were out of the reach of the street girls and their families.

One hot day, whilst walking to collect flowers, Elena found an empty hut and went inside to shelter from the sun. It was abandoned and neglected but solid. The windows, doors and shutters were sound. The roof didn't leak and there was no sign of vermin. It was cool inside and outside was the remains of a wall round what would have been the yard. There was even an old water pump. From the hut, she could see the streets of houses on the fringe of the town, where the factory and dock workers lived with their families. Day by day, Elena cleaned and patched up the hut. She moved out of the bordello and instead of working through the night, started to go out in the early morning, before the sun blistered and picked her flowers. She spent the rest of the morning plaiting, twisting and shaping wild rose and honeysuckle into decorations of beauty and allure. Then she would open her shutters and the customers would come. At first, it was the town girls and their families but as time went on, the local residents would come to her at times of fiesta and carnival as well as family occasions. She called her shop 'Flowers of Love.'

Elena was now able to send word back to Anna that she was fine. She had her own shop, lots of friends and enough to eat. Soon Elena was able to build another room at the back where she slept and had a small kitchen. There was enough money to buy ribbons and coloured yarns for binding instead of grass. She combined pins, combs and beads, discovered the times when the ships bringing flowers from the islands were coming into dock and would purchase a few to combine with the gathered ones. Elena's shop always had the wonderful scents of hot summer. Her reputation spread and respectable women began to seek her out to buy a little something for a rare tryst with a lover or in the hope of giving some encouragement to an elderly husband.

One day, as Elena was closing her shop before siesta, a well -dressed young man arrived. This was unusual as flower shops were seen as the province of women. This young man, however, was gentle and well-spoken, not at all like the sailors who used to pay for her services. Elena didn't think he had used any woman's services; he seemed a total innocent.

'I am sorry to come just as you are closing. I have had to get here from my office on the other side of town. But I have heard about you and think you may be able to help my sister.'

Elena was intrigued. 'Of course,' she said, 'Come in.'

His name was Luis and he seemed so shy and hesitant that Elena could tell he would be slow to explain. She put on a pot of coffee and gave him time to tell his story.

'My family has been well known here for generations. My father owns and manages a large engineering company; they specialise in irrigation systems. I work in his office. My sister, Alma and I have had a very privileged life with good tutors. Alma has been doing some voluntary work at a charity hospital and has fallen in love with one of the doctors. I have met this man, Daniel. He is a kind, generous person, but somewhat older than Alma. He is not from a wealthy family and he had to work to pay for his training, so it took him years to be qualified. Now he works in the charity hospital where they cannot give him a high salary. He wants to marry Alma but they are afraid my parents will not agree.'

'A doctor is a very respectable profession. Why would they object?'

'Because he is poor; he is older, nearly forty and because I think, my father in particular, would prefer Alma to marry the son of one of his business partners. My mother is more sympathetic.'

'But it is Alma's choice. She's the one who has to live with the man she marries.'

'Yes, I know but she is very loyal to my parents and would prefer they give their blessing.'

Elena was intrigued and puzzled.

'How can I possibly help?'

'My parents have agreed to meet Daniel. They have invited him to dinner tomorrow evening. In fact, it was my mother's idea. Daniel and Alma will explain how they feel and hope they can persuade my father to agree to an engagement. I would like you to provide flowers for the table and the house. Perhaps decorations for my mother and Alma to wear as well? I have heard talk among the women in our office about the effects your flowers can have on a hot night. I want my father to be in the best possible mood.'

Luis then offered Elena a fee she could only have dreamed about.

'If I could afford to, I would do this for nothing as I'm so impressed by your love for your sister.' She agreed to accept half.

Elena knew a ship was coming in next morning with flowers in its cargo and she would easily be able to afford blooms in their prime from the generous fee she and Luis had agreed. She couldn't get to sleep that night, partly because of the airless heat but mainly because she was planning the flower combinations and arrangements in her head. She also found it hard to stop thinking about the sensitive young man who had appeared from nowhere and the last thing she remembered before falling asleep was an image of his dark eyes and shy smile.

Elena was up before the sun had time to be more than warm. She chose flowers at the docks, picked wild ones from the lanes and set to work. By siesta time, they were all finished and it had been arranged that Luis would drive to her in the family car to collect them all.

'These are wonderful,' he said, burying his nose in a table display. 'My mother will love them.'

'Let's hope your father does too. Please let me know how it all goes. I hope it will be good news. Then I'll offer a gift of flowers for the wedding.'

Elena was desperate for a siesta after the bad night and the morning's work but there were interruptions from her old friends. A tanker had just docked and the girls knew they would be busy. Elena's flowers made them so irresistible, they could charge more. Elena couldn't refuse her friends and with the help of coffee, laughter and gossip, she found the energy to twist wire, ribbons and petals while they wondered why she had a rather distracted look.

Later that evening, there was a tap on Elena's door. She hadn't expected it so soon. She had the wine ready but not lit all the candles. Luis came in full of excitement like a child at a birthday party.

'It was all perfect. It worked like magic.'

'Of course. But how did you get away so early?'

'When I arrived home with the flowers my mother was arranging the table but already dressed for the evening so I gave her the corsage and she pinned it on immediately. She was most impressed with the flowers for the vases and the table arrangements. My sister was still taking her bath. When my father came home, my mother poured him a drink and asked him to sit down with her in the conservatory. She gently but firmly explained how Alma and Daniel would be really happy together and he ought not to make Daniel too nervous tonight. Did he not remember how nervous he had felt when he had approached her own father? Then she kissed him and he gave her a look which said he was powerless to deny her anything.'

Elena was impressed by how the shy, stuttering man who had come to her only the day before had acquired such honey-tongued confidence. He went on.

'When Alma came down, I gave her the flower braids for her hair. She breathed in the scent and was delighted with them. Daniel arrived and stood beside her. The hair braids were level with his nose. When we were all together before dinner, he took a deep breath and didn't give the long meandering speech of the nervous suitor. He spoke to my father respectfully but clearly, said how he and Alma felt about each other, touched briefly on his work and lack of prospects but he hoped my father would agree to their marriage. All in three eloquent sentences. My parents were so impressed my father agreed immediately. You really worked a miracle.'

'No,' said Elena, pouring the wine, 'Daniel is obviously a man they can respect and it's clear he is going to look after their daughter well. That's all they want. But I didn't expect you quite so soon. Didn't you have dinner?'

'Yes, dinner went really well. The conversation never stilted and over liqueurs, my father offered to make a large donation to the hospital. I couldn't believe it. He kept looking at my mother and suggested they shouldn't hang around boring the young people. Then he led her up the stairs. I felt uncomfortable then, left with the two lovebirds but Alma asked Daniel if he would like to walk in the garden and I saw them making their way to the summerhouse. As I was left to my own devices and it wasn't very late, I decided to come and thank you.'

'Good,' said Elena. 'Enjoy your wine. Let's drink to love.'

The very positive 'Yes' Luis spoke in reply surprised Elena. He emptied his glass, stood up, bent over and kissed her. She took his hand and led him to the back room where she opened the shutters to let in the moon. He saw she had strewn rose petals over the pillows and pinned jasmine flowers to the mosquito net. She untied her headband, letting her hair fall and pulled off her sash.

'There's no rush. No one at home is going to miss you tonight.'

Luis allowed himself to sink into the pillows after the hot, packed day. By the dawn, after Elena's skilful tongue and feral fingers had done their work, Luis knew he could not live another single day without her.

Elena and Luis extended the shop. They bought the land at the back and cultivated their own flowers. They built a hot house. Luis' father designed a state-of-the-art irrigation system. Through the family's contacts they found corporate clients keen to put floral decorations in boardrooms where deals were to be struck. They were in demand for society weddings and events. Elena always stayed true to her friendships with the street girls. One of their first employees was Carla, who turned out to have green fingers. Some of the other girls came to work from time to time and Elena always donated flowers to their family celebrations.

This was all a long time ago. The port expanded. The neighbourhood was developed and the remaining ground swallowed up by flats, houses and supermarkets. But the old shop called 'Flowers of Love' with its gardens and hothouse is still there. If you should walk past it, you will see an elderly couple sitting outside as they wait for customers. At siesta time, they close the shop and retreat inside, where Elena will pour wine and strew rose petals over their pillows.

The Ledge

John Heap

'I'm freezing,' said Mike, 'and you told me not to bring my bag. If I'd agreed with you, I wouldn't even have my jacket! Fast and light, you said, fast and light!'

Chris couldn't help himself, 'Emphasis on the *fast* Mike. Let's think about this and how *fast* you were getting out of the tent this morning and how *fast* you were getting your shit together. At every belay you had an excuse to slow things down. We should have been off hours ago; if I'd known you were so incompetent, I would've left you behind.' Chris drew breath, but too late; it was said.

Mike looked away, pulled out his cigarettes and with a slow and careful movement, he lit one up, sheltering it like a loved thing. Chris envied the release it brought, the immediate composure.

Mike turned and said, 'Suppose I was a bit hung over this morning. We shouldn't have brought that wine up to the tent.'

'Perhaps.'

They both looked out. The rock was sheltering them from the worst of the weather, but periodically they would be blasted by an aberrant gust. Snowflakes, the quintessential image of softness, gravel hard, ricocheting down their necks.

Mike continued, 'But then again it was probably all that ale the night before; that was a night, eh? I tell you what, though. You were on a promise with that Michelle. She couldn't take her eyes off you.'

'Possibly,' Chris allowed himself a smile, as he thought about her, that night, the drink, the plans, the warmth, especially the warmth.

Chris used to have romantic notions about alpine bivouacs, with the beckoning lights of the valley emphasising the distance from the familiar. Not anymore. All he saw was grey, dusk grey, mist grey, nothing grey and despite the drop below, he felt strangely claustrophobic. He wished for the night, for then he wouldn't be able to see what he couldn't see.

The snow drifted up behind Chris' shoulders, but trying to dislodge it made it fall behind his back pushing him further from the cliff and making his seat feel even more precarious. For the first time, Chris wondered whether this could get serious, whether their discomfort could shift into something more dangerous.

'I'm glad I didn't get off with that Michelle,' said Chris.

'What? Why's that?' Mike was irritable again.

'Well just imagine the inquest. What it would do to Sue, if Michelle was the last person to see me alive. That'd be hard for her wouldn't it?'

'For God's sake Chris, what inquest? Don't you worry. I'll be there. I'll give them their statement. I'll tell them how you were a miserable pessimistic shit right to the end, OK?'

'OK. But I'm still glad.'

The night progressed slowly. They were getting colder and their ability to do anything about it was diminishing. There was a little water left and Chris decided they had better drink it, before it froze completely.

'Mike. It's time for a drink.'

'What?' He opened his eyes with difficulty.

'Here, drink some of this.'

'You sure?' Mike took a big mouthful and then another.

'Hey. Not all of it!'

Mike looked at the bottle, it seemed to take a long time to register, but eventually he shrugged and handed it back.

'Chris, we've been mates for ages haven't we? You know, really close.'

'Hmm,' said Chris with suspicious ambiguity.

'Well, you know, Sue. Well there's something I should tell you.'

'What's that then?'

'Well, it's really about me, as much as her, I suppose.'

'What the hell are you trying to say, Mike?' Chris demanded suddenly alert.

'Forget it, if you are going to be like that,' and then to Chris' frustration Mike leant back, his arms folded, his eyes closed.

'Mike!' Shouted Chris, but to no avail.

Chris watched and waited for some time before turning off his lamp, he was then immediately alone again, and in solitary a person can lose their mind.

He sat there, playing with the remote, going over and over his relationship with Sue, rewinding and replaying the little vignettes of their life together. His first thought was 'Sue wouldn't do anything like that, not to him,' but then immediately added, 'Would she?'

Had he been entirely oblivious? Chris remembered an occasion when he'd arrived home from work, expecting Mike to come around for an evening session on the wall, but he was already there, waiting. Wasn't there an awkward feeling about that? And the way Sue came breezing into the kitchen saying 'You two ready for the off?' And hadn't she stopped complaining about the amount of time he spent climbing? That didn't feel right either. Suddenly it was all clear; it wasn't 'Would she?' but 'She would, and with him.'

Chris looked across towards Mike, trying to resolve his shape, black against black. He felt a base loathing and immersed himself in it. He punished himself with the most graphic images he could. He wanted to feel the pain. He needed to feel it, to feel the emotion, to fan the hatred. He imagined their bodies together, their mixing of fluids; he forced himself to totally understand the implications, to no longer hide in foolishness.

Chris' thoughts were rank with putrid despair; they bubbled and formed, shifted and sank, and then rose again. They came from a place that Chris didn't know, but a place he recognised as his own. They frightened him, but he welcomed them. They were solid, they were dependable, they were real.

There was another side to Chris, a calm side. One that knew he was on a ledge suffering in the cold, attempting to deal with the snow, and trying to cope with the worry and fatigue of an unplanned bivouac. But this quiet side had been relegated out of his body; it could only witness from afar the louder, brasher and more passionately alive side. The side that was about to unclip Mike's rope and drag him to his death.

Nobody would know. It would be a mistake, a mishap, a death by misadventure. And when Chris somehow got back to the valley, nobody would blame him. They would look after him, comfort and counsel him; there would be sympathy. Sue would hold him in her arms, and then in the warm darkest part of the night, he would whisper into her beautiful ear, two simple words, 'I know.' That would be enough; it would be her turn to suffer. She too would have doubts and then, she too would be certain.

'I know,' would be enough.

Chris switched on his light and looked at the screw gate that held Mike to various points of the rock; it wasn't far away. He could lean over and reach it and in the darkness, slowly move the lock anticlockwise, a few turns only, and let the sling fall silently from the gate. A quick tug and it would be over. Chris practised the movements in his mind; seven seconds of courage would be enough. He just had to reach across.

'You all right, Chris?' asked Mike, roused by the light.

'Just go away and die won't you,' replied Chris and turned off his torch.

Cowardice and self-disgust are hard habits to shake off and even as Chris was practising and planning, he knew that he wouldn't do it. He knew it was all bullshit, a fantasy. He knew he would just sit there, useless, in the dark.

The Ledge

A few hours later and dawn was approaching. The weather was calmer and so was Chris. He now knew what he'd known all along, that he had just favoured the comfort of the status quo, over the difficulties of confrontation. He now knew he was free; he knew that there were many beautiful places to see and only one life with which to see them. He knew it was time to move on.

He looked over at Mike, who turning his head towards him, affected a Monty Python voice and said, 'I'm not dead yet.'

Unprepared, Chris accidentally smiled and then said, 'Let's get out of here; I've things to do, places to see.'

Together they sorted the ropes.

Town and Country

Vicky Turrell

The geese in the field shrieked. A chill wind had sprung up. The wisteria tendrils clung on more tightly to the front porch and the early hanging blooms shivered.

A sleek red car came down the lane, screeching back at the geese. Its brash colour stark against the subtle greens of the countryside.

Olivia had come to see her aunt and she had brought Ben along to proudly introduce him. She had spent happy times here as a child but as she grew up, she began to despise the emptiness of the countryside where all her family lived. She had never cared for getting her hands dirty with gardening and could not bear the poultry with their never-ending need to be cleaned out and fed.

It was safe for a child here, but she soon began to feel suffocated. It was as if the tendrils of the wisteria were surrounding her, trapping her in this boring green wilderness. Olivia had wanted freedom and adventure, and as soon as she could get a job in the city, she left.

Ben rapped on the door as the wisteria swished above his head. There was no reply. Olivia knocked again and again, but there was still no reply. Aunt Daisy knew she was coming; they had arranged it all by letter. Annoyingly, there was no mobile phone signal here and certainly no broadband. There was a landline phone, though, and now Olivia wished that she had rung this morning, just to check that it was still fine for them to come.

The door was firmly locked, so Olivia hunted round and, sure enough, the plant pot was still there from all those years ago. It was full of daffodils now; she lifted it up and there was the key. It was a big brown one to match the door.

They went in apprehensively. There was silence inside the cottage apart from the tapping of the wisteria branches on the window. They tiptoed warily and listened to the echo of their footsteps on the stone floor. They shouted, 'Aunt Daisy, Aunt Daisy,' but there was no reply. Then Olivia spotted the note, scribbled on a piece of torn-off paper, on the table.

> *Dear Olivia and Ben,*
>
> *Welcome to Wisteria Cottage. Sorry I am not here. I have had a fall on the kitchen floor, just as I was going to get your tea. Managed to call an ambulance – am going to the local hospital.*
>
> *Help yourself to anything you want. There is plenty to eat.*
>
> *Love, Aunt Daisy.*

Olivia rang the hospital. Aunt Daisy was fine now that her arm was bandaged and no bones were broken. And she felt even better being looked after and having a cup of tea. She had to rest that night but they could come and pick her up tomorrow.

Ben and Olivia were relieved and then suddenly realised that they were starving. They searched the kitchen for food. But they couldn't find much. They couldn't find a fridge or a freezer. They found homemade bread and tea bags. Butter and milk stood in the cool north facing larder, but nothing else. They had toast and a cup of tea and then went to bed to get warm; there was no central heating.

'I don't understand how she manages to live here,' sighed Ben.

On the way to the hospital, in the morning, they went to the supermarket and filled the boot of the car with food and a bunch of exotic flowers for poor Aunt Daisy.

Aunt Daisy sat bemused in her living room, the gaudy flowers already wilting in a jug. She was surprised that the logs had not been burnt to keep the young couple warm last night – maybe they didn't feel the cold like she did. She carefully walked to the kitchen and stared at the bright boxes and tins of food on the table.

She was puzzled, because the garden was bursting with vegetables, ready to be eaten, there were home grown apples and potatoes stored in the shed and the geese in the field were surprised that their eggs were overflowing in their nest box.

'I don't understand it,' thought Aunty Daisy as she took in the sweet scent of the beautiful wisteria flowers wafting through the air.

Far and Away

Wendy Lodwick Lowdon

I am the seventy-seventh colonising flight. I've taken a one-way ticket. There were fifteen flights still logging, blogging, blobbing their experiences when I entered my ship, Far Seeker.

It has been 27,000 hours since I was launched from the Jupiter space station and I have had no further information about the other flights. I only know how I am doing in this ship on my own. On my own because, they, the powerful in Earth Biosphere Foundation (EBF), informed by techs and psyches, decided marooned was more conducive to survival than companionship. For almost fifty flights, they'd sent crews of four, three or two but all proved to be vulnerable to the psychosis of one (and there was always at least one); misery likes to share and to bring down the roof on all not just itself. Thus, I am, all on my own, an observer on a Robinson Crusoe (RC) colonising vessel. I suspect the silence from the other ships is a planned separation; after all comparisons are odious and I must admit before I took my seat, I was getting jealous and tetchy about a couple of the pilots before me stealing all the best lines.

I have no duties but to record my physical and emotional well-being; or unwell-being. Part of the selection was to discover how attached one was to 'a room of one's own' and the fluidity and lucidity of one's stream of consciousness. I have always liked my own company because I appreciated the opportunity to pursue my own imaginary interests which turned out to be a fit for being sought for the Far Seeker expedition.

I am separated from the engines and the recording equipment; this became the procedure after three space flights were disrupted and two destroyed by RCs who began to imagine they were not alone. It was made very clear when I interviewed, and at every training session thereafter, that for the purposes of the journey, my role was to be human cargo. I have no access to any of the controls. A third of the ship, which I call home, is almost wholly given to the hydroponics farm which provides my food. I am also expected to grow my clothing. The ship has a built-in climate control of a mere fifteen-degree differentiation over the course of twenty-four hours and nakedness is mostly comfortable. The thinking is that any work to ensure adequate body covering, which is a preference rather than a necessity, is handy as occupational therapy. Similarly, if I want a pack of cards or body paint or a dice, I must make my own.

Estimated arrival time for Far Seeker is eleven years. I am detached from the movement of the sun but the light and heat in my ship waxes and wanes in a regimented routine. Large numbers getting gradually smaller were the calculations more suitable for my mind set; I preferred cricket and basketball to the tedium of celebrating one goal. Indeed, I find I eschew the whole concept of years here and I tell you, at this moment I have, 92,720 hours to landing on ES3.6. And so I progress hour by hour to the destination.

I hope to get there alive but the survival percentage for Robinson Crusoes, though longer than ships with multiple occupancies, was in the low twenties when I was launched. My death would only be a disappointment, but a minor disappointment, especially since pilots have been deemed unnecessary and all personnel are unable to access engines or navigation. Far Seeker RC77 would remain in good order without me and it would continue on the mission without me.

Should I buck the odds with my continued existence by being alive in 92,719 hours' time, when RC77 lands, I would have the ability to facilitate the speed of the colonisation. In the event I do not make it, a mechanical spreading machine would be activated which would perform all that was necessary. EBF assured my they would miss my reports which provide the nuanced human knowledge and observations about the site. Once I was accepted for the Robinson Crusoe programme, I had to graduate in a number of related sciences, studied with an electronic tutor, before I was considered for the post. I suppose they would not have made me spend all those hours studying, if I really was superfluous to the mission.

My long-term life options, even if I make it through, will be tied to the ship as this planet will not be very hospitable for mammalian life. They told me it would be a one-way ticket. The rewards are to be reaped by my family; a breeding permit for five over three generations and status elevation with education and purpose. Obtaining influence will be up to them but however much they gain, they will not be in a position to bring me home.

There was a period of time on this voyage when I forgot who had made the choices to become an observer and I was convinced it was thrust upon me. Despite all the years of training and preparation, I ended up thinking my family and EBF had connived, conspired and tricked me into being here. I thought like this for a couple of weeks. I was very angry about their cruelty and I recorded my rage. After a while, I was so exhausted and bruised and voiceless, I could not sustain my attacks about their unjust imprisonment of me in this tin can.

I became calm and then felt colourless. My sense of commonality with other people had been so eroded the distance, and the distancing, deepened. Of course, that was to be expected. I had read the electronic dairies of several of my predecessors, which were censored, but they all wrote about being distant and lost; they repeatedly used words like pariah, outcast, exile and hermit. Their blogs recorded themselves as being marooned, ship-wrecked (and unhappily for some of them this came true!) and abandoned.

I described myself as unhitched. In the months following the two dreadful, raging weeks I recorded how I was unhitched, unhitched, unhitched again. I screamed I was unhitched and said I was unhitched while I banged my head against the floor.

I did think, now I am past the worst, that it would take a little longer before I lost the plot. I had anticipated at least 35,000 hours. After all, my profile was considered very promising given my disposition for introverted activities and general lack of interest in other people. I was also not a genius nor someone with a super focus nor given to deep introspection. Geniuses were among the first sent on Robinson Crusoe ships but they died early from diseases associated with lack of personal hygiene and hunger, though they were meticulous in making readings and formulating intricate, mostly ridiculous, theories. Most were dead within 15,000 hours.

Now I find hunger very motivating.

I can hardly bear to write about that time of horror and distress a mere 27,000 hours into the voyage because I fear it will engulf me yet. I am terribly aware my condition is volatile. I confess I have times when I curse them that took engine, direction and steerage control away from me; I curse them for several hours. I roll up in my rug and sleep and I wake to curse them all the more. There are times when I tend my plants and grubs, my hands shake with anger and I have mashed them wantonly. At odd moments, which take me by surprise, I scream and scream and fling myself from wall to wall. And then I cry but these distressing episodes do not last.

When my breathing is back to normal, I am not shaking and I am not sighing or crying, the years of hours I planned upon surviving still seem possible. It is not as if there wasn't preparation for these despairing episodes, once I was selected.

I had applied because my study grant had dried up and I was about to be housed in the dormitory with no allocated desk space. I hate the puerile mutterings of people and I hate it even more in close-up. Also, I knew my cousin was in line for breeding but she was close to thirty and then she'd be spat out of the programme. EBF likes several motivational reasons for applying for the RC programme. They liked my profile for the stubborn isolationism I consistently displayed and they infused it with the necessity for routine.

I have been on the bike. It is my preferred form of exercise: no wheels just pedals and resistance. Well, there are wheels but currently they are in use in the spinning wheel. Expertise in making paper and cloth from fibre was another part of the training thus I can scrutch and ret with the best of them. I don't switch on the wall screen. I have become unconnected to stories about a world I no longer belong to.

The weekly rationed sleeping pill is five days away so if I want to sleep, I need to be tired. Sometimes sleep evades me even when I achieve a state of exhaustion.

My preparation was primitive, literally. The computer would do all the calculations and control every aspect of the flight and the landing. My role is to survive as an effective entity so I can supplement the purposes of the biome release. It involved training as a farmer for the most part. I raise vegetables and grubs. I am fond of my witjuti grubs. They grow in the roots of the Wanderrie Wattle plantation (twenty-five square metres). I also raise flax on another twenty-five square metres on the gallery above, which provides seed and oil for me, food for my grubs and the option to make paper and clothing. The rest of the farm, this year, is planted with potatoes, beans, spinach and rosella. Active fungi were considered too opportunistic as evidenced by what happened to RC31. The water tanks take up the most room but they are run by the computer, to which I have no access: the water is sprayed, filtered and recycled and sprayed again.

I have no access to the bio-tanks either. Only when I arrive at ES3.6 will the doors to three of the chambers become available and I will have a small influence over the manner and placement of the robotic delivery of their contents unto the world: chlorophyta one month, phytoplankton the next and then flatworms. My final delivery after two phases of the year – yes they expect me to live that long – will be zooplankton.

I am to mother the most basic and primitive of life forms under a new sun.

Rosetta

Kirstie Edwards

Rosetta lived in a small cottage on a cliff, which overlooked the shore. She had never known her father. Her mother she remembered as young and beautiful, with long wavy, auburn hair. Sometimes she thought her mother was there with her, but it was hard to tell. She knew that she lived on the very edge of a tiny village, but she did not know its name.

Rosetta was trapped. She could see into the past of her own life. She could also see into the future, but she could not see or understand anything happening in the present. Her actions were not controlled by her own will, but by some other force. She could not account for her actions and yet afterwards, she knew exactly where she had been and what she had been doing. This is perhaps hard for the reader to understand, because we live in the present and everything we do is in the present. Rosetta did not know of the present. Occasionally she felt something, a queer power trying to open up her senses to the present, trying to make her alive. Perhaps these were the moments when someone outside of her was trying to reach inside, trying to understand her, trying to communicate.

The villagers pitied her and prayed for her. The fact that she did not talk or communicate to them in any way classed her in their minds as mad. Her actions had no purpose and she made no effort to help anyone understand her. She never spoke and she never looked directly at anyone. She behaved as though nobody was there. She was described by the villagers as 'not quite there.' However, she was not locked up or cared for, because she survived without harming anyone, even when they tried to communicate with her. She mostly kept herself to herself, living up in the cottage on the clifftop. One or two kind hearts in the village occasionally took a loaf or other simple food produce up to her cottage and left it there for her.

Often, she was seen standing on the cliff, leaning over the very edge with no fear of falling. At other times, she was found standing on the beach, whilst the tide came in around her. The water would ripple over her pink toes and deepen until it covered her ankles and knees. Then, when the waves were washing around her waist, she would walk away to climb the rugged path up the cliff to the cottage.

Her mind was full of pictures. Flames danced high around her. Then she would see a picture of her mother. A beautiful young girl running through woods and along pebbly shores and climbing cliff sides. Unconsciously, she was seeing herself acting out romantic but purposeless feats.

On one particular occasion, she became very aware of something unfamiliar to her natural life-sequence. She saw pictures of herself with a man. He hit her hard across her face. He was making loud noises but she could not interpret his meaning. Nor could she understand his violent gestures.

The man was a stranger to the village and passing through he had happened to see Rosetta clutching a large stone in one hand. Her grip was so tight that the sharp edge of the rock was cutting deep into her flesh, so her blood flowed freely. However loud he spoke to her, Rosetta did not seem to hear nor even look at him directly. Assuming that she was blind and deaf, the man tried to take the stone out of her hand, but she would not let it go. He hit her to bring her to her senses, but the stone remained fast in her grip.

Rosetta tried to understand. She screwed her eyes up tightly and willed to understand, to be there. She knew what she was looking for now, something in between, not in her head, but she couldn't find it. She screamed, for she could not speak. Then, the power which controlled her so completely took command once more. Later, whilst standing on the cliff, she saw a scene in her mind. She saw herself kill the man. She had hurled the heavy stone at him. It hit his head and he fell instantly to the ground. The blood from two souls now covered the stone.

Rosetta found herself crying. Emotion flooded her soul. She was reborn but had never been alive before. She was still fighting a power and swinging between the past and the future, but the power was weaker now. She felt free. She could see and feel a present.

Hearing a mumbling noise outside the cottage that night, Rosetta went out. There, for the first time, she saw real live humans and she understood life. She saw that they were trying to communicate with her. They were trying to make her understand something.

The village folk saw the blood stains on her dress and hands and full of superstition and pagan beliefs, they dragged her down to the village and burnt her at the stake.

Rosetta watched as the flames danced higher and higher around her. Then she saw into the future; she saw her own ashes lying where the fire was now living. Then she saw those pieces of dust, all that remained of her body, being lifted by the wind and scattered towards the cliff and out to sea. She felt an even greater freedom. She looked back at the people's faces around her, the villagers watching her burn. How serious and frightened they looked gazing at her. It made her feel trapped again, more so than ever before, for she could not tell them, she could not make them understand that now she was alive.

Package to India

With apologies to E.M. Forster.

Ronald Turner

As the plane dipped towards Delhi the sun rose and by the time the formalities were completed at the airport it was bright day outside. Margaret followed the others through the air-conditioned building and out onto the forecourt where the minibus waited. The heat outside took her breath away; like opening the door of an oven and stepping in.

Passing through the suburbs Margaret could not at first accept the reality of what she saw: cows ambling undisturbed along the highway; women in colourful saris carrying piles of bricks on their heads; a barber and his customer squatting opposite one another on the pavement. These still seemed like images on her TV screen at home, rather than the real world just a few feet away. She began to feel slightly nauseous: partly with weariness after the long flight; partly from the suddenness with which she had been whisked from the late winter gloom of west London, but mostly because she found herself, for the first time in more than twenty years, in a foreign land without Philip by her side.

Margaret, at forty-two, was easily the oldest member of the group. Several times during the journey she began to wonder why she had joined them. Her entitlement was obvious. This was the height of multiculturalism and the trip had been arranged by her local education authority for those who taught in schools with a high proportion of pupils from families with an Indian background. Margaret was head mistress of such a primary school in her borough, but she knew she was not like most of the others in the group, who were apparently already experts on India. They kept in touch with the politics, they knew all the statistics, some of them had already begun to learn the language of the area they were to visit. Margaret's India, on the other hand, was an amalgam of *Jewel in the Crown*, a very popular TV series at the time, *A Passage to India* recently filmed, and the cultural snippets she had absorbed from daily contact with her pupils and their parents during the last six years at her school.

Next day, they left Delhi and headed north, crammed into an even more dilapidated minibus, jolted along terrible roads, faced frequently with extinction as huge, highly decorated trucks thundered towards them in clouds of dust and waited until the very last second before moving over to let them pass.

The other, younger members of the party had already formed relationships so Margaret found herself sitting next to their guide, Mukat Singh, a tall broad Sikh with a thick black beard and matching eyebrows hiding most of his smiling face. She had been disturbed by Mukat from the moment he had taken a fierce grip of her hand at Heathrow and introduced himself. He was altogether too big, too loud and jolly; like a dark brown Father Christmas. She thought of slim, dapper Philip, setting off for his office in Shepherd's Bush.

As they progressed northwards across a vast fertile plain, crossing wide rivers, passing fields of maize or plantations of banana and papaya, squeezing through crowded villages or stopping for 'chai' while the ancient minibus cooled down, Margaret discovered that Mukat was good company. He was intelligent, knowledgeable, gentle and charming. He had lived in London for many years, while studying for an engineering degree, before returning to his native land to pass on his technical know-how and lead groups of foreigners on visits such as these.

When they reached the village where they were to experience the real India, Margaret felt immediately at home. It reminded her of the fenland village where she had spent her childhood. There was the same higgledy-piggledy cluster of buildings surrounded by a windbreak of trees, like a little island on the vast sea of the plain.

Margaret wandered about the village, watching the older women repairing walls with a mixture of mud and dung, or the younger women bringing back on their heads enormous loads of straw from the surrounding fields. Wherever Margaret went she was followed by a pack of skinny children with distended stomachs, watching her every move, giggling and chattering or trying to persuade her to photograph them. She looked at these children and thought of their counterparts in her school. Which were the happiest she wondered? She noticed one child in particular, a girl of six or seven, with a beautiful face but runny eyes surrounded by buzzing flies. As Margaret took out a handkerchief and wiped the little girl's eyes, she felt a twinge of yearning for the child that she and Philip had never had.

Mukat had disappeared since they arrived at the village. He had important meetings to attend; many things to arrange. But on the third evening he joined them for their meal and asked if anyone would care to accompany him on his evening walk. Only Margaret agreed.

They set off for the edge of the village where there was a little shrine among the trees. Mukat padded beside her in silence. When they reached the shrine, he put his palms together and bowed briefly in prayer.

'This is a Hindu shrine. Of course, I am a Sikh. But God makes no such distinctions.'

Margaret paused too, but only to appreciate the beauty of the evening. She had been brought up in the Church of England but had abandoned religion many years ago. Philip's recent conversion to Catholicism and her own refusal to join him had in fact caused a slight rift between them.

Night fell swiftly as they turned back towards the village and fireflies appeared, dancing round their path. Suddenly Mukat blurted out.

'Are you married, Margaret?'

She began to tell him about Philip, but he interrupted her, 'I am married, but I do not live with my wife. She lives with our children – they are grown up now – in England. She would not return with me to India. Perhaps one day my children will come home.'

'I don't have any children,' said Margaret. 'My husband didn't want … Then I became so busy with my career. Now it's …' She stopped abruptly, her heart thumping. What on earth was she doing telling all this to someone she hardly knew?

In the darkness, Mukat took her hand and gently stroked it and she felt immediately calmed. They walked on, side by side, as stars began to crowd the velvet sky. That night Margaret hardly slept, partly because of the patter of drums celebrating the wedding of a village girl, but mainly because this place seemed to be unwrapping years of habit and leaving her vulnerable to disturbing feelings.

By now the rest of the party had succumbed to various ailments and the main topics of conversation had become lurid descriptions of the symptoms or lengthy discussion of possible remedies. Margaret began to feel quietly superior as she remained healthy. In fact, she had not felt so well for years. She did not mind the heat now that the first shock had worn off, and she loved the spicy vegetarian diet which would have been her own choice anyway, but Philip loved his meat and it had always seemed too much bother to cook separately for herself.

Margaret did not see Mukat again until they began the next stage of the tour. Then, as they travelled northeastwards, he sat beside the driver, chattering away in the local language. As she studied his broad back and nodding turban, she wondered why he seemed to be avoiding her and wondered equally why she cared.

The plain ended abruptly and they began to climb into wooded hills which rose higher and higher. The minibus began to complain as the road climbed in spectacular loops. They crossed a narrow bridge and glancing down Margaret saw a river boiling fiercely over huge boulders far below. She closed her eyes and wondered how she could possibly describe all this to Philip.

Two days later they reached an ashram high among the Himalayan foothills. It was a place of peace and stillness. Margaret joined the others in meditation but felt restless and silly. She walked alone among the pines, listening to the cuckoos and found that her eyes kept suddenly filling with tears.

Again Mukat disappeared, except at mealtimes. He did not make direct contact with her even then, but sometimes when Margaret glanced up from her food, which they ate sitting on the floor, she would catch him looking at her before he could turn away. No, she decided, that was just her imagination. Mukat was interested in everyone and everything. He had something to say on most subjects and delivered his opinions in a deep bass voice that commanded attention.

One afternoon Margaret was sitting on a low wall, writing a postcard to Philip, when she became aware that Mukat was standing behind her. She quickly dropped her card into a pocket as he spoke softly.

'This is a very special place for me, Margaret. When I came back to India I was in a terrible state of mind. It was not so much that I had left my family behind, but that I didn't really care. I felt this tremendous sense of waste, realising that I had lived half of my life without really knowing what I had done with it. Apparently, this was one of Gandhi's favourite retreats. So I stayed here and began to make some sense ...'

He broke off suddenly, took Margaret's arm and lifted her up. 'Watch!' he commanded, pointing northwards. She looked as directed and saw nothing at first, except the usual veil of cloud which had covered the northern horizon since they arrived. Then the cloud began to drift away, like a stage curtain drawing aside and behind it a whole new landscape began to emerge, of gigantic, sunlit snowy peaks. Margaret had thought they were already high up but now she found herself lifting her gaze higher and higher to take in those sharp summits of rock and ice. She felt slightly faint and leant back against her companion. He opened his arms and she relaxed momentarily into his comforting grip, then quickly disentangled herself, as the cloud reformed over that staggering scene.

Next day they moved on to their final destination; a small lakeside town that had been a hill-station during the Raj. At first glance they could have been in Switzerland, with steep wooded hills slanting into a jade lake, but closer inspection revealed the ramshackle state of the buildings and the smell at the lake's edge was definitely un-Swiss.

Once they had booked into a dilapidated hotel Margaret set off to explore. She took a well-worn path which wound among rocky outcrops as it followed the shore of the lake. She remembered taking a similar track in Scotland on her honeymoon. It seemed a very long time since she and Philip had walked anywhere together.

She stepped around a large rock and froze. A group of big, black and white monkeys, stood like assassins, staring her out. What would they do if she tried to pass them? Would they leap after her if she turned back? Suddenly a familiar voice boomed behind her.

'Don't worry, Margaret. They won't hurt you. But they do look fierce, don't they!'

She turned and gave Mukat a relieved smile. They walked on together.

'I was looking for you. The others said you'd come this way. There is something I particularly wanted you to see. Come!'

They walked on round the lake until they were almost back in the town. When they reached the place Mukat had no need to tell her. Margaret exclaimed, 'Good God.' For here, among these Himalayan foothills was an English village church, surrounded by a little churchyard, with perhaps a hundred long-neglected graves, such as you would find anywhere in rural England. There were even large blackbirds, which might have been crows, cawing among the dark pines.

Margaret walked slowly among the gravestones, fascinated, reading the names of English officers, their wives and many, many children, who had ended their lives in this far-off land. She did not object when Mukat took her arm. He began to speak slowly, solemnly, half to himself, she thought.

'First you English invaded our land. Now we have invaded yours. It seems we are destined forever to be linked. Yet we are so different. Will we ever really understand one another? Sometimes I think we do not even like one another, yet ...'

Margaret withdrew her arm, then turned and hugged her big companion, pressing her head against his chest. She did not know what would happen next. She did not care. In a few days she would be back in South Harrow, back with Philip, back at her school and the long, slow flow of her normal life would be re-established. But in the meantime, she was further away and higher up than she had ever been and she had seen, briefly, another world, even higher and further, beyond the clouds.

The Bend in the Track

Trixie Roberts

Approaching Abbotsmere station, the track curves sharply to the left so the speed of the already slow-moving train becomes a crawl.

I am on my way to a school reunion, the first time I've done this journey in fifteen years. Then, I took the train every day until the post-exam world called. I knew the journey would not have changed; the same hills, the same townscape beyond the grassy railway banks. And now, edging towards this bend, the same deceleration, the brake squeal and the whole train listing to the left. On this evening of high summer, I knew the bank by the side of the bend would look different.

He was always there, every day during my final year. The smart, dark suit, briefcase and *Financial Times*. As anachronistic a caricature as a *Punch* cartoon. Around exam time, when the war in Afghanistan was at its most vicious, I noticed he wore a black armband. One morning I stood near him in the crowded train as we neared the Abbotsmere bend. He moved towards the door, too soon for the station and pulled down the sash window. He put his hand in his pocket and with a single, swift movement, withdrew it and thrust it out of the window. As his palm opened, a quantity of what looked like black dust hung momentarily in the air before allowing the breeze and slipstream to scatter it over the bank.

Now the train is inching towards the station. At the bend it leans over as if to salute the display of brilliant red poppies clothing the bank, vibrant in the evening

Overheard in a Café

Vicky Turrell

Have you a toasted teacake?

Sorry sir, no toasted teacake.

Why not?

No toaster.

I'm on a diet, my wife is brainwashing me into eating healthy.

Good for you.

She didn't give me breakfast and now I'm starving. Butter us a teacake, love.

No can do.

Why not?

No teacakes.

Give us a mug of coffee then and I'll think about it – not easy when you're watching your weight.

Milk or cream, sir?

Cream.

Sugar?

Two please.

Anything else sir? I can recommend the chocolate cake.

Oh, go on then, a big piece of cake.

Do you want custard with that sir? I can heat it up.

OK then. You've twisted my arm.

There you are, sir. Enjoy.

I will. You can't starve, can you?

Sorry we didn't have any teacakes, sir.

Good job really. My wife said I have to get my weight down.

Geraldo the Great

Bernard Pearson

I see dead people. Well you would too, if like me you worked in a crematorium. Not that we see everyone, that we are, how can I put this, providing a service to, but well you know mishaps occur, particularly when we are short-staffed as we are at the moment. It's not always accidents when we get to see the deceased. We had one chap who was chairman of a double glazing firm and he insisted on a very ornate sarcophagus made entirely of glass. Apparently, he had fallen out with all of his family so he had 'BOG OFF' engraved on the lid.

Then, of course, there was the case of Geraldo the Great, the escapologist, and a rum business it was too. You may remember Geraldo according to his publicity, 'No chains can bind him! No prison can hold him! No tomb can contain him!'

You see the one thing about cremation is it is there to provide certainty; I mean you know what with a 9,000-degree heat and an eight-inch urn to take away with you, you can be pretty sure your loved one ain't going to walk through the door and ask why their tea isn't on the table, or so I've always thought, until that is old Geraldo came along. He had according to reports passed away peacefully at a conference of escapologists in Blackpool. His doctor, a man named Culpepper, an old friend and amateur magician who happened to be attending the same conference, had written on the certificate 'Natural causes consistent with a pre-existing condition.'

Any how, it were a big do, his send-off. The car park was full and many of his friends from his years in the circus were there. I could see them, some in costume, as I was putting the bins out. Now I know what you're, thinking: bins at a crematorium? Well it doesn't all go in the incinerator, you know.

Anyway, where was I? Oh yes, there was Maurice the Strong Man there and Angelique the Bearded Lady plus several of the clown troop in full make-up. There were others in civvies so to speak. Geraldo's widow of course, a woman of somewhat craggy aspect, and then standing a little way off was a tall striking woman of indeterminate age, dressed in a beautiful, red dress with a black shawl around her neck …

Being 'Johnny on the spot' due to the council cuts and covering three people's jobs, I had to go back into where the magic happens and begin to get the ovens up to regulo seven, so to speak. Geraldo was our first customer that day, just as I got to the door, I came across the young clergyman who was to perform the ceremony.

Now you get to know all sorts of clerical gentlemen in my line of work. There are those who love a good funeral and those who get in a filthy temper about the fact people only come to religion when there's an occasion but for the rest of the year don't touch God with a barge pole. But this young chap were different; he appeared to me to be a troubled priest.

'Morning Reverend,' said I.

'Oh hello,' he replied. But he wouldn't look me in the eye. He just continued wringing his hands nervously looking down at his shoes.

'I'm Father Robin.'

'Nice to meet you,' I replied. 'I'm sorry but I can't help noticing you seem a little troubled.'

'Well, I shouldn't really be telling you this, but by spiritual supervisor, Bishop Norris, is coming to observe me officiating today and I happen to know, the one thing he absolutely hates, is when "funerals become blasted circuses" as he puts it,' Father Robin said, casting a doleful eye over the assemblage in the car park, just as Wanda the Bareback Acrobat arrived on her snow-white steed, dressed in little more than a sunny smile.

'Look, I'm sure it'll be fine,' I said trying to calm the poor fellow down a bit.

Geraldo the Great

One has to say, as far as I could see, proceedings got off with due decorum. The congregation appropriately trouped into the building. It was my job at this point to be doorman to ensure no stragglers disrupted the service once it had started. There were no latecomers but just before things got really underway, the beautiful woman in the red dress came out and asked where the ladies were. Then the music started. Geraldo must have had a bit of a sense of humour as it was an instrumental version of the Engelbert Humperdinck classic, 'Please Release Me.' Everyone in the congregation smiled, apart that is from Bishop Norris, a large dour-looking man under an even larger dour black overcoat. He sat at the back of the room like a thunder cloud waiting to do its stuff.

However, he was upstaged when about halfway through the eloquent eulogy – by Waldo the Wild Knife Thrower to the Stars – the fire alarm went off.

'Oh gosh, dreadfully sorry about this,' said Father Robin. 'Perhaps we'd better just pop outside. I mean it could be a technical fault.'

'Right! Everyone follow me in a calm and orderly fashion,' I heard the old bishop roar.

Well, of course I immediately thought electrics and went to check in what we called the 'oven suite.' Of course, I know this wasn't following the fire procedure, but we have occasionally suffered with a bit of 'after burn,' if you know what I mean and those smoke detectors do tend to be a little oversensitive.

The fire brigade arrived six minutes later, adding somewhat to the carnival atmosphere of things. However, Geraldo's widow looked less than impressed and I had the distinct impression she wanted to get on with saying her fond or otherwise farewells to her hubby. Eventually the mourners trooped back in for the rest of the service, after it had been established that one of the 'Break glass' fire alarm points had been broken, probably by that gang of kids who seemed to take pleasure in desecrating the place. If I ever get hold of any of them, there'll be a few more funerals added to our rota, I can tell you.

Things went relatively smoothly after that. I was detailed to stand guard outside the room where the service was taking place in case any of those little terrors tried to pull another stunt. Father Robin mumbled through a few more prayers and there was a moving duet by The Human Lighthouse and Master Tomb Thumb of *All things bright and beautiful, all creatures great and small.* Then, multitasking as ever, we took the coffin and placed it on what we in the trade call, 'Brucie's conveyor belt' and the curtain came down on Geraldo for what supposedly was the last time.

But here's the funny thing. At the end of the service, Maurice the Strongman called me over and asked whether we had a first aid kit, as his friend, who it turned out was the beauty in the red dress, had had a mishap and cut her elbow. Nasty it was; he said she'd taken a tumble but she must have landed on glass. As I helped dress the wound, I noticed little shards glinting in the morning light. Was she the alarm raiser? Maurice thanked me profusely. Two other things struck me as odd: one was that we were missing two of the large potted rubber plants from our garden for floral tributes. It struck me that they would have weighed approximately the same as a corpse in a coffin and would certainly have been too heavy for any kids to have nicked. The other curious thing was that I could've sworn there were only five in the troop of clowns when we'd gone in but now as I watched them drive away, waving from the back of a minibus, I could swear I could see six, plus the beautiful woman in the red dress.

Last Orders at the Library

Trixie Roberts

'May I order a book? You don't seem to have it on the shelves.' Malcolm, the ever-obliging librarian was always willing to send out searches to other libraries in the county for requested books.

'Certainly, Miss Parker. I'll get the forms. You're just in time.' Malcolm, the librarian pointed to a notice above the desk:

> *Last orders for books from other libraries is Friday 1st March.*

'Oh dear, I see what you mean,' said Rose. 'But why can't I order books after Friday?'

'The library's closing at the end of March,' Malcolm explained. 'It takes two weeks to get a book on order. Then you have it on loan for two weeks. That takes us to the end of the month.'

'I didn't realise the library was closing.' Rose looked shocked. 'They certainly kept that quiet. What about our petition to the Mayor, all that campaigning? The Mayor said the council would "reconsider." We didn't hear anything so I thought it was still being considered and that the new financial year may help by bringing in some new money.'

'They certainly did keep it quiet,' said Malcolm. 'I only got my redundancy notice on Monday. Thirty years I've worked here. I doubt I'll get another job now and certainly not in the library service. They're cutting back everywhere, not just in Foxbridge.'

Rose worried about this all the way home. She and her neighbour, Jenny, had organised the campaign against the library closure. They called it, 'Foxbridge Library Action Group,' or 'FLAG.' They had presented the petition signed by the majority of people they had asked to the Mayor, Silas Pincher, at the Town

Hall. It had been a well-orchestrated campaign; press photographers and regional TV cameras had turned up to publicise it. FLAG was told the petition would be given 'due consideration.' It had clearly been ignored.

'Why didn't they let us know?' Rose asked Jenny; she had gone straight round there to tell her the news. Jenny poured tea.

'It's a deliberate ploy to keep it quiet till the last possible moment. Then the public can't take any further steps to try to reverse the decision.'

'That's very underhand.' Rose was still shocked.

'Well, that's Pincher and his brand of local democracy for you,' said Jenny. 'He's got form where dirty dealings are concerned; he pushes schemes through on the quiet and before anyone can do or say anything, it's too late. Remember that scheme to sell off the school playing field for a car park?'

'Yes, I do. Remind me what exactly happened. All I remember is that it was about to go ahead and then suddenly stopped.'

'Yes, well some of the parents were on a city break and they spotted, and photographed Pincher going into one of those "massage parlours." One of the parents happens to be a lawyer and spoke to Pincher "man to man" about the inadvisability of proceeding with the sale.'

'You mean, blackmail?'

'Charles the lawyer just called it "Gentle Persuasion." After all, Pincher does promote himself as an upright family man. Charles would have been very careful with his words.'

'How do you know all this, Jenny?'

'Charles is my son-in-law. When you're dealing with these characters, Rose, you sometimes have to be as underhand as they are. As for the proposed library closure, I'm sure we can still get some of the original FLAG members together and brainstorm to see if we can do anything. After all, we've still got four weeks.

I could ask Charles along to make sure any action we take is legal and to check out if anything Pincher is planning isn't.'

The next evening, Jenny's kitchen table was surrounded by militant library users, all of whom had been active in the original campaign. They were incensed that not only had the views of the public been ignored but that no one at the Town Hall had had the courtesy to inform them of the closure decision.

'Right,' said Jenny in the chair. 'We have two issues: the library building and the library service. Let's look at the building first. We strongly suspect Pincher has a plan to sell the building for development.'

'... and get a back-hander for himself,' chipped in a big man who had just walked in. 'Sorry I'm late.'

'You may think that, John. I couldn't possibly comment,' laughed Jenny and ironic chuckles broke out all over the room. 'Anyway, whatever his motives, he shouldn't be allowed to get away with this. Charles here, is going to use his contacts to look at getting the historical grading of the building assessed. That may stop him. Meanwhile, we have to preserve the library service – the community's thirst for books. We have a plan but we need the skills and know-how of all of you.'

She addressed this in particular to Bill, the postman, John the haulier, Maggie who ran a print shop and Geoff and Ellie who ran the scout and girl guide troops. Jenny was an excellent chair. She had already come up with proposals and assigned tasks relevant to the skills of the individual members. Rose was going to work on Malcolm.

Malcolm had never been asked out by a young woman before. When he thought about it, he reckoned it would have to be one as dynamic and forthright as Rose to ask a man out. He knew she was both dynamic and forthright as he'd seen the books she'd borrowed: *Feminism and Fate* and *Self-Determination for the Modern Woman* had stuck in his mind. Despite working everyday with these books, the changes in gender equality of the last thirty years had completely bypassed

Malcolm, who still preferred the world of Jane Austen and The Brontës to real life. In truth, he found Rose a bit frightening. Then he thought of the wordless days of redundancy stretching ahead and wondered if Rose may be worth cultivating: a sort of hobby.

Rose's motives were very different.

'I'll pay. I asked you here,' she said to Malcolm after ordering at the local tea rooms. It was very early, hardly anyone was in the café. Rose had led Malcolm to a quiet corner. She knew that Malcolm hated the thought of the library closing but as a paid public servant was in no position to do anything about it. She let him talk.

'It's not the money. I was an only child and my parents left me the house and some investments … and I'll have my redundancy. But I've no idea what else I can do.'

'Then perhaps I can offer you an alternative. Here, let me explain while you eat your teacake.' By the time their plates and cups were empty, Malcolm had a conspiratorial smile on his face.

'There will be no risk to you, your redundancy or your pension,' Rose reassured him. Just don't breathe a word to anyone and behave normally on the weekend the library closes. Just trust us.'

It was a sad day for Foxbridge, when the library closed: Saturday 30th March. Malcolm locked up as usual. With it being a Saturday afternoon, there was no one at the Town Hall to accept the keys so it was arranged he should keep them over the weekend as he always did.

On the morning of Monday 1st April, Mayor Silas Pincher was in his office thinking how smoothly the library closure had been. He had expected some last-minute trouble from that FLAG lot but it all appeared to have gone without upset. Later on that morning, he was scheduled to be showing a property developer around the library building.

What he hadn't seen was John the haulier's van drive to the back of the library after dark on Saturday. John had met Malcolm in a quiet spot and then a number of willing Scouts and Girl Guides. The High Street shops were not open on Sundays so there weren't many people around to see the unusual level of activity in them and the many deliveries, nor Malcolm running from one to another with index cards and lists. Silas Pincher had spent Sunday on the Golf course. He hadn't seen Maggie delivering a box of printed material to each shop, nor the Guides and Scouts working hard with each shopkeeper, all of whom had been asked to co-operate.

'So what's in it for me if I squeeze a bookshelf into the back of the shop?'

'Readers are browsers,' Rose explained to the owner of the gift shop. 'If they're looking for books, they'll look at your goods as well. They have to pass them on the way to the bookshelf at the back. You'll sell more and this scheme is bound to increase footfall on the High Street. The library is at the far end, near the bus station. Many people come into Foxbridge just to go to the library. If they have to walk along the High Street to get books, it's bound to increase trade. Anyway, if our plan works, it may only be temporary.'

Silas Pincher hadn't seen the historic buildings experts being let into the library over the weekend to make the initial assessment that could potentially halt any further plans. He hadn't seen Jenny and Rose go from one shop to another with cakes, nor had he been aware that, at the end of their day's work, Malcolm had been persuaded to reopen the library one last time and all the volunteers enjoyed a celebratory glass of champagne.

'I'll pick you up in the morning and take you to the station,' Jenny said to Malcolm.

'That's kind of you, Jenny. It was a good idea of yours for me to spend some of my redundancy money on a holiday in Scotland.'

… and in case any awkward questions were asked, Jenny thought.

The Mayor was preparing himself for the visit of the property developer when his phone rang. It was a representative from the Historic Buildings Association informing him that Foxbridge Library was of significant historic interest and he would be writing to arrange more further detailed visits. Meanwhile, nothing was to be done to alter the fabric of the building in any way. He was a jocular man and could imagine Silas Pincher's anger as he spluttered on the other end of the phone.

'I'll be in touch then, Mr Mayor. You never know, sir, your library may have a regal body in its basement.'

The property developer arrived. Pincher and other council representatives joined them in making their way to the library. The council representatives gasped in astonishment to see all the shelves were empty. In fact, some of the shelves as well as all the books were missing.

'You have been very prompt in clearing the building. Well done,' the developer said.

'Oh, well,' the Mayor thought quickly, 'We don't want any unnecessary delays.'

'Well, to be honest, I fully expect things to take some time. I have only just heard this morning about the strong local opposition to the "Change of Use" status of the building alongside the investigations into its historic, architectural grading. Also, as I always like to have a flavour of any place where I wish to invest, I walked along the High Street this morning. I had a very interesting conversation in the gift shop.'

Silas Pincher was nonplussed. He replied,

'Shall we arrange a further meeting when these minor issues have been ironed out?'

The property developer looked doubtful but suggested they keep their appointment for lunch at the Grand Hotel, so it was well into the afternoon before Silas Pincher was able to make his own enquiries. By then, the whole of Foxbridge knew about the

People's Library. Pincher's deputy on the council came into his office.

'What a brilliant move, Silas. You kept that plot quiet.'

'Er, sorry, Tim, I've had a strange day.'

'The word's got round. It's brought more people into the town centre than I've seen for months. There's a TV camera crew out there, now. Did you compose this too?' He handed the Mayor a flier. 'This is in every book in all the shops.'

The Mayor looked puzzled.

'Books in the shops.'

'Yes. Didn't you plan to get them all out so quickly? It's genius, moving the library books into the shops so people can browse while they're shopping.'

The Mayor looked at the flier. It read:

> *This book, along with all the books from Foxbridge Library, has been liberated. We are the property of the people of Foxbridge. Although the library has closed, you may still borrow books from High Street shops as you did from the library. The Popcorn Toy Shop will house all the children's books. As arrangements are fine-tuned, we shall let you know which type of book will be in which shops. Look out for the posters!.*

For once in his life, Silas Pincher was speechless.

The Bend in the River

Vicky Turrell

Kath and Ray stood on the old bridge looking at the rapids. They were on the grey stone bridge which matched the sky – Kath could feel tiny drops of rain going down her neck. It was a shame because she had just had her hair done ready for tonight; it would be spoilt. She looked at Ray with his camera and huge lens.

'Oh, hurry up Ray, for God's sake.'

'I have to get this just right.' He was pointing his camera lens and focussing carefully.

'Why have you got to be messing about with that great big camera when everybody else is using their phones to take a picture?'

'I've always wanted a Cannon EOS; they're the best. You know how I've saved for ages for it and ...'

'For goodness sake, Ray! Time's moved on while you were saving.'

Ray screwed the camera onto his tripod, taking no notice of his wife. He had to get the adjustments right – now what 'f' number should he use? He wanted quite a good depth of field, but he needed plenty of light for the action – he sighed – it would have to be a compromise.

Kath put her hood up.

'Oh, just shoot and let's go!'

'Ah, you can't do that if you want a good photo.'

'Why don't you put it on automatic like everyone else?'

There was no answer because in the distance Ray spotted the raft. There were, in fact, three inflatables, strong but flexible for white water rafting.

'Look at the rafts and in front the safety canoe!' Ray shouted excitedly; this was just what he wanted.

Kath craned her neck, disappointed now. Ray would be at least another ten minutes and her hairdo was getting squashed under the hood.

'Here they come!' he shouted above the noise of the rapids.

The safety canoe appeared first, through the haze of foam and cloud – down between the teeth of the dark rocks, through the waiting jaws and out at the end, its oar raised in triumph. It pulled to the side, away from the huge logs and mass of branches. They had been brought down by the winter storms and lodged at the bend in the river.

Then came the rafts – all full of excited red hard hats, like ladybirds swarming thought Ray. Like dreadful drops of blood, thought Kath. They disappeared and rose time and time again, foam flying, spray shooting. Oars raised in triumph before they rowed off under the bridge and downstream.

'Brilliant!' shouted Ray raising his hand in an echo of the oars.

'It's in the can.'

'No one says that nowadays, Ray,' shouted Kath heading off, hoping he would follow.

At last, they were in the crowded tearoom with a pot of tea and scones with spray cream, which looked like the frothing foam from the river.

'Look at these,' smiled Ray pressing the arrow for the next frame and admiring the pin-sharp photos. 'You couldn't get that definition with a phone camera.'

Kath glanced down stifling a yawn. He had taken hundreds; how boring.

'Just a minute – there's one missing.'

'It won't matter, you've got plenty more.' She poured another tea. 'Eat your scone.'

'No, I mean a person is missing. Look! Nine hard hats before the falls and only eight after.'

'It's probably a different boat or one is hidden from your camera. Drink your tea.'

Back at home, Ray slid the SD card into his desktop – and looked at the photos again on a bigger screen.

'There *is* one missing.'

'There can't be. They'll be tied in or something.'

'They weren't. Look! They are all over the boat.'

'Well, they'll have life jackets.'

'Might not have been fastened.'

'Oh, come on Ray! They would all be checked.'

'One might have come out and got caught under the branches and trunks.'

'You're letting your imagination run away with you. You've done that before – you always make things sound dramatic Do you remember when you couldn't find your car in the car park and called the police and then realised that you'd gone on the bus.'

'Look there's the red helmet under the branches. Just a minute, I'll zoom in – there!'

'Ray, that looks like a reflection to me. Leave it now; you will have to hurry if we are going to get to John and Debbie's in time for dinner.' She patted her hair into shape as best she could.

'I expect you are right, dear.'

Ray shrugged, closed his computer down and then went to get ready for a dinner with friends. He could not help thinking, though, that it had all happened so quickly and that it didn't seem to be a very organised event. Come to think of it, he hadn't seen them do a head count at the end. But what could he do? Kath was usually correct about most things.

Debbie greeted them at the door. 'I'm really sorry,' she said angrily, 'but John's not back yet. He went out with some new mates; it's just not on, him leaving me to do all the preparation for this evening's meal.'

Outside, the rain continued to pour. It was like a cloud burst and Kath and Ray were beginning to feel like drowned rats standing there.

'Oh, come in and dry off. Sorry, I don't know what I was thinking.'

'Why don't you phone him, if you are worried, Debbie?' asked Ray.

'I have done. He didn't pick up, so I left a message. He must have forgotten that you were coming. I didn't remind him and I bet he's gone to the pub after some outing or other. It's what he usually does.' Her voice was harsh and angry, but they eventually all sat down at the dining table.

'We'll start without him,' Debbie suggested.

The meal was wonderful – chicken and all the trimmings with a glass of white wine to finish.

'Not too much now, Ray. Remember you're driving,' said Kath leaning forward and tapping him on the knee – and we should be setting off home soon.'

'Just watch the *Ten O'clock News* with me and have a coffee,' urged Debbie looking more worried now. Her brow furrowed.

'I don't know where John can have got to. I am so sorry.'

They settled down in front of the TV. There were the usual war stories and sex scandals. Then Debbie's phone rang from the hall.

'That'll be John now,' said Debbie as she rushed out to answer it.

The local news came on.

'The police have found a body at the bend in the river. It is believed that the man fell out of a raft and became trapped in the debris and the rising water. Police believe that he lived for some hours and struggled in vain to free himself. Investigators are looking into why no one reported the man as missing. It is thought that he could have survived had anyone noticed him in the water ...'

Debbie's scream from the hall echoed all over the house as she dropped her phone.

Two's Company

John Heap

Margaret closed the front door behind her. She paused in the hallway, steeling herself before facing her sister; whatever state she was in.

'Hi Margaret, you want a cup of tea?'

Eyebrows raised in mock surprise, Margaret's eyes narrowed in suspicion, but after quickly checking against her mental catalogue, nothing seemed to be missing; all seemed to be well.

'OK. Thanks.' She placed her bag on the patterned carpet by the settee and sat down. The clock in the corner chimed six as she slipped off her black shoes and rubbed her feet. Secretarial work may be classed as sedentary, but she'd been on her feet most of the day and felt tired. Raising her voice to the kitchen, Margaret asked Louise if everything was all right.

'Everything's fine,' said Louise as she entered the room with the tea tray. Recently showered and wearing a faded pink track suit, she looked young and bright compared to her older, careworn, sister.

'Here you go, Margaret; I've got Tartan biscuits as well, your favourites.'

With a half-smile Margaret took a biscuit, sat back, closed her eyes and just enjoyed for a moment the delicious sweetness of it.

They were both quiet. Conversation was often best avoided.

'Shall I be mother?' said Margaret as she began to pour the tea. She realised her mistake and looking up saw the cheery smile fade from Louise's face and tears begin to well up in her eyes.

'I'm sorry Louise. I didn't mean anything.'

'I know. But it still upsets me to think of Mum sat in that chair by the fire. She always seemed pleased to see me, no matter what I'd done, but now she's not here. She was always so cheerful.'

'She wasn't always that cheerful, believe me. Remember whilst you were off gallivanting, I was looking after her. She could be a right madam when she wanted. That was Mother: lovely to visitors but …'

These things had been said before.

Louise didn't like Margaret talking about Mum like that, but today instead of protesting, she reached for her tea and wrapped her hands around her favourite mug. Margaret had a cup and a saucer.

There was another silence, but this time it was brimming with unsaid things.

Margaret was the first to break.

'You've tidied up as well?'

'A bit, before my shower.'

'But you never tidy up,' Margaret looked around and thought, 'and hardly ever shower,' then aloud again, 'and you're not watching television?'

'I wanted a change. I've been watching too much recently. I need to get out, do things, positive things.'

This unnerved Margaret.

'Louise, what's going on? Have you taken your medicine?'

Margaret never used the word methadone.

'No, I haven't. I've stopped taking that.' Louise was wide-eyed, as if scared and excited at hearing herself say this.

Margaret placed her cup and saucer back on the tray.

'Now Louise,' she said, 'what did we discuss?'

Louise kept silent, staring at her mug, with her knees close together hiding the tension in her body. Every muscle was straining against another. She tried to relax, to stay calm.

'No? Well, we discussed the fact that you could only live here if you continued to take your medicine. We are not going back to the days of your lies and thievery. And what will your friends at the Monday Club say? Now come on be a good girl and take your medicine! I'll put the dinner on.'

'I've thrown it out; it's all gone. I haven't got any.'

'What, where?'

'I don't need it, Margaret. If you'll just let me explain. Louise was getting agitated; she made to stand up, but then sat down again.

'At the Monday meeting, you know I sometimes have a one to one with a counsellor. Well, yesterday I had a chat with a new guy, Derek.'

'And what exactly did Derek say?' asked Margaret

'He said, methadone is a management regime, not a cure. It may not be the best thing for me.'

'But it keeps you off the streets and out of prison.'

'Yes, that's good, but Derek said that that's even better for society than for me. You know, I'm not a problem anymore, so … so they leave it at that. I'll be on methadone forever. But I don't want that, I want to be free of it.'

'But you haven't been for years; I have to look after you.'

'Margaret, I need your support. Don't you want me to succeed?'

Margaret started sorting out the tray, ready to take it back to the kitchen. She stood up over Louise and held her hand out for the mug.

'Of course, I want what's best for you, you know I do. It just upsets me to see you get your hopes up.'

Louise looked up, was about to speak, but just nodded and passed Margaret her mug.

Margaret took the tray out of the room to the kitchen, saying 'At least things are more manageable now; we haven't had any trouble for months.'

Louise got up and started to follow Margaret.

'I thought you'd be pleased. What after all those years of looking after Mum, then so soon after she … you know. Well then you had to start looking after me. Once I'm over this and feel stronger, I can get a job, and then my own flat and a life and everything.'

There was a clattering of crockery from the kitchen.

'Louise will you just listen to yourself. This Derek has filled your head with nonsense. Get a job? Who's going to give you a job? Now sit down whilst I get dinner together, steak and onion pie do you?'

Suddenly angry, Louise came rushing into the kitchen her fists clenched. She was aware that her finger nails were biting into her hands, but right then she needed and wanted the pain. Margaret turned, kettle in her hand and gave Louise one of her 'I won't stand for any of your nonsense' looks, and Louise, subdued, sat down at the kitchen table.

In charge again, Margaret talked calmly as she filled up the kettle.

'Listen, Louise; look at yourself, you're all tense and fidgety, you look as though you are about to explode, this really isn't doing you any good.'

Sure enough Louise was fiddling. She didn't seem to be able to sit still. Her hands were picking obsessively at the cork backing of a place mat. Margaret took it out of her hands and placed it back on the worktop.

Louise, with less confidence said, 'Derek says that I need to remember who I was before I was an addict, how it felt and how in control I was.'

She stood up and spent some time regarding the calendar, then continued, more brightly.

'And if I make it to the next meeting, it'd be fantastic. Don't know how long it'll take, but you know, a week at a time. I'll talk to Derek next Monday; he'll be really pleased.'

Margaret was losing patience again. She put down the potato she was peeling and pointing the vegetable knife at Louise, said vehemently:

'This Derek doesn't know what you're like. This Derek hasn't taken you into his home and looked after you for years. This Derek hasn't made the sacrifices I've had to make. I'm going to ring up the centre tomorrow and find out exactly where this Derek is coming from. You won't be speaking to him again, I promise you.'

Perhaps it was the way that Margaret had pronounced 'Derek' with such derision and contempt, or the way she had emphasised his name with a stab of the knife in her direction, but to Louise it felt like an assault and she sat down again, this time in tears of fear and frustration.

'Derek trusts me, and he trusts me to trust myself and you are being horrible. And I don't know why. I'm trying to make a change, become self-reliant and you're putting me down. Derek says I can do it and if he says so, then I can. I've thrown all my methadone away, so I have to do this.'

'Don't lie to me and don't lie to yourself! We both know you haven't got rid of your drugs.'

Louise stopped sobbing immediately and looked up at Margaret suspiciously. 'What do you mean?'

'Who does all the tidying up in this house? All the dusting?'

'What are you getting at Margaret?' Louise asked slowly.

'This,' she spat and with a quick movement Margaret reached above a kitchen cabinet, pulled a small silver foil package from behind it and slapped it down on the kitchen table, right in front of Louise.

Louise looked at the package in horror. Her hand moved out to reach it, but then pulled back. Not taking her eyes off it she asked,

'How long?'

'Long enough and I know where the rest are. So let's stop all this self-reliance bullshit, shall we? Brave words when there's emergency stashes all about the house. Just like your mother, you'll never make it on your own. Never.'

'I hate you,' said Louise.

With a grunt Margaret turned around, opened the oven door and busied herself with checking the pie. She caught a movement and then heard the front door close.

Margaret stood up, removing her oven gloves.

The wrap of foil was gone.

'Soon be back to normal,' she said, setting the table for two.

'Just the way we like it.'

Woman in the Moon

Celebrating the fiftieth anniversary of the first moon landing.

Ronald Turner

In the last summer of the sixties, when those intrepid astronauts set off on their long journey to the moon, Brian Jenkins went fruit picking in Herefordshire. He had this romantic view of rural life based on reading *Cider with Rosie* at school and seeing *Far from the Madding Crowd* four times at the Finchley Empire, so when he saw this advert in *The Observer*, 'Students wanted for fruit picking,' he quite fancied the idea, but it was his mate Mike who convinced him. 'All that fresh air and scrumpy,' he enthused over a second pint. 'That'll get the birds really randy. You'll be well in there, Bri.'

That rosy view of the countryside began to fade as Brian – having missed the only bus – walked the eight miles from Hereford to Upper Crabley weighed down with a bulging rucksack on one of the hottest days of that long, hot summer. Any remaining rosiness died out completely when he reached the village to be told that Manor Farm lay two miles further on.

As he trudged down a seemingly endless driveway, Brian began to see bright red double-deckers which dissolved in the heat haze when he tried to stop them. At last, he heard the sound of a real vehicle and turned to see a Land Rover approaching in a cloud of dust. When it braked beside him, the driver asked where he was going and offered him a lift. If the devil himself had been driving and demanded his soul Brian would have accepted, but closer inspection revealed that this driver was an angel.

The woman at the wheel, in her late twenties perhaps, was tall and slim, with honey coloured hair neatly coiffured and large blue eyes that matched her expensive suit. When she spoke, it was with the faintest of foreign accents, perhaps Scandinavian.

'You are here for the picking?' she asked as she expertly manoeuvred the heavy vehicle down the rutted lane. Brian wasn't sure whether this was a statement or a question, but her mellow voice excited him and he was disappointed that their journey together would be so short.

By the time they reached the farm she had inspected him thoroughly, taking in his tall frame, broad shoulders and fashionably long brown hair. He felt himself blushing under her scrutiny as she learned his name, age and where he came from, without revealing anything about herself.

She braked hard in the cobbled courtyard, scattering cats and chickens, directed him to the farm office and gave him a delicious smile before striding off towards the large farmhouse.

Glyn Evans, the farm manager, was Welsh, dark, short in body and temper. He growled at Brian the fact that he was later than expected, but showed him where to erect his tent, where the very basic amenities could be found and which field he should go to at eight o'clock next morning.

By ten o'clock the following day Brian was covered in sweat, his back felt as if it would never straighten again and his punctured hands were stained with blackcurrant juice. But there were compensations, like the view, which was magnificent. From the field where he stood the land fell away steeply and a whole patchwork of multi-coloured fields, dotted with toy farms and cottages, stretched across to the Welsh hills. And the view closer by became equally pleasing as the other pickers, mainly female, revealed more and more tanned flesh as the day grew hot.

At ten thirty a whistle blew and they all took their pickings to a collection point where Glyn weighed each offering and recorded this against the appropriate name. When he saw Brian's pitiful contribution he laughed aloud. 'Bloody 'ell, man! You picking fruit or just dirtying the basket?'

Woman in the Moon

'There's no need to be coarse, Evans. Everyone has to learn.'

It was the angel again, dressed this time in immaculate riding gear, standing beside a stout, crimson-faced middle-aged man, who wore a tweed suit and carried a shotgun under his arm. The young woman gave Brian another of those enchanting smiles before taking the man's other arm and walking away.

Brian gazed at the retreating couple until Evans came up and whispered menacingly, 'You watch it boy. That's Major Wacton's wife you'm gawpin' at.'

'You mean,' gasped Brian, 'she's married to that ...'

'Aye, lad and just remember, the Major owns everything round 'ere.'

At the end of that first day Brian collapsed into his tent, too tired even to undress but as the evening cooled, he recovered sufficiently to feel hungry and incredibly thirsty. He joined the others round a campfire, downed a pork pie and a jar of local cider, while he studied the females of the group. Several were quite pretty and all were friendly. Brian knew that girls found him attractive and that if he played his cards right, he could probably take his pick, but he could not get the image of Major Wacton's wife out of his head.

The moon above was full and bright. Someone remarked, 'I just can't imagine men walking about up there.'

'Well, they ain't actually took off yet, 'ave they?' added another.

Brian had never drunk homemade cider before and as he finished his third glass, he began to wonder which of the moons they were talking about. Feeling totally exhausted he staggered to his tent and fell into a deep sleep. When he woke again in the early hours and stumbled out to pee, the moon still blazed above them, untroubled as yet by mankind's temerity.

After a few days, Brian began to get the hang of things and felt less weary each evening. He looked forward to sharing cider and stories round the campfire. One of the girls had a transistor radio and kept them in touch with news of the astronauts who by now were well on their way. Brian tried to be interested but his mind was filled with more personal developments. Was it just coincidence that each time the Major's wife appeared she seemed to single him out for one of those heart-stopping smiles? So when talk turned to the moon and Brian glanced upward he did not see the cratered surface of Earth's nearest neighbour but the smooth, smiling face of the land owner's wife.

The next night, when Brian returned to his tent, he found a note pinned to his sleeping bag. The paper was scented and when he read the note with the help of a torch he could just discern the shape of a pair of lips under the few words.

'Meet me on Devil's Anvil tomorrow night at ten.'

The following evening someone suggested a walk down to the village pub for a change. Halfway down the drive they were overtaken by the Land Rover, going far too fast, forcing them off the road and smothering them with dust. Brian caught a glimpse of Glyn at the wheel, scowling as he accelerated away. Beside him was the Major's wife, looking cool and beautiful as usual.

'Our Glyn don't seem too happy these days,' said one of the group.

'Perhaps Mrs Wacton's roving eye has found another target,' suggested someone else and this set them all sniggering.

Brian did not understand why they all turned briefly to look at him or why they all burst out laughing again when he asked what the Devil's Anvil was. They pointed out the ancient earthwork, rising clearly beyond the village as a silhouette against the setting sun.

'They do say,' said one of the lads in true storytelling fashion, 'that if a young man stands on the Anvil at full moon, the devil himself appears in the guise of a beautiful woman and lures him to his doom.'

'Ah,' said another, picking up the tone, 'and the moon be full tonight.'

They all roared with laughter this time.

Woman in the Moon

When they reached the Ploughman's Arms they found the entire clientele huddled round a small, black and white television watching the *Nine-O'clock-News*. Apparently the American rocket was now in orbit round the moon and soon the lunar module would be attempting to land on its surface.

After a couple of pints Brian felt the need to relieve himself and went through the saloon bar to find the toilets. On the way he noticed Glyn sitting in a corner with the Major's wife and having what appeared to be a smouldering row. When Brian returned Glyn was alone. He rose from his seat and blocked Brian's path.

'Don't think I haven't noticed,' he spat out between clenched teeth. Brian opened his mouth to ask what it was that Glyn had noticed but the farm manager turned and stormed out.

Just before ten Brian excused himself and set off for the Devil's Anvil. Raucous laughter followed him into the still, warm night.

He did not have long to wait on that strange, turfed mound before all was revealed. The woman who had filled his thoughts since the day he arrived suddenly appeared, wearing a short white dress which appeared luminous in the moonlight.

'It is time, my dear Brian, that we became better acquainted.'

She rapidly discarded her dress, under which she was wearing nothing but a healthy tan and a luscious smile. At first Brian was transfixed, partly by her extraordinary behaviour but mainly by the firm beauty of her naked body. This was not Brian's first sexual experience but it went way beyond his usual inept fumblings. This woman knew so many ways to pleasure her partner and herself.

When it was over, she quickly pulled on her dress and hurried away. Brian lay, exhausted but content, looking up at the moon, which suddenly slipped behind the first cloud that had appeared in the sky for almost a week. Brian shivered, dressed rapidly and set off down the hill.

It wasn't long before he knew that he was lost. In the sudden blackness he groped his way into a thick copse which clung to the slopes of that prehistoric fortress. Suddenly an unseen branch caught him on the chin and the shock sent him stumbling backwards. The branch, if it was a branch, seemed to follow him, catching him forcefully on the side of the head, then in the chest and finally in the solar plexus. He gasped and swayed, winded by that last blow. He tried to straighten up and saw a shadowy form against the first flicker of lightning and a sudden breeze seemed to whisper, 'That'll l'arn you, boyo!' Then another blow exploded on his chin and he seemed to float down the hillside into a deep pit. Halfway down he lost consciousness.

When he woke, Brian was soaked and frozen. He didn't know how long he'd been lying there, but the storm was well advanced, with frequent flashes of lightning and echoing growls of thunder dimmed by the clatter of torrential rain.

By the time he reached the farm it was almost day. The storm had passed but heavy clouds were still racing across the dawn sky. All he wanted to do was to dive into his tent, strip off his wet clothes and sleep, sleep, sleep.

But his tent wasn't there. Or rather it wasn't a tent anymore. Someone had slashed the canvas and snapped the poles. He didn't need to ask who had done this and knew there was no point in complaining so he salvaged his rucksack from the ruined tent, stuffed it with his belongings, stuck a warm sweater, which had stayed dry under the tent canvas, over his soaked shirt and set off down the drive.

As he approached the end of the drive, he heard a familiar sound and turned to see the Land Rover speeding towards him. His mood lightened as he thought it might be the Major's wife coming to rescue him, but the vehicle swept past, showering him with muddy water. Oh yes, she was in the Land Rover, sitting beside the Major who was in the driving seat, but she didn't even glance at Brian as the vehicle sped on.

When he reached Hereford, Brian made straight for the station, thankful that he'd purchased a return ticket. With his last few coins, he bought a cheese roll and a newspaper. Its banner headline proclaimed, 'A giant leap for mankind!'

The First Thing I'll Do

Wendy Lodwick Lowdon

Jan sat down again. The pace, turn, pace and turn performed hundreds of times had served only to emphasise how small the lift was. She jammed her teeth together to stop the scream; the muscles of her jaw were getting the most exercise.

Despite her determination not to look at her watch again, as she had already done so more than a hundred times, she tilted her wrist so the sullen sodium light showed a whole seven minutes had passed and it was now twenty-three minutes past four in the morning. Jan had been in this steel coffin for five hours and ten minutes, stuck between the eight and the ninth floors. She was only two floors away from the comfort of her own flat.

Jan shook her head violently in an effort to shake away the lyrics of Glen Campbell's Song, 'By the Time I Get to Phoenix,' which mocked her situation because she wasn't rising an inch. It was an ear worm which was rapidly turning into a mole.

She focused on reassessing the list she had created which was all about the first thing she would do, imagined in exquisite detail, when she was released from her prison. Four hours ago, she thought the first thing would be to have a huge glass of cold Pinot Grigio followed by another larger one. Two hours ago, she prayed for release so she could go to the toilet, but another hour had passed without rescue, and she had had to succumb to the pressure on her bladder and had urinated as close to the lift door as possible. The consequent stench in the lift had been worse than that in the underpass to the Tube from The Red Lion and, for a short few moments Jan had felt so ashamed she was reluctant to be rescued. Then reason reasserted itself, she became less aware of the smell and the desperate desire to get out of the lift surged. She fought for composure by picturing the

183

long hot shower she promised herself as the first thing she would do once she got out of this awful, awful situation.

Jan stared at the emergency button. It was the one she had pushed when the neon lights failed and the lift shuddered to a halt. The button had accessed a robotic voice which informed her the emergency had been registered and she could expect engineers to open the lift in the very near future. That was all! Jan had pressed the button six times in the course of the first hour and the message had been the same and no engineers came to her assistance. The frustration about not being able to beg or demand or persuade the listener to organise a faster response had burned like acid; she felt so powerless. She decided she hated answering machines with a vicious intensity. The first thing she vowed she would do was to make sure all of her future interactions would be with a real person.

Jan looked at her mobile phone which she had placed carefully on the top of her bulging bag. It was turned off but she could make out its rectangular shape by the insipid floor lights. The signal in her sweatbox was intermittent and she had very little battery left. When she was still stuck in the lift after midnight, Jan managed to ring Cathy. She had had to balance on her bag, which she had stuffed with her jacket and shoes, to achieve enough height to get signal. In course of a short and shrill conversation, Jan had been told the power failure had affected so much of North West London that the emergency services were overwhelmed. Cathy had taken the details of the lift services and said she would get in touch with them for her. It seemed an eon – of struggling to stay on the bag and hold up the phone so long her muscles burned with fatigue – before the phone rang.

On the end of the line was a kind voice with an attractive accent who'd been alerted by Cathy as to Jan's current stuck-in-a -lift situation. Jan made an oath in her heart that the first thing she'd do once she had got out of the lift would be to order kind, lovely Cathy flowers and chocolates and theatre tickets. The real person, who really understood what it was like to be stuck in a small, dark, smelly lift, asked Jan to answer several questions. Was she alone? How old was she? Did she have any medical conditions? Jan had tried to make a joke about how she had nothing at the moment but she expected to get an ulcer. The voice, whose sibilant hiss seemed suddenly more pronounced, had informed her that, as she was a healthy young adult, she would have to wait several more hours for rescue. The scratchy voice had been sure she would understand and she was not to worry about being endangered by fire as all of the high-rise buildings affected by the power failure were being monitored.

Then the voice had disappeared and Jan had sobbed and wailed. It had been a long, frightening time before she was able to regain control. She had called Cathy to tell her the news of her not-so-imminent rescue and she had not been able to keep her voice from wobbling. Cathy's sympathy had brought more tears and choked gulping; but the screen on her mobile had gone dark and Jan had had to say she must go while assuring Cathy that she would probably sleep. She'd save her battery and she would ring again at seven. Hopefully, Jan had thought, by then she would have organised the flowers, had her shower and tossed down the two glasses of wine.

Jan had not slept. Her limbs were beset by tremors and her lips kept twitching. Her mind had been seesawing between imagining the stuffy heat in the lift was due to fire in the tower block and the film *Freefall,* which sessions of frantic exercise had not expunged.

Jan sagged against the lumpy bag. Her eyes were sore and she was thirsty; the first thing she would do when she got out of this horrible tin can would be to drink a bottle of water.

Shampoo

Vicky Turrell

When my daughter Sophie was at home, my shampoo bottle was always empty. She has lovely hair and she washed it every day with my special shampoo. It's expensive shampoo – luxurious and rich. It has all the things that my life has lacked and it has always been my only treat. I have never had much money to spend on myself – I have always spent any I had to spare on Sophie. It's not that I have ever really begrudged her anything. In fact, I have tried to give her everything she wanted, so maybe it was my own fault that my shampoo bottle was always empty.

And maybe it was my own fault that I had to bring Sophie up on my own. You see, I wasn't careful enough when I fell for Mark. We were young with our whole lives stretching ahead of us – we were so very much in love and flying high. What could go wrong?

What went wrong was that I fell to Earth with a bump. Mark fell out of love with me, left me for someone else and I was left with another bump that turned out to be Sophie. Not that I am complaining, you understand. I loved her as soon as I saw her and I knew then that I would do anything for her and give her everything I could. The trouble was I did not have much money. My job in the local supermarket didn't pay a great deal but I loved buying Sophie little gifts like sparkly slides for her beautiful hair. The smile on her face and her warm arms round my neck made it all worthwhile. She grew into a very pretty little girl.

The years seemed to speed by and in no time at all she was old enough to go to school and I know that I am biased but when she set off, she looked so lovely in her uniform with her glorious curly blonde hair shining out like a halo round her head. I had washed it with my special shampoo that very morning.

She looked just as lovely when she went to the High School and then on to college, although now she had long smooth hair falling like silken threads that swung in unison when she moved her head. Of course, she washed her own hair by now and, of course, she still used my special shampoo. I did not mind too much, because I didn't want her to feel that she couldn't have nice things just because I wasn't earning a great deal. Her absent dad was no support at all, but I wanted to give her the best things in life.

As she grew up, I found it ever harder to earn enough money to give her all the things she wanted. The clothes she chose were so expensive, and even though I worked more and more hours at the supermarket I was permanently broke. There was always that special party and later that special club that she was going to and of course she wanted the latest trend. She could twist me round her little finger.

'You wouldn't want me to look stupid next to my cool friends, would you?'

'Oh Sophie, don't exaggerate! The last silk top and leggings I bought you are still fine and you've only worn them once.'

'The top doesn't suit me anymore, and in any case it's not what they are all wearing now,' she wheedled and I gave in, I always did. I never said 'No' to Sophie and I did not know how to; maybe I never would.

Then, as soon as she was old enough and had passed her test, she wanted a car. I drove a very old one myself and took her wherever she wanted, but she had lots of good reasons why she needed a car of her own and she was very persuasive.

'Mum, I will need it when I go to uni. You won't want to be taking me backwards and forwards all the time, will you?'

This was the first I had heard of her wanting to go to university. I thought that it was a wonderful idea and I was so proud of her. How could I resist now? In any case, my car was so unreliable it would not take her backwards and forwards anywhere, let alone the distance to our nearest university. And

Shampoo

who was I to say that she would choose the nearest university? She would want to choose the best one, of course. So, it wasn't long before we were on our way to the car showroom in town.

But the car she wanted was not just any old car. It had to look good and there was a little red one on show that she spotted as soon as we arrived.

'Oh, Mum. Isn't this just so cool? Doesn't it just suit me?'

'It's not a fashionable top we are buying Sophie. A car needs to be reliable. Never mind what it looks like!' But I had to admit that she did look really attractive sitting there in the plush seat, flicking her hair back to show her big doe eyes pleading with me to buy it for her. The salesman tried to show her other suitable cheaper cars, but no, it had to be this one. In the end I gave in just like I always did and I had to take out a loan to finance it. I don't think that she even noticed how much it cost me to buy that car and make all the arrangements; she just wanted to drive it.

Sophie drove her new car with the window open so that her golden hair billowed in the wind. I sat beside her and shrugged at the salesman. He smiled at me and shrugged back as we drove away. I tried not to think about the loan I had taken out and instead I thought of how proud I was that Sophie was going to university.

But Sophie didn't go to university after all. She decided she wanted to be a hairdresser instead and she left her college and went off to live in a flat with some of her friends. And with a quick flick of her newly styled hair, she waved me goodbye. I was so disappointed but smiled as best I could and watched her rapidly disappearing car. I stood there alone and I knew that upstairs on the bathroom shelf would be sitting my empty shampoo bottle. She would have used my shampoo before she left.

Later, I found out that I was right. The bottle was as empty as the feeling I had inside me. I had given her everything and now she had left to start a life of her own and I had nothing –

not even shampoo to wash my hair. And at last, I realised that I had brought her up to be selfish.

I thought long and hard about what I should do about it as I tried to get on with the rest of my life, although it was very difficult at first. Then one Friday, out of the blue, she rang. She wanted to come home for the weekend.

'No,' I said. The word was out of my mouth before I had time to think. I could hardly believe it when I heard myself say 'No' to Sophie. I had never done it before. You see, I had a plan to change the habit of a lifetime and I was hoping I could stick to it. I didn't want her to come that weekend and I told her very gently why but I could tell she was shocked and she snapped her mobile off quickly, the mobile with internet and all the apps, which of course I had bought her.

I didn't hear from her for quite some time. It was hard for me and I often went to pick up my phone to ring or text her but I always managed to resist. I wanted to say 'sorry' that I had said 'No.' But I didn't. I stuck to my plan even though it seemed to get harder by the day. Then, after what seemed like an age, she rang again.

'Mum,' her voice was tentative.

'Sophie!' I practically jumped down the phone I was so pleased to hear her. She asked again to come home for a few days and this time I agreed.

I was glad to see her looking so well. Her hair was cropped now like a little bright cap on her head, short at the back and longer at the front. She had highlights too, I noticed, and I also noticed that she still used my special shampoo during her stay. I had bought a little bottle only a few days before but it was rapidly emptying. You would think she would use her own by now, wouldn't you? I know she has some of her own, just like mine (but a bigger size of course), because I have seen a full bottle in her wash bag. It made me sad, but I didn't say anything. She hadn't changed the habit of her lifetime even though I had tried. I said 'Goodbye,' to her just now and felt her warm arms round my neck and saw her smile. It was lovely, just like when she was little but I could hardly hide my disappointment. She has a good job in that very posh hairdresser's in town – I have never been able to afford to get my hair done there – and I bet she could buy her shampoo at reduced rates, but she still used mine. I saw my bottle on the shelf in the bathroom last night and it was almost empty.

Then tonight, when Paul and I went up to bed and I went in the bathroom, I saw my shampoo bottle was full. I blinked in surprise and then blinked again as joyful tears filled my eyes and spilled down my cheeks. Sophie must have poured some of her shampoo into my little bottle before she left. So instead of my shampoo bottle being empty, it is full to the brim.

And I am brimming with happiness too. You see after I bought Sophie the car, Paul from the showroom called round to see how it was running (well he said that was the reason) and we have started a new relationship so I don't feel my life is empty without Sophie anymore. When I said 'No' to Sophie, it was the first weekend Paul and I had spent together. I didn't want Sophie at home because I wanted to concentrate on Paul. I wanted things to go well with me and Paul and, thankfully, they did.

Now, thinking of her filling my shampoo bottle, I'm sure that Sophie has, at last, realised that I have needs too and that relationships need give as well as take. It was such a little thing but it means so much to me. Maybe the best thing I have ever given Sophie was saying 'No.' I did her a favour, which I should have done long ago. I am even more proud of her now.

And because I am so proud of her, I am going to celebrate and book an appointment at that posh salon in town for my hair to be shampooed and styled. I am going to ask if that special stylist, Sophie, is available to do it.

I hope she won't say 'No!'

Tricks of the Memory

Kirstie Edwards

You couldn't imagine a young boy dying in your arms on such a day. It was a hot, blue-sky, no worries kind of day. I was a little rushed because we'd spontaneously invited friends for a barbecue. It would be one of those Sunday afternoons when the fuzziness of wine and sun slowed time down. Standing in a queue at Sainsbury's, I glanced impatiently at my watch.

'Good morning. Do you need help with your packing this morning?' the checkout girl sang robotically to a concave pensioner with wrinkled skin.

'No,' the elderly customer replied resentfully, frowning folds into her forehead. She emptied the contents of her trolley as though each item were an anchor, heaving them up onto the conveyor belt one by one. Two customers in front of me threw up their eyes in despair. I glanced at my watch again. I only had twenty minutes. Perhaps we could manage without the extra beer; we had plenty of wine. The old lady stacked her precious heavy-weight purchases into flimsy orange bags; they surely wouldn't hold. The assistant chatted to her patronisingly, pretending to affiliate. She was giving her client the full shopping experience. A group of youths were laughing just outside. I recognised one with a peak cap; he'd rushed out past me as I entered the store.

'Seventeen pounds and fifty-three pence, please. Do you have a Nectar card?' the cashier finally trilled, but the old lady couldn't find her purse. Her bag was a Tardis of zips and pockets, but her purse was not to be found. The man in front of me abandoned the queue and marched swearing to the self-service till. The elderly lady became distraught. Someone had stolen her purse. The cashier slammed her till shut and rang a bell. The lady was crying now and a manager, who appeared from nowhere, bellowed to a plump, spotty young store assistant:

'Get a chair over here and fetch a glass of water!' The boy dropped the fabric softener he was stacking, scrambled down from his ladder and ran off to complete his orders. Wine it would be, I decided, feeling thwarted.

I abandoned my basket still full of beer cans and rushed out into the sun, where a boy flew up into the air and floated horizontally for a thousandth of a second. His body turned gracefully, his peak cap falling away from his jet-black hair, before he landed on the bonnet of an old Volvo, where his head thumped backwards and he fell to the ground.

Staring at the limp figure on the road, I fumbled in my bag for my mobile. Trembling, I tapped 999. The driver, a tall broad-shouldered man in his eighties, heaved himself out of the driver's seat. He wore a long grey coat, traditionally buttoned up to the top, even on this searingly hot day. He leant over and reached down close to the boy.

'No! Don't move him,' I shrieked. People emerged from nowhere and started to gather around us forming a perfect circle.

'I don't know where he came from; I just drove into the car park and he came from nowhere,' the old man stuttered. I felt sorry for him. His head was shaking; he muddled his way towards the store. I wasn't sure whether to call him back but I guessed someone would look after him in the store. His blue Volvo with its dented bonnet and open door had an abandoned air. The boy's friends stood helplessly, not knowing what to do.

'Give us space! Does anyone know first aid? Can anyone help?' My voice sounded strange to me.

A rotund woman with a shocking red streak in her fringe lowered her bulk down next to me. Relieved that someone was doing something, I watched her feel for his pulse. Relief was brief. There was no pulse. I watched as she pumped his small chest; the counts between pumps seemed endless. I folded my precious silk scarf to tuck beneath his head. Time slowed so that I was convinced the emergency services were not responding to my call. I rang three times in the eleven minutes it took them to reach us. When they arrived they declared the boy dead.

A carpet of flowers grew across the car park for weeks and the boy's death was declared a tragic accident, caused by age-induced incompetence. Eventually, Sainsbury's put up a small remembrance plaque and re-opened the car park. The elderly driver who killed the boy that day was sentenced to serve twelve hours of community service. A small price for a boy's life.

*****

Four years later, I was in Portugal with my husband, in a small market town called Soulée. After the hot drive up the narrow zigzagging lanes to the summit, where Soulée was perched, we wandered through the deliciously refreshing indoor market. Outside, under the maple trees, gnarled elders proffered their bunches of equally gnarled twigs of rosemary and thyme.

We joked about buying live crabs for dinner and which of us would dare to cook them. When I was little, my grandmother had told me that you could hear crabs scream as they fell into boiling water. The stall holder deftly wound elastic bands around their claws and dropped the now suffocating, lethargic crustaceans into a bag.

I'd seen the posters but hadn't paid much attention. Everywhere a tourist went these days, there were warnings about pick pockets. The lad was no pro. As I jostled between the shoppers' bags of ox tails and stinky fish, I felt two fingers crawling, sickly, into my pocket. We tried to keep up with him as he weaved out of the market hall, but we were hindered by the growing crowd and disoriented by the echoes of shouting hagglers. Outside, the intense sun was painfully blinding, slowing us down.

I soon refocused, but to an ugly scene. One of the withered herb ladies held the boy by the hair. He was screaming and twisting under her grip. She was kicking his shins raw. A second woman punched him in the stomach. He gasped and my purse fell from his hands to the floor, its value now lost to me. The penance was too cruel for the crime.

Confused, we rushed over. The eldest lady, with grey hair scraped back into a hairnet, thrust the purse at me. She was unable to mould her hardened face into a smile. I was unable to thank her. The boy ran away. He must have been eleven; his peaked cap lay between us in the soil, splattered with his blood.

My husband thanked the women, offering them money, but they shook their heads and returned to sit on the cushions behind their dead, colourless herbs. Henry bought some to demonstrate his gratitude and we escaped to a café, where we could sit in the shade of the maples to recover. Old men played petanque in a glade to the side of us. The clicking of the balls seemed strangely comforting.

I sat silently, while Henry described what he could do with the crabs and the herbs, but I could only see the boy with the bloodied shins. But I saw something else too. I saw the boy in Sainsbury's car park. I saw an old man in a long overcoat, buttoned to the top, leaning over Sainsbury's cold meats counter and pulling himself up when the young lad in the peak cap ran out of the shop to join his friends. An elderly lady, oblivious to the young lad, had continued with her trolley, slowly, slowly up the aisle, stopping occasionally to squeeze a vegetable, testing its ripeness, oh so slowly. The old man hadn't joined us at the till, but I remembered the old lady, who was two in front of me, when I queued to pay. She thought someone had stolen her purse.

'What are you thinking about?' Henry pulled me back to the present under the maple canopies. 'You're upset about those ladies beating the boy, aren't you?'

Henry knew me well.

'It wasn't very nice,' he said, 'I was shocked myself, but I suppose he won't steal again.'

Tricks of the Memory

'Two wrongs don't make a right.' I paused. 'Henry, do you remember the day the boy died in Sainsbury's car park?'

'I thought you were over that now?'

'I am. But something's worrying me.'

I explained about the boy running out of Sainsbury's to his friends, the youths laughing outside, the old man never buying anything and the old lady losing her purse.

'Well, what's so unusual about that?' Henry squinted as the sun rose higher. 'If the lad took the old lady's purse, he certainly won't steal again will he?' Henry sounded uncharacteristically cruel. My change of mood was annoying him. An hour before we had been happy holiday-makers.

'No, but the old man who hit him – he bent over the boy, while I was calling the ambulance. He took something. Could it have been a purse, do you think?'

'You think he knocked the boy down deliberately? You think he was trying to stop a pick pocket?'

'Possibly ...'

'That's rather far-fetched.'

We sipped our drinks silently, lingering over this macabre thought.

*****

Back home, I browsed the online archives of *The Ferrows Star* for any reference to the earlier tragedy. There was a short report on the date and a longer piece following the inquest. An eighty-eight-year-old gentleman had hit a young boy, while driving into Sainsbury's car park. I rang Sainsbury's to see if they kept records of thefts in the store. They did, but they had no record of any theft reported on that date.

Again, I saw the boy floating above me, the car facing me at the entrance to the car park in front of Sainsbury's. But I no longer pitied the driver. He hadn't just arrived. I'd seen him bending over the meat counter when I first arrived. He'd left without buying anything. He'd waited in the car park. I'd seen him bending down for something when the boy was dead and then return to the store. Just like the herb ladies, he had returned something to its rightful owner.

Playing Host

Bernard Pearson

Reverend Meurig Morgan had over three hundred marriages on the clock and almost as many funerals come to that. His church, St Iltydd's, was falling down around him; damp rot, dry rot, death watch beetle and then there were the atheists, of course. In his darker moments after one of his more lack lustre evensongs, he would ponder on such matters. God alone knew why they came, to church; it seemed such a waste of time, both his and theirs.

Mind you, given half a chance he'd have been an atheist too but then there were the visions. It's difficult to deny the existence of the Supreme Being when He's sat across your breakfast table or making Himself at home on your settee watching Match of the Day, while you're trying your best to put the finishing touches to a sermon on 'The Transfiguration.'

The odd thing was the Reverend Morgan could not quite put his finger on when it was that the Lord put in his first appearance, but it must have been a good few months ago now. If he remembered rightly, it must have been after he'd held an emergency meeting of the parish council around his kitchen table. Our Saviour was not present then. The only person there who put the wind up him that evening was Owen Coalville Jones, the treasurer, shaking his head like Banquo's ghost every time the church's heating bill came up for discussion.

St Iltydd's was a parish on the outskirts of Cardiff. It was quite a mixed parish, covering several long streets of detached suburban housing built between the wars. Most of the front gardens had been tarmacked over and were taken up with two, sometimes three family vehicles and the back gardens reduced by conservatories of varying designs. The houses were mainly occupied by young professional couples who worked in IT or the media. One or two were still owned by elderly, often widowed professional people and it was they who made up ninety-five percent of Reverend Morgan's congregation.

Then of course there was the estate, pebbled dashed and all painted in what his mother had called 'that condensed milk colour.' Reverend Morgan had long since given up the battle here. Some of them came, of course, but only for weddings, funerals and christenings, waiting outside the church until just before the service to come in, as if they might catch something if they loitered too long on sacred ground.

The Way Centre however was a different matter; here they gathered every Sunday, six to seven hundred at a sitting to hear 'Pastor Max' and generally have a good time. Both the young professionals and the unrewarded poor stood and swayed hands aloft in the kind of communion now only associated with the most fervent of football fan.

The 'better be on the safe side brigade,' as the Reverend Morgan liked to refer to some of his flock had been coming to church for longer than many of them cared to remember. They kept the place clean, organised the Christmas fayre and the summer fete in what were laughingly described as the church grounds. They were good people; he accepted that but the church served now as a kind of social club and his services had become peripheral events mostly, to be benignly endured.

So when did it start, this sharing the vicarage with one's Maker? Ah yes, he remembered now; it all began when he got back from his summer retreat. Well 'retreat' was how he referred to it when speaking with his congregation. In fact, it was more of a holiday with Felix, his old friend from theological college days. He'd turned in his dog collar years ago and now ran a cat rescue centre just this side of Evesham. Felix was a flamboyant, well-connected character who'd lost his partner, Troy, several years ago. He was a superb cook and raconteur and liked to spoil his old friend. Morgan for his part, would listen patiently to Felix's tales of woe, usually involving council bureaucracy over the housing arrangements of his cats, or his growing neurosis about the effect of ageing on his appearance.

'Meurig, darling, there was a time when even a certain member of the royal family wouldn't have been able to trust themselves in my company,' Felix would boast.

The two weeks spent with Felix every year usually set Morgan up for the rest of the year. His waistline expanded somewhat causing comment among some of the more observant ladies of the church, while the men found their vicar more amenable to their many suggestions on how the life of the church might run a little more smoothly. His apparition appeared after one such suggestion, centred around the need for a fire evacuation plan for the church proffered by the aptly named Ivor Pugh.

'The thing is, Vicar, if we were all burnt alive it's the vicarage door they'd be knocking on.'

The man, Pugh, had been a thorn in his side ever since he came to the parish. He was pompous and a prig and worst of all, he was usually right about most things.

Morgan returned home fuming that day and was petulantly drawing up an evacuation plan involving 'Hell Fire Exits' and signs saying 'Keep all Infernal Doors Open,' when he noticed a figure in the garden bending over to smell his delphiniums. The figure certainly appeared to fit the description of the Son of God: long hair, white robe, sandals, soulful facial expression; less Max Von Sydow, more Robert Powell. He threw his spoof evacuation plan into the waist paper basket and went out into the garden to investigate. Once out there he could find hide nor hair of any deity, only next door's cat doing something unspeakable in his herbaceous border.

He returned to his study, which seemed cold although it was mid-August, and pondered on what he might have just seen. The only explanation he could come up with at that moment was that he had mistaken 'Billy the Fag,' a local vagrant, for Our Lord. Billy had lived on the streets after a bad trip on LSD back in the late seventies. He believed that all property was theft and therefore gave himself pretty much the run of the parish. His dreadlocked hair had last seen shampoo in 1995. And however much Meurig Morgan tried to find it in his heart to love Billy, he could not say that he did.

When he did come to Billy's aid, it usually meant bailing him out financially or pleading his case with the local constabulary. This was usually a way of assuaging his guilt for the fact was the only emotion Billy invoked in Meurig was that of envy. How, he wondered, had a man so successfully managed to avoid the yolk of any kind of personal responsibility for so long. If it had been Billy in the garden, he'd certainly spruced himself up a bit, which was probably a good sign.

Over the next few months, the visitations became more regular, sometimes in the vicarage and sometimes in the church. On one occasion, he'd been lighting the candles prior to Sunday worship, when there in a pew right at the back of the church was the Messiah, down on his knees in prayer. I mean the whole thing was getting exceedingly awkward. Thankfully, when he delivered his sermon, the apparition had disappeared; otherwise it would have really cramped his style, not that the sermon had been anything to write home about as it was.

There were other embarrassing moments such as when Dilys Williams had invited herself to tea, ostensibly to discuss the flower arranging rota. But Dilys had recently been widowed and was, as they say, hormonally challenged. Meurig had seen the way she looked at him and he had to say he was not averse to giving her the occasional sideways look back. Her neat little figure and gamine features gave her something of the look of a 'late period' Audrey Hepburn.

Well things came to a bit of a head over the Viennese whirls when, bold as brass, Mrs Williams had crossed the room with said biscuits and puckered up for a kiss and possibly more. Well, Meurig was on the point of responding, when he looked over and there in front of the sideboard was his spectral companion leaning on the sideboard smiling at him in that annoying way He had. At this point, the Reverend Morgan reigned in his carnal desires, sat Dilys down and proceeded to listen for the next two hours – yes two hours – to his parishioner's tearful recounting of the thirty years of married life, cut short due to her Charlie's demise while attempting to escape a bunker on the thirteenth hole of the local municipal golf course.

'He was under par of course,' said Dilys.

'Well, that would probably explain it,' Meurig (who was not up on the niceties of the game) replied.

Throughout his ministry, Meurig Morgan had suffered what now would be called compassion fatigue. The trouble was that people were so good at getting themselves killed. There were the drink drivers, of course, wrapping their cars round lampposts on the road out of the city, the drug addicts often from supposedly good homes expiring in some squalid squat down near where the docks used to be and then there were those irresponsible middle-aged individuals, who insisted on eating themselves into an early grave, when half the world hadn't got enough to eat. Their relatives would all come to him tearfully wanting confirmation that heaven awaited their dear departed. In a funny way, he had more respect for people like Colonel Ackerman, whose daughter Jenny had thrown herself in front of a train at Queen's Street station.

After this, whenever Ackerman saw Meurig, he would mutter something along the lines of 'Still peddling your fairy stories are we padre?' before stuffing his pipe firmly between his gin-soaked lips. The thing was, what could you say when something so tragic occurred. Jenny Ackerman had been twenty-one, just come down from Cambridge with a first, but her undiagnosed depression was so all-invasive that taking her own life seemed by far the best option. Morgan's platitudes had fallen on very stony ground on the day of her funeral. The Colonel had, however, grudgingly accepted a photograph of Jenny on a millennium Sunday school outing she had been on to Minehead, which Meurig had dug out.

It was no good; he would have to talk to someone about his problem. It wasn't as if his Jesus was the talkative kind. He couldn't talk over church business or pastoral matters with Him as he got nothing back but the same quizzical half-smile. The Bishop was his chosen port of call: a corpulent, eternally cheerful character, who preferred to be called Glyn than Your Grace. He listened to Meurig and then advised.

'Well buddy, if I was you, I would see it as a blessing. In my forty years of wearing a frock and the last ten a funny hat to boot, I haven't caught sight of so much as a whisker of Our Lord. But for the moment, I would keep it between you and him: we don't want to scare the congregation off, do we now?'

The only other person Meurig shared his visions with were his friend Felix, who was very sympathetic but assured him that his cats were on the right track in knowing that it was they alone who were masters of the universe.

'That's why the ancient Pharaohs worshipped them, don't you see darling. Anyhow this spectre of yours sounds rather dishy to me.'

The trouble was Meurig was beginning to find that he was practically never alone. At an otherwise acrimonious meeting during the week for Christian Unity, Pastor Max had taken him backstage to see the new sound system at 'The Way Centre.'

'You see, we can relay to the overspill outside with a flick of a switch and we lose no auditory quality whatsoever,' said the Pastor.

Meurig, who had been studying the beaded necklace round his colleague's neck, then became aware that God was sitting at the drum kit backstage, gently beating out a rhythm.

When he got back to the vicarage, Billy the Fag was waiting for him. He'd found a place to live but needed bond money in order to secure it.

'Five hundred quid would cover it man. I've met this chick, see, and anyway we got it on and …'

'Yes, yes I think I get the picture … five hundred pounds though, um, I'm really not sure I've got that kind of money spare.'

It was then that Billy the Fag's doppelganger appeared, robed unlike Billy, all in white sitting in the vicarage summer house grinning, in that way of his.

'Well look,' said Meurig, 'I might just be able to help.'

'Cool man!' said Billy the Fag. 'Her name is Drusilla by the way; one witchy woman, I tell you man.'

'I'm sure she is Billy. Now if there's nothing else, pop around the vicarage tonight and I will have been to the bank.'

'Got you man! Hang loose, now, you hear?' With that he was gone just leaving a faint trace of skunk and patchouli hanging in the air.

Meurig looked over at the summer house, thankful to see it empty and returned to his office to await a meeting with the treasurer, Owen Coalville Jones, about the church's charitable giving. Owen began by lecturing Meurig.

'We have to cut our collar according to our cloth, Vicar.'

The annual donations St Iltydd's makes to Doctor Barnardo's, Save the Children, and

UNICEF. None of them local charities as you know. I suggest a cut of fifty percent. Present levels are, I am sure you will agree, unsustainable.'

'Yes, but fifty percent! I mean.'

'Vicar, I've always applauded your unworldly approach, but I'm afraid we need to be realistic.'

'I'm sorry, but I don't see Jesus in all this,' and then, as it happened, he did. He was in the kitchen sitting on one of the units' legs, swinging to and fro, looking as if he hadn't a care in the world.

'I'm sorry Owen, but I'm afraid I can't sanction any cuts in this budget.'

'Well, I hesitate to say it, but …' responded Jones.

'Oh, spit it out man! You consider me biblically one of those foolish virgins!' said Morgan testily.

'Are you ill by any chance, Vicar?' enquired Coalville Jones hopefully, as he'd never liked the man and his way of running the parish. He had even flirted with the idea of becoming a Methodist for a while.

Well as it turns out, Meurig's health did begin to cause him concern, after the incident down on the council estate. He had set out on a pre-baptism visit to Jonty and Tess Caxton and little Abigail. They lived on the parish boundary, where the houses were all detached and burglar-alarmed with integral garages and front gates that opened with the flick of a switch.

Feeling a little weary that day, he had taken a short cut that he had taken hundreds of times before, involving a footpath which ran along a stream and then over a bridge and passed the playing fields and bob's your uncle. However, inexplicably, he turned off the footpath too soon and found himself slap bang in the Summerfield estate. He was normally familiar with the area, as in the good old days, at least some of his congregation would hail from this part of town. But today it all looked strange and the day was turning out to be hot. He rubbed around his dog collar with his finger and mopped his reddening brow with what turned out to be an old service sheet. Then, after a few seconds, he blacked out completely.

'He won't 'urt you, just wants to be friendly like,' said a disembodied voice. There was nothing disembodied about the large pit bull terrier who appeared now to be pinning him to the ground.

'Cyclops come here, you old sod! Let's get you upright. A man of the cloth, I see. Been at the communion wine, is it?'

The voice, it was now clear, was coming from a small man in a leather jacket sporting one of those pigtails, where a few strands of hair were constricted into what could hardly be described as a bunch by what appeared to be several rubber bands.

'I'm Leighton, by the way, but people do call me Leight. All right?' said Leighton.

'Yes, I think I am now,' said Meurig.

'Come on! I'm still not happy with you. Come over my place and the missus will make you a brew.'

Leighton led the way. His house was on the junction of two roads so his garden was bigger than some. A number of other dogs of a similar tonnage to Cyclops were tethered in one part of the garden, while the rest was taken up by various vehicles and a caravan that had seen much better days. Leighton guided Meurig into the kitchen.

'This is her in doors. Tracey say hello to Reverend Morgan.'

'Hiya,' said Tracey, who was a very large lady wearing a very small T-shirt and a pair of pyjama bottoms with a motif involving Yogi bear doing something disgusting to Boo Boo. However diverting this may have been, Meurig's attention was once again drawn to another presence in the room. Sure enough, it was the Lord himself sitting out on Leighton's patio under an umbrella that appeared to have once been the property of The Royal Oak public house.

'Tea, or something stronger for the shock. I know, a Pernod perhaps?

'No, no I won't, thank you.'

Again, a curious smile came from the figure on the patio.

'Well, tea would be lovely!'

About three hours later, after two cups of tea, three large glasses of Pernod and four slices of Pizza, and when he'd heard all about Leighton's wrongful arrest for drunk driving, Tracey losing her job for throwing up while pregnant at her distribution warehouse and how their boy, Grant, had been diagnosed with OCD and Crohn's disease, the Reverend Morgan suddenly remembered where he should have been, at Jonty and Tess Caxton's. So hastily supplying Leighton and his family with various helpline numbers and relevant websites and saying he would call again in a couple of weeks, he made his way to the door.

'I'll walk you home, Reverend. It's time I took the other mutts out for a walk. Here, Brawler! Here, Attila!'

He telephoned the Caxton's soon as he got back to the vicarage.

'Well yes, I'm terribly sorry … and I do realise you need your quality time as a family and perhaps we can rearrange … yes … yes, I quite understand why you must think about it and yes I'm sure little Abigail was upset …'

Abigail upset! She was six months old, for God sake. She wouldn't know a christening from My Little Pony, thought Meurig.

The appointment for the brain scan came through relatively quickly. Meurig's GP had said it was probably nothing, but just to be on the safe side, he'd make a referral. Meurig had been to the vast Heath Hospital on many occasions, but always visiting his parishioners. Today it was his turn and 'probably nothing' turned into an incurable brain tumour deep rooted and inoperable.

The consultant explained that more black outs, visual distortions and hallucinations would possibly follow.

Meurig decided to keep his biblical companion secret from the medical staff. There seemed little point in broadcasting it as there was nothing to be done and in fact, if his medical team had put an end to the visitations by means of sedation or whatever, he began to think he would miss his mute companion, now sat at the end of his bed doing up his sandals.

A steady stream of visitors arrived, some bearing gifts. Owen Coalville Jones came with some cheques for Meurig to sign, a card and a houseplant from the parish council. He didn't like to tell Jones that he wouldn't be returning to his house, so had little use for a houseplant. Dilys arrived one day with some grapes and a bottle of Pernod.

Apparently, she'd been approached by a man in a leather jacket and long hair tied up in a kind of bun. Said he didn't think he'd be allowed in the main building unless he was on his deathbed because of a misunderstanding he'd had in Accident and Emergency one Friday night and besides, he'd got the dogs with him. Billy the Fag sent him a postcard from Mexico thanking him for the five hundred quid. He and his 'chick' had decided rather than get a flat, they'd go travelling with the money. They were now both working in a drug rehabilitation clinic in Tijuana. Poacher turned gamekeeper, thought Meurig.

Felix came down from Evesham and started to weep as soon as he arrived at the old priest's bedside. Meurig held his hand, something he had learnt from the many dying people he had visited: it was they who often brought comfort to those left behind.

The vision was still there, of course, but it seemed to the Reverend Morgan that it was beginning to fade: the Lord's features were becoming more and more indistinct, merging with other faces in the rest of the ward.

Bishop Glyn took the funeral service. The rundown little church of St Iltydd's was full and on this occasion, as happened at 'The Way Centre' every week apparently, there was an overspill into the graveyard outside. Jonty and Tess Caxton were there hoping to catch a word with the Bishop regarding little Abigail being put on the waiting list for the local 'Church in Wales' School.

Owen Coalville Jones read the lesson appropriately from the *Old Testament Book of Numbers*. He was surprised to see Colonel Ackerman outside the church after the service as he knew there was 'history' between him and the vicar.

'Colonel, I didn't think you were a church man these days,' said Coalville Jones.

'I'm not,' said the Colonel, but I remembered the ladies at the church always put on a good spread after these kind of do's.'

'Oh, hello Colonel,' said Dilys, 'it was so good of you to visit the vicar the other day. It meant a great deal to him.' She squeezed Ackerman's arm.

The Colonel spluttered his response and turning to Coalville Jones said in a half whisper.

'I was at the hospital anyway, do you see; appointment with the trick cyclist.'

'I'm sorry?' said Coalville Jones.'

'Psychiatrist. Pleasant enough chap, I suppose. Not from these shores, though. The fact is recently I've been having these … well, I suppose you'd call them visions.'

The Ben Harding

Trixie Roberts

'Excuse me, are the four-leafed clovers still in the skipper's cabin?'

Arthur stares at the young woman, bemused. Has he seen her before? She looks familiar, especially round the nose and mouth.

'They were in a wooden frame on the wall by the berth.'

'I'll go and see, Miss.' Down below, Arthur lifts the frame off its thirty-year-old nail and wonders. How can this young woman know about the contents of the skipper's cabin? It was only ten years ago, when he became first mate that he'd been in the cabin and seen the clovers even though he'd worked on The Leopard since he left school.

Waiting on the dockside, Pam looks sadly at the gutted trawler. Rust shows through the dingy paint. Workmen are everywhere, crawling over the decks once covered in cod and haddock. Like a corpse in a funeral parlour, The Leopard is being stripped before restoration for public consumption. Once she defied the North Sea gales to provide fish for Friday dinners. Now, in her after-life, she is to be a floating restaurant on the new marina. Her function will be to provide comfortable surroundings with scampi to visiting executives.

Pam remembers her first sighting of The Leopard as a child. Waiting on the dockside for her to sail in. There are lots of lights in the distant black.

'Dad, why are there lampposts in the river?'

'They're not lampposts, they're lights on lots of ships, all like Granddad's, waiting for the tide.'

'Will the tide take long?'

'No, they'll be coming in soon. That man in the uniform says Granddad's will be in first.'

'Good. Why?'

'Because The Leopard's coming back from her first trip. They call it the maiden voyage.'

A white mass floats towards the dockside. A giant four-leafed clover is painted across the bows. Soon, the trawler is so close and so huge, Pam can't see anything but metal and ropes. People cheer and shout. Music is coming from a squeeze box somewhere along the dock. Then she has a new vantage point from her dad's shoulders and sees her granddad high up at the wheel, steering the ship. He waves his cap to her as he glides past.

People start to move and soon Pam is being carried up a ladder, across ropes and the slimy wooden deck. She can smell the fish which is being lifted in crates from the ship on to the dock side. Then a dark, narrow staircase into the smallest bedroom she's ever seen. It's also the most crowded. As well as Dad and Granddad there are other men she doesn't recognise. They are talking and laughing and someone opens a bottle of whisky. Granddad kisses her.

'Here you are, Princess.' He balances his cap on her head and passes round glasses. Everybody laughs. Will Dad be able to hold her and the brimful glass? There is a framed picture on the wall at her eye level. It's a letter with some four-leafed clovers pressed to the paper. Pam has learned to read enough:

> *Dear Mr Harding,*
>
> *I found these during my school holidays. I would like you to have them for The Leopard and hope they bring you good luck.*
>
> *Yours sincerely,*
>
> *Joanna Bewes*

'Who's Joanna Bewes?' Everyone goes quiet. One of the gentlemen with whisky, the one who seemed very pleased when

'A good trip' was mentioned turns to her and smiles from above his smart, blue overcoat.

'Joanna is my niece. The four-leafed clover is The Leopard's emblem so I suggested she try to find some for my new ship.'

Pam is confused and jealous. She has never found a four-leafed clover. And, despite what this man says, this is Granddad's ship. He's been out at sea in her for three weeks. She saw him steer her into the dock only a few minutes ago.

*****

Arthur looks at the clovers in the frame and the letter. He remembers Joanna Bewes. When he was growing up, her uncle built a number of new trawlers including *The Leopard,* where he got his first job. There hadn't been many new trawlers built since the war so there were always press photographers sniffing around the docks and photos of the Bewes family in the papers. But this woman isn't Joanna; she's too young but she does seem familiar.

'How do you know about these clovers?'

'They were my granddad's. I was brought here after *The Leopard's* first trip. I remember them on the wall of his cabin.'

'Your granddad?'

'Yes, he was the skipper then. Ben Harding. Did you know him?'

Now Arthur remembers. The profile is Ben's and he realises he must have seen her at the skipper's funeral.

'Everyone on these docks knew Ben Harding, Miss. I worked for him on this ship. He taught me how to find fish all over the North Sea. Here you take these ...'

Pam hesitates. She very much wants to but somehow feels they belong on the ship.

'... I'm sure Ben would want that.'

'Yes, you're right. Thank you and don't call me Miss.'

*****

The Red Lion is quiet. Too early for Saturday night crowds and too late for happy hour.

'Lucky you came by today. They've been through that ship like locusts. I reckon there'll be no fixtures and fittings left next week. They only let me on board because I used to sail on her and because they've seen me hanging round the docks for weeks looking for work.'

'It was lucky for me, indeed. I'm just back visiting my mum for the weekend. My work is hectic at the moment so weekends have to be grabbed when I can.'

Once Arthur has got over the shock of having a woman buy him a drink, he is forthcoming about The Leopard's recent history.

'I can tell you lots, Pam, but the nutshell is, the big decline in the trawling trade. Old Mr Bewes died leaving his fleet, such as it was by then, to Joanna. She lives in London with her city husband. They're not remotely interested in a declining provincial fishing fleet. Bit by bit they've been selling it off. The Leopard's last skipper retired and I no longer had a job. The new marina is being developed so Joanna and husband saw an opportunity to make a profit out of what was once the flagship. It's been sold to a local opportunist of a businessman who intends to open it as a floating restaurant. That's why it's being restored.'

Arthur spends his free time hanging around the docks. He can't come to terms with not going to sea. He's not alone. At any time of day there are men, some alone, some in groups staring down the river. There's the dock tower. In years past they peered for a glimpse of it over the horizon as they sailed home with the tide. Now they stare at it. From this side they can't see anything beyond. No clear horizon. No one rushes any more. The morning market bustle is reduced to a few crates. The docks are sinking and not much drinking is done at The Red Lion.

The Leopard's reincarnation is complete. Arthur and Pam have kept in touch but Arthur can't bring himself to suggest eating there. He can't be sure of how he'll react with petite portions of nouvelle-cuisined cod. He knows what has to be gone through to get it to the table. Pam backs off too. She still has the childhood memories of the happy faces and the whisky glasses. She remembers the crowded cabin and how everyone laughed when Granddad's cap fell over her eyes. Now the cabin is the restaurant manager's office with a computer that prints out VAT receipts.

'No air conditioning was ever needed out on the North Sea,' grumbles Arthur to Pam during one of their phone calls.

Then a recession begins to bite. A succession of unusually severe gales damages the marina and The Leopard. During the weeks of repair, the owner's other business interests start to fail and he is implicated in a local corruption scandal. There are cases of food poisoning in the town with the hint that they originated from The Leopard's kitchens.

The headline reads, 'Floating Restaurant Boss Bankrupt.'

Pam phones her mother

'What's happening to The Leopard, Mum?'

'It seems she's to be auctioned. That's if they can find anyone to buy her. There's talk around here that she's jinxed. No one I know would go and eat there.'

'Let me know when the auction is to be, Mum. I may come up and take a look.'

*****

Arthur's brother, Mike, a carpenter, has been made redundant. He and Arthur spin out a half-pint and try to calculate how they'll manage the mortgage on the house they share.

'Of course, there'll be a lump sum. We could pay it off; then at least we'll own the roof over our heads.'

'Will it be enough?'

'Doubt it.'

The drinker at the next table leaves. Arthur reaches for his abandoned newspaper and sees the same headline Pam read earlier.

'Will it buy us a trawler?'

Pam hits roadworks on the motorway and by the time she reaches the auction rooms, it's all over. She dashes to The Red Lion. Arthur and Mike are there, drinking jubilantly having bought The Leopard for a song. They have already met an advisor from the local Enterprise Board and plan to tap the Heritage Trust for whatever's going. They will sell the restaurant fixtures and fittings and fit out The Leopard as a live-in mobile workshop. Mike will make furniture and wooden items, which they will sell at marina fairs up and down the coast.

'I may even try my hand at serving tea, coffee and cakes too,' Arthur volunteers, 'Trawler Teas.'

Pam hands Arthur the framed four-leafed clovers.

'Take these; don't you agree they belong on The Leopard.'

'Yes and no,' replies Arthur. 'We need all the luck we can get but we're re-naming her The Ben Harding.'

The Silence Before

Vicky Turrell

Have you noticed the silence just before the kettle whistles? There is an eerie stillness just before a storm, the quiet fall of the snow before it smothers, the expectant gap between lightning and thunder.

Eleanor stood on the end of the pier staring into the black merciless sea below.

She knew that she could not carry on; she had to end it, but how? There was no easy way.

Her thin coat whipped around her and the blast suddenly iced through. Her body was cold, but her mind was boiling, like the turmoil of the waves as she watched their insidious climb up the harbour wall.

It was now or never; she held her breath and the whole world seemed to do the same.

The eagle-eyed gannet froze over the water; the open-mouthed gulls stopped their screams and the waves stilled at the very top of the pier. The fishermen stopped their angled rods and statue-stared into the distance.

Silence now.

Waiting for the inevitable, the moment before the tide turns.

Then, in the blink of an eye, the waves recede, the gannet dives, the gulls call out, the fishermen cast their rods and Eleanor makes her move, at last.

She decides that from now on she is to be called Ellie and she strides off briskly to face her parents. She will leave her well paid job at the bank – the one her mum and dad are so proud of and she will take up that place at Art College. She will follow her dream of being an artist. But she must tell her parents first. Her dad will be angry and her mum will put the kettle on the Aga.

And they will all sit still and wait in that awful inescapable silence before the furious whistle.

Kindred

Wendy Lodwick Lowdon

The buggy pivoted on its wheels and Lady Sarah slid against the left-hand side of the vehicle. She pressed her lips together to hold in a hiss of pain. Jim urged the old chestnut mare up the rough track.

'Get on wi' ya,' and he slapped the reins on her skinny flank.

Lady Sarah held as strongly as she could to the leather handle with a knobby hand encased in suede gloves as the buggy lurched up the track. 'Quite out of the way, Jim,' she commented.

'Yerse, m'am. The Evans family done lived here since 1850 when the cottage were built.'

'Must be hard on their horse and cart getting up and down this lane,' said Lady Sarah.

Jim tossed a bit of a look over his shoulder. 'Owen Hughes never had no horse. No Hughes could afford a horse.'

Lady Sarah felt the heat in her cheeks; of course they didn't. 'I've not been up here before,' she offered by way of an apology.

Jim grunted. 'Didn't have no need,' he pronounced.

'No need, indeed,' said Lady Sarah in a whisper. 'Well, things change and we must get on with it,' she said in a louder voice so Jim could hear her.

'Yerse, m'am.' Jim wrestled the head of the old mare out of the grass by the hedgerow and urged her to continue up the hill.

Lady Sarah considered other changes. Lydia was married and living in Chester and she hadn't been able to travel to see her daughter at all this summer. Harry had taken his commission with Shropshire Yeomanry in 1914; he'd rounded up half the estate's horses and successfully urged many of its men to go with him. They'd ended up kicking their heels with The Welsh Mounted Border Guard for a year before they'd been sent to Egypt as part of the 4th Dismounted Brigade. Bertram, determined to be in the forefront of the action, had taken his commission in 1915 with the Kings Shropshire Light Infantry, along with conscripted older men some of whom were from the estate. Lady Sarah shook her head over the wilfulness of her younger son.

With the boys gone and Sir Peter in a wheelchair, Lady Sarah had reluctantly assumed an active role in the management of the estate. Sir Peter and the ancient Mr Black, dragged out of retirement, poured over the books trying to balance a shrinking income by mothballing rooms in the Hall and selling silver on a glutted market. They were unable to physically travel about the estate to visit the tenants.

'Needs must!' Sir Peter had declared to his protesting wife the previous summer. 'With Bertram gone we must have some eyes on the ground. It keeps up morale too, my dear. And it reminds the slackers to keep their noses to the grindstone.'

Lady Sarah wondered, as the horse slowly crested the hill, why her husband had begun to speak like a cross between the newspaper headlines and nursery rhymes. He refused to allow her any time to retreat to her small study but quashed his doubts and anyone else's by booming on about 'the cause' and 'backsliding.'

Ruby was slowing down and Jim whipped her rump with a switch. Lady Sarah felt her eyes fill with tears. Poor old thing; another creature brought out of retirement. She and the old Clydesdale were hardly able to fill two of the roles left by the emptying of the stables let alone that of five men and a dozen working horses which were now pulling artillery guns. She shook her head to clear it of unhelpful sentiment and dabbed at her eyes.

Kindred

She could see the cottage now. A small rough red stone building with no windows on the south side faced the track. A dog barked and Lady Sarah frowned.

'The oldest boy keeps a dog. Uses it for rabbiting and it is good with the sheep. He asked the master and he give him permission.'

Jim seemed to have read her mind, which was not surprising as they had been making these visits to cottages on the estate for two years now. Lady Sarah felt her eyes grow wet again. She still mourned her darling dachshund bitch, Biddy, which had been one of the first dogs led away to be knocked on the head.

'Can't have a useless animal eating up valuable provisions,' Sir Peter had explained. 'Besides, woman, it is a German breed and it just won't do. What sort of example would we be setting our people if we kept our dogs while we made them kill their dogs? Even old Ralph will have to shoot a few of his collies.'

Lady Sarah gritted her teeth. She deliberately moved on the leather seat so the lance of pain in her hip would block out the current train of thought. Instead, she remembered climbing back on after falls from her horse and all-night dancing in spite of sense and pain; she wondered what her heedless younger self would think of this wreck of a body. 'Didn't think, just was mad to do!' she murmured to herself. 'Just like Harry and Bertram.'

Suddenly the present was overwhelming her again; the war had consequences beyond the usual punishments for gallivanting of reckless youth. Lady Sarah could feel her chest contracting and she was beginning to breathe in puffs and pants.

Jim didn't have to rein in the mare; as soon as they reached the yard outside the cottage she sighed and dropped her head to her knees. Lady Sarah wished she could so block out the world. She steadied her herself, took as deep a breath as her stays would allow, and looked towards the front door of the cottage.

The door was flung open and children boiled out onto the step whispering shrilly to each other. Lady Sarah was astonished by the number and energy; there seemed to be so many more than the five she had been told lived in the cottage. The children fanned out to either side of the stone scrubbed threshold of the cottage and a stocky woman stepped out of the gloom.

'You be Lady Sarah? Had word you be coming.' Her words were delivered brusquely. For a few moments the two women stared at each other in silence until the jingle of Ruby's harness as she shook the flies away from her eyes broke the silence. 'Well, you best be seated on the bench here and I'll make you a brew.' And with that the woman turned and went back into the dark of her home.

Lady Sarah looked at the hard wooden bench with dismay and wondered for a moment if she could just stay in the buggy but she gritted her teeth and Jim helped her climb painfully and stiffly to the ground. Throughout the difficult manoeuvre the children had watched silently. Even the dog, sat close to the bare feet of the tallest child, was silent. Once she had regained her balance and fiddled with her heavy olive-coloured travelling dress until the pain had subsided, Lady Sarah looked at the gathering with more interest.

'Jim, let them tell me their names.'

A girl, her hair tugged off her face by a tight braid, then broke the silence. 'Tom, Ben, Mattie, Milly and I be Jane,' she said so quickly and in such a broad accent it took Lady Sarah by surprise. Jim repeated her words.

'Is this all of the family,' Lady Sarah asked Jim regarding him in the same fashion as she did her Italian interpreter in those halcyon days before there was war. Jim managed to find out there was another girl working in the armaments bunker on the edge of the county and a boy in the army in France. Lady Sarah shivered and felt her eyes well with tears. 'And the father?'

Jim looked at her with disapproval; she flushed as she tried to grasp for the synopsis of the Hughes family which had been given to her at the onset of the journey.

'He's dead!' declared the child flatly and Lady Sarah had no trouble understanding her.

Mrs Hughes was at the door with a tray, which she placed on the bench with a horrible sort of care and turned to her visitors. Her mouth was turned down with bitterness and the words were forced out over a shaking jaw.

'Yes, dead! Dead in a filthy war! And for why? So, such as you can come to give me notice now I've no man?'

'Oh, dead! He is dead! My son, Bertram, is dead too! He was on the lists this week. It is so dreadful and I am so empty. Harry's still there, still there in that awful, awful place.'

The two women stumbled towards each other and held each other in a fierce grip. They wept together: whispered their grief at their losses so hard felt and told of the fears so deeply hooked into every waking moment. Gradually, with much patting of each other's faces and slowly sliding reluctant hands along each other's arms, they became two people once more.

Lady Sarah felt as if a fog had lifted; someone who could understand. She patted her friend on the shoulder.

'I am here to tell you, Mrs Hughes, you and your family will stay until our sons return home to us.'

Manaslu

In Sanskrit: Mountain of the spirit.

John Heap

We knew there was too much snow before we had even started to climb Manaslu North. But the North East Ridge is such a beautiful line, it was still very much pre-monsoon, and we were there. What else was there to do?

We were preparing to leave our third bivouac and Mick was looking up at the ridge as if it had just insulted his mother.

'Right, Phil! Let's do this bastard!' he said.

'OK,' I replied unconvincingly, still fumbling with my rucksack, having had to repack everything I'd forgotten the first time around. I was tired, I had an altitude headache and I was getting frustrated at my apparent ineptitude.

Noting my clumsiness, Mick was away quickly; swearing quietly as he once again sank through the icy crust that had formed on the deep snow.

Mick was a boulder of a man, solid, determined and straight talking, but a bit grim. He had little sympathy with my more romantic approach to the mountains. I remember Nanga Parbat in 2004 and asking him to take a summit photo only to be told that, 'I should save all my bloody posturing till we'd got back down.'

But in our quiet way we got on.

Mick had paused about fifty metres above me, beneath a large bosse of snow.

'We're going to have to belay,' he called down as he stamped himself out a ledge and started to sort out the rope.

Fifteen minutes later I had joined him. The steep snow was certainly too soft to climb, so we had to go around it. Mick pointed right, to a possibility on the west side of the ridge, where a promising groove led up to a small snowfield that would get us back on route.

'I'm going to lead this section; you haven't got it together yet,' he said.

With restrained heckles, I set up an admittedly poor anchor. Mick looked at it, then at me, raised his eyebrows and nervously began his exposed traverse, out over the massive drop to the Larkya glacier. Once he reached the groove, his movements became more fluid, revelling in the fact that for once he wasn't knee deep in snow and soon, with a victory whoop, he had planted both his tools in the snowfield above. Kicking himself a belay perch, he shouted for me to follow.

I had taken him off belay when I heard the muffled cry. Looking up I saw an area of snow, including Mick and his tethered axes, slowly moving down the face. I glanced at the rope connecting us, by the time it became taut Mick would be moving fast and inevitably, a moment later, so would I.

With a theatrically drawn out 'Oh shit ...' I launched myself down the opposite side of the ridge. Unfortunately, the rope didn't catch immediately and it was a tense and bruising few seconds before I stopped.

There I waited, fearing another fall; I had cracked some ribs and injured my right wrist, but all was still and I had survived. Out of sight, Mick was shouting for me, and once communication had been established, he reminded me to keep the tension on the rope as whilst my side of the ridge was climbable, his side was too steep and he needed a fixed rope.

My progress was slow; my right hand was useless and my ribs made breathing difficult but eventually I gained the small shoulder where the rope had embedded itself. I made the rope safe and looked down towards Mick. He wasn't far below and seemed to be climbing steadily, so I was shocked when he eventually flopped down beside me. His face was covered in blood and he could only lie on his back, his eyes closed, fighting to control his breath.

'That was hard,' he gasped after a while and seeing the concern on my face continued, 'Oh this, don't worry; it's only skin deep.' He grimaced as he tried, unsuccessfully, to wipe the blood from his face.

He then became serious. 'Philip, I lost my sack, it's gone.'

There was little I could say to that. In his sack had been the stove and without that we had nothing more to drink than the water we'd melted the night before. Still, I knew that we'd been in tight scrapes before and I had absolutely no doubt that we'd make it this time, so I was surprised when Mick grabbed me and said,

'We'll make it, I know we will.'

I looked at his blood-stained face. 'Of course we will, don't we always?' I said, but I saw something in his eyes I'd never seen before, a vulnerable uncertainty that stung me into action. I shouldered my sack and said, 'Keep close Mick, we've got to go.'

Our descent was to be down the Normal Route climbed by the Japanese in 1956. However, from here it entailed a long traverse east and as soon as we were off the ridge the difficulties became apparent. One-handed it was slow and tiring work and every few yards I would sink to my thighs in the deep snow. Mick was also moving slowly, but when I asked, he just shrugged and encouraged me to continue. After five hours we had to stop. We were both exhausted.

I retrieved some chocolate from my sack and offered half to Mick.

'No thanks, I've got these,' he replied pulling a packet of jellybeans from his pocket.

The chocolate made me thirsty and guiltily I took a mouthful of our precious water. Mick declined; he said he was OK and selfishly I was glad.

We surveyed the distance we had come; Mick was the first to voice it.

'We won't make base camp tonight and you don't want to be amongst that in the dark either.' He pointed down to the Manaslu glacier where the last kilometre was a maze of seracs and crevasses.

By the time it was dark we had moved to an area on the slope that was a little proud of the avalanche chutes and we prepared to bivouac. Mick had to make do with my duvet and rucksack for warmth but, as we settled down for the night, he said generously,

'Getting across that slope in your condition was pretty heroic; you've been strong today.'

'Yeah, it was tough' I replied, 'but it'll soon be over.'

With an affirmative grunt, Mick fastened up his hood, folded his arms and huddled himself further into the slope.

My ribs were aching, my wrist throbbed and I was thirsty. Mick was right; it had been difficult, but I didn't feel very heroic. Most of the time I'd been cursing him. I was angry at having to break trail, angry that he had fallen, angry that he'd lost his sack, just angry at him, at this mountain and at all this bloody snow.

I was grateful when the next day dawned clear and soon we were making good progress down the slope. All my anger was forgotten and encouraged by the sight of the tents below, my conversations with Mick became much more positive.

When we reached the confused mass of ice cliffs and crevasses, Mick's mountaineering sense came into its own. When faced with what seemed an insurmountable obstacle, Mick would confidently indicate which way to turn, and sure enough, a way around would be found. Soon we were through the most broken area and encountering much easier ground. As we came up a short rise, we saw two climbers coming up to meet us. The relief was incredible and despite my ribs, I embraced Mick enthusiastically.

The first of the climbers took my sack, introduced himself as Tom and then helped me down to his tent. I collapsed onto his mattress and childlike I allowed him to take off my crampons and boots. I was tired of having all the responsibility and now it someone else's turn. Tom made me some tea and I slept.

When I woke, I was alone and found myself thinking about Mick. I was in the porch struggling into my boots when Tom came over with another brew.

'Nice one,' I said cheerfully standing up to take it.

His climbing partner was approaching the tent and told us that the helicopter should arrive later that evening.

'Thanks,' I said. 'How's Mick?'

He looked a little taken aback and, looking only at Tom, said softly.

'Hey, sorry man, but he's still up there, where you fell. Look.'

Avoiding my eyes, he pointed up the mountain to where still visible, was a body, hanging from a rope on the far side of the North East Ridge.

Teetering

Wendy Lodwick Lowdon

Bella, swaddled in motley, jiggled her cup on its saucer. She didn't like the tone of the Streisand song. 'It's so whiny,' she muttered knowing it would have brought a sigh of nostalgia from her mother if she'd been listening.

The waitress loomed. It took Bella a long blank moment before she assured the raised eyebrows that she had not been signalling, thank you very much. 'Off down memory lane,' she offered with a smile but the waitress only saw the too-even false teeth and turned away with a flick of her ponytail. Bella quickly drank the last inch of milky coffee. She found her embossed, red leather purse at the bottom of her capacious print shoulder bag, laid four gold coins on the paper bill and hurried out of the café.

The easterly wind, which had taken possession of the county for several days, was in total control of the High Street and shoved shoppers along the dank pavements. Bella huddled her paisley cashmere shawl more closely about her person but it still flapped wildly. Her long white hair flicked painfully across her cheeks; it was as bad as being sandpapered on a windy beach in Barmouth. Normally Bella would idle her way to the bus stop via the other charity shops on Wyle Cop but the wind and the earworm moaning of Barbara's lyrics made her decide to get home as quickly as possible.

The small, terraced house was a shrunken version of the home she had shared with Ted. It had been her residence for six years but she was still bewildered by the raft of changes his death had propelled her into taking. When she opened the front door, she was greeted by the yowl of her ginger tomcat. She flicked on the hallway light and his eyes glowed green and round and his fur was flecked with white. Bella felt her heart contract as she realised that Watcher was old.

By the time Bella had hung up coat, shawl and extra cardigan, she had shrunk in size by almost a third. She leant down and stroked her cat which followed her into the lounge. She remembered when Ted had held a ginger scrap of fur in front of her eyes.

'Wotcher think of this, Bella? Reckon he needs a home.' Ted had given a beery burp. 'Wotcher reckon we keep him.'

Bella had huddled the kitten into the crook of her arm and tucked him under her heart. The cat had not turned out to be as cuddlesome as Bella had wanted but he took on his role as guardian of their household with attentive commitment.

The gas fire was soon lit and flooded the lounge with heat and Watcher took up his position of the back of the sofa onto which Bella slumped with a sigh. She reached up and scratched him under his chin and wondered, as usual, if he would have been more placid if he had been neutered. She smiled as she remembered Ted's face when she proposed giving Watcher the chop. He had protected the cat's gonads as if they had been his own.

Her gaze skittered around the cluttered shelves of the room. Normally she would find one or other of the pretty objects she had rescued from the charity shop would reinforce her sense of having appreciated its quality and saved it.

'It's a form of beachcombing,' she would tell friends who sighed at being presented with another piece of china to admire or a whatsit to ponder over.

Today, though, the growing feeling of disgruntlement led Bella to consider tossing today's catch back in the cardboard box and delivering them back to the sad shops from whence they'd come! The itchiness of dissatisfaction was so strong Bella got up. It required a grunt and a heave and her feet still ached from being reshaped by the non-leather court shoes.

The cup of tea she made herself warmed her hands and her throat but the lump of despair and loneliness didn't shift; it even seemed to have its own groaning soundtrack. She wandered around the four small rooms which made up the ground floor of her house. The pegs in the hallway were so overwhelmed by layers of coats and scarves they dropped them on the floor yet she still could not bring herself to remove the three which had belonged to Ted. The kitchen was tidy but there was little in the way of a clear surface where she could easily work without a plethora of things fouling her efforts. The old cookbooks had been her mother's. The enormous tin breadbin had been used to house loaves for a family of eight and Bella remembered how it had been empty a little too often for comfort. The condiments and glass encased herbs lined the bench because they had been unable to fit into the cupboards which protected her great aunt's tea service and collection of willow patterned plates given to her by a dear friend. The pile of plastic boxes in the corner on top of the fridge, with their cascade of ill-fitting lids, were a necessary evil though their ugliness constantly offended her. Although she knew she definitely did not require six trays, she could not decide which four could no longer be given house room. By the electric kettle there were half a dozen old tea caddies each of which housed a different tea.

The kitchen was so beset by clutter it was failing in its proper function. 'Not that cooking is very interesting anymore,' Bella explained to herself. Yet even she baulked at trying to shoehorn in the latest, and fifth, teapot. Also, it was really too big for her to comfortably lift on its own let alone fill with boiling water. It would make an ideal garden ornament she decided and felt a small surge of contentment that one problem was solved.

Still holding the cup, designed to proclaim the beauties of Porthmadog, which had been their regular holiday retreat in the working years, she went into the tiny dining room. It glowed with glass; the overhead light lifted diamonds and rainbows out of the crystal. Bella's spirits rose but eventually she had to look at the heavy, recently-acquired, green glass bowls squatting like diseased mushrooms on the corner table. 'Why did I buy that large bowl and its six matching relatives?' she asked her cat which was supervising her ramblings. 'Yes, yes, it is identical to the one my grandmother owned.' Bella continued to look at the green glass objects with a jaundiced eye. 'But I didn't like it much then then and I didn't much like her; in fact, I wonder if Nanny liked it herself? Well, they will have to go!'

That decision gave her a spurt of satisfaction, which lasted until her return to lounge. Bella sighed as she slumped onto the sofa. Swans were jostling each other for space on the mirror table; some she had selected but too many were ugly versions given by friends. Bella became more aware of Barbara Streisand's voice in her mind; a warbling pushing for more space and attention. Watcher leapt onto the back of the sofa and Bella was offended by how lumpy her fingers looked as she scratched him under the chin. 'I could do with a bit of fur to hide these unsightly bumps; it'd disguise the patchiness of my skin too. I'd be a tortoiseshell, me,' she informed her old cat.

Within a few seconds Bella was back on her feet and back in the kitchen to make another cup of tea. 'I'll do it properly in a pot and have a biscuit with this one,' she told her cat, which had taken up his overseeing position in the cane basket on the utility bench. 'It'll cheer me up.'

The roar of the kettle filled the small kitchen space and then subsided with a choked wheeze. Bella poured the boiling water onto the tealeaves in a poppy-decorated pot. She placed it carefully on the tray beside a small white jug of milk. She had put a chocolate and ginger biscuit on one flowered plate and several cat treats on another.

'It's that bloody song! It's been needling me for hours,' she suddenly declared to the cat. 'All that nasal, self-pitying carry-on about 'Second-hand Rose.' I feel like she is singing it at me; running me down. Making me feel small, making me feel like I've missed out just like the woman Streisand was wailing about. They oughtn't to play songs like that where people are minding their own business. It's … it's,' Bella struggled to find the words. 'It's pushy and uncomfortable to make people hear things when they're not ready and strong,' she finally blurted.

Teetering

She carried the tray into the lounge and carefully placed it on the table in the centre of the room. 'Well,' she announced to Watcher, as he delicately ate his biscuits off a fine china plate decorated with cornflowers, 'I'm not going to go to that café anymore where a person can be ambushed liked that.' She switched on the television and a brisk conversation between two heads filled the room and cleaned snobbish Barbara and moaning Rose out of her head. Bella felt suddenly stronger and more positive, 'Mind you, the green glass will have to go and some of those swans but the teapot is staying.'

I See No Ships

Vicky Turrell

Chloe is blind. But Chloe was not always like this. She remembers being able to see when she started school, but gradually her sight deteriorated, so gradually, in fact, that no one noticed initially.

She found herself turning her head to bring objects into her field of vision. It was no big deal, at first, but as time went on there was less and less that she could bring into focus. Her mother noticed when they were out birdwatching together. Chloe had always been good at describing species and identifying them. But, sometimes now, she didn't even spot them at all. Off they went to the doctor.

Doctor Moon was very kind and he stared into each eye, in turn, with a light so strong it would have blinded her, if she had not already been going blind. Chloe thought his name was very suitable because he had a big white moon face which beamed out reassuringly. She had always liked the moon. She thought of the moon having no light of its own, but always reflecting the light of the sun, showing that all is well even in the darkest night. But all was not well.

'How's the birdwatching going?' asked Doctor Moon. He was the family doctor and knew all about her hobby, well passion really. Chloe was a keen birdwatcher and did regular surveys of bird populations in the fields surrounding her home.

'Really good,' she enthused, 'we had a flock of waxwings last week. They were eating the mountain ash berries. Waxwings are so unusual with little feathers sticking up on their head like a cheeky cap. They have such beautiful colours and they take your breath away when you see them.' Chloe spoke breathlessly trying to make sure Doctor Moon understood how important this sighting was. She smiled at the memory of these visitors from another country. Of course, she was describing the waxwings from memory, she could not see them clearly enough now to see their unusual appearance in such detail.

'Hmm,' said the doctor and for some reason Chloe suddenly shivered and her smile disappeared. Perhaps it was just that she was cold; it was the winter, after all, and she never wore the warm clothes her mum was always holding out for her.

'You'll catch your death of cold,' said her anxious mother.

She hadn't caught her death of cold, but by the look of Doctor Moon's face something really bad was going to happen to her. And for the first time Chloe could see that his shining reassuring face had clouded over.

He sent her for tests and made an appointment for her to see a specialist.

The specialist said that Chloe was about to go blind. Well, he didn't say it as bluntly as that but you knew what he was saying really. Phrases like 'deteriorating, degenerating, debilitating' kept jumping out of his mouth – all wrapped up with words like 'research, rehabilitation, readjustment.'

'It's surprising how fast modern research is moving on,' he tried to smile. 'There is so much we can do to help.'

'It's marvellous what they can do these days,' said Mum trying to smile in the same way but all Chloe could think was reject, refuse and relegated. It was an inherited condition apparently – a recessive gene and she had drawn the short straw.

Then she set her jaw stubbornly and made a resolution. Never mind faulty gene or short straw. If they thought she was going to lose her sight they had another thought coming. Chloe was going to get on with her life – reject what the specialist had said and refuse to go blind and she would not be relegated to the empty darkness.

She exercised her eyes, she looked into the distance at the far away blue hills to calm them and rest them and she used soothing eye drops. But it was no use, the darkness kept on falling like a curtain at the theatre when the play is over. Except that at the theatre the lights come on after the show and no lights came on for Chloe.

She was angry.

'Why has this happened to me?'

She went up to her room and slammed the door. It remained slammed shut and even her mum's tentative knocking brought no reply. Her meals were left on a tray outside her room, but they stayed there and went cold.

'You need food to keep healthy,' coaxed her mum. But Chloe did not answer.

How could she live if she could not see? How could she watch birds? How could she do anything?

She knew now that she was doomed to spend the rest of her life groping about in darkness.

Then one day her friends came round and, at last, she ventured out of her room and went off arm in arm with them. Her parents were happy, at first, but that happiness soon turned to despair because night after night, Chloe came back drunk.

'Blind drunk,' she laughed, a loud forced laugh, thinking in her stupor that she was clever and funny. It helped her forget what had happened to her, for a short time. She groped her way upstairs on all fours and then stumbled into a dreamless sleep. She couldn't even see in her dreams now.

The next day, her dad tried being jovial.

'When Nelson lost one eye, he used it to his advantage, do you remember? He was ordered to retreat when the enemy ships came into view, but he held the telescope to his blind eye and said, 'I see no ships,' and so he went on to win the battle.'

'At least he could see with one eye. I can't see at all. Spare me the jollity, please,' was Chloe's sullen reply. Her father looked at his wife and shrugged helplessly. But he tried again.

'Well, I have always heard that if you lose one sense, the others develop more, to compensate. So, people who cannot see have better hearing.'

'That's rubbish and you know it – there is no scientific proof for that – it's just an old wives' tale,' she replied with contempt. Her dad gave up.

Now it was her mum's turn.

'Look Chloe – I know how much you like birdwatching.'

'Liked,' corrected Chloe.

'Well,' persisted her mum, 'I have been looking into this and there is a birdwatching group for the blind, and, as it happens, it's not too far away from here.'

'Yeah, like music appreciation for the completely deaf.'

'Well yes, people who are hard of hearing can hear music, but sometimes in a different way.'

'Don't be so stupid, Mother!'

With that Chloe stumbled upstairs to her room again and slammed the door.

Her friends stopped coming round.

As winter droned on, an awful black silence fell around everyone in the house and it was nothing to do with the short days. Her mum and dad felt that they, too, were in the dark and were at their wits' end and didn't know how to help. All their efforts to be positive failed and all their efforts to get more help failed because Chloe simply refused to accept help. Even at her regular check-ups, she ignored advice.

Chloe was getting more and more angry unable to accept that life, as she knew it, was at an end. She felt that she was living in an alien world without light. She couldn't do anything that she wanted to do. She knew that she must look awful. She could feel that her nails were jagged and broken, and her fingers were sore where she had crashed them into something that she didn't know was there. The exciting life that she used to have had been snatched away from her.

I See No Ships

Then finally, in desperation and reluctantly, she said that she would try the stupid idea of birdwatching for the blind. Her mum let out a sigh of relief and went with her as her sighted partner. They all met in a nearby woodland and were told that you had to identify the birds by their song.

'That's a woodpecker, a wren, a wood pigeon ...' Chloe rattled off the songs she recognised in monotone, whilst her mum hastily scribbled the list. At the end of the session, the leader was very impressed.

'Well done, Chloe; we've listed lots more species than we normally do.'

Chloe shrugged; who cared? This wasn't real birdwatching. Her mother was pleased, though, and thought that, at least, it was a start. They went together every week bird listening and when spring crawled in, new species started to appear.

'Chiffchaff, curlew and cuckoo ...' muttered Chloe, 'everyone knows that one, but you don't often hear a cuckoo these days.'

Meanwhile, her dad had her desktop computer adapted so that it spoke to her and read out as you moved the cursor. Chloe took to it easily. Time edged on and now summer surprised in. But Chloe still spent most of her time alone in her room and only went out to her birdwatching for the blind. She still found no joy though, and never smiled. She did so miss seeing the birds especially their bright colours; it seemed second best, if she could only hear them. If only she could do something where her lack of sight wasn't a problem, she thought.

Then, one day, she suddenly had an idea. It came from nowhere, but she knew it was good and decided on a plan. She ordered a little machine from a shopping website on her computer and when the parcel arrived in the post, she grabbed it and went upstairs. She had to work out how to use this machine, but that was easy because the instructions were on her computer and it spoke them to her.

Then, that night, she went outside, without bothering to put a jacket on, of course. She groped her way into the orchard. The moon was shining a bright light, but Chloe didn't know that. She sat on the old wooden seat and switched on her machine and waited.

And there they were! She could hear the things of the night – pap, pap – tack, tack – clack, clack. All sorts of different noises came out of her bat detector. It was picking up the silent sounds they made, unheard by the human ear. Even sighted people wouldn't be able to tell which bats were flitting overhead, in the dark, without the detector. And Chloe wasn't worried about seeing the colours, because they were all black. She was on equal terms with a sighted person, at last. There was a pipistrelle, there was a horseshoe bat, there was a whiskered bat – each one had a different sound.

'I might even join the bat watching club; no need to be blind or sighted; in the dark, we are all the same,' she thought.

Clouds came and hid the moon from view but, of course, Chloe did not know that.

Then it started to rain.

'Come on in now, Chloe, come inside – it's raining,' called her mum. 'You'll catch your death of cold.'

'As if I don't know that it's raining,' thought Chloe, 'I am blind but I can still feel the rain dripping down my neck.' But she didn't reply to her mum with her usual nasty retort. Instead, she put an imaginary telescope up to her eye and said,

'I see no drips.'

And, at last, Chloe slowly smiled.

Author Biographies

Kirstie Edwards

Kirstie Edwards is a writer, editor and tutor of writing and founder member of Leaf by Leaf Press. Kirstie completed her MA and PhD studies in writing at Sheffield Hallam University and has since lectured and tutored writing skills in higher education in the UK and Belgium. Apart from her research publications, Kirstie has published poetry, flash fiction and short stories in *Oswords,* a local magazine of the Oswestry Writers Group and in *Reflections*, a collection of writings on the Meres and Mosses in Shropshire edited by Gladys Mary Coles and Simon Fletcher. 'Crossing Paths at Christmas,' which is included in this anthology, won the *Oswestry and Border Counties Advertizer* short story competition in December, 2015. Kirstie works with independent authors, either copyediting their manuscripts or tutoring them on how to copyedit themselves. Kirstie's primer to help independent authors copyedit their own novels will be published in 2021: www.kirstieedwards.org.uk

Ronald Turner

Ron Turner, a founder member of Leaf by Leaf Press, is a Shropshire lad. He attended Goldsmiths College London, studying Speech and Drama. While there he wrote a play which won the London University One Act Play festival and went on to win the South East England Festival. For many years writing had to take second place to providing for his family. When he retired from teaching, he began to write again, including a full-length play, produced locally, a story read on the radio and several prize-winning poems. He has written two historical novels, one published on the internet, and is working on a third. Not content with this, he has gone on to publish *A Perfect Alibi* and *Murder on the Moss,* two fast-paced contemporary crime novels, with Leaf by Leaf Press.

John Heap

John Heap was born in Rochdale and after completing a degree in Zoology, went on to work in computer programming and the hi-tech industries. Although still working in IT, John combines this with climbing and walking holidays with his wife, Sara, and dog, Dennis. He has written for magazines and edited and contributed to *Oswords,* a local magazine of the work of the members of Oswestry Writers Group. The title of this anthology, *The Call of the Sea,* is taken from a spellbinding short story of his included within these covers.

Wendy Lodwick Lowdon

Wendy Lodwick Lowdon is a founder member of Leaf by Leaf Press. She grew up in Australia, studied history at the Australian National University and took an MA in English Studies at the University of Birmingham. Though retired from teaching, she maintains her abiding interest in reading, writing and reviewing. In 2018, she published *Here and There* with Leaf by Leaf Press. She draws on material for her short stories, young adult novels and poetry from her experiences in Australia and Great Britain but focuses her reviewing on science fiction writing: www.wenlowdwhispers.wordpress.com

Bernard Pearson

After his career in human services, Bernard has spent much of his time writing either on his own or in collaboration with other writers. Bernard has penned a memoir of his father's life, *Steaming Light,* which was published by Book Midden Publishing and a collection of poetry, *In Free Fall,* which was published by Leaf by Leaf Press in 2018. Bernard's poetry and prose are available in many ezines, magazines and journals both nationally and internationally. He won second Aurora Prize for poetry in 2019. Bernard is married with two grown up children and after a somewhat itinerant life, now lives in Oswestry.

Trixie Roberts

Trixie Roberts lived most of her life in the North West of England but moved to rural Shropshire in 2010. She started to write in her forties and was drawn to the short story form. She has won prizes for her short stories and poetry, had her work broadcast on radio and included in a North West Writers anthology. Her first collection of stories 'Bananas' was published by Leaf by Leaf Press in 2018. Trixie enjoys writing short stories because of the necessary economy of language and believes the best ones use dialogue to develop plot and reveal characters' reactions to experiences and events. Interaction between characters is crucial in revealing life's hiccups, joys and puzzles. She can often be found eavesdropping. When not writing, Trixie enjoys her grandchildren, singing in a local choir, competing in quizzes and living in a very busy village where she helps to produce the community magazine.

Vicky Turrell

Vicky Turrell is one of our founder members of Leaf by Leaf Press. She grew up in East Yorkshire and her family were from farming and fishing backgrounds. After retiring from a successful career in education, she set about writing a memoir of her rural childhood in the forties and fifties. Following the success of *It's not a Boy!* Vicky has written a sequel to this book, which is a moving account of her complex relationship with her mother, entitled *Me and my Mam*. Vicky has also been a regular columnist in the *Oswestry and Border Counties Advertizer,* describing in vivid detail the natural world. Compilations of her nature notes are available in two illustrated books entitled *Robin on my Teacup* and *Ducklings on my Doorstep*. More recently, Vicky has been writing a regular column for the *Shropshire Star* called 'With Vicky Turrell,' which is illustrated with photographs: blog.nestcottage.co.uk